The AC

Cover design by Stephen H. Provost
Front cover collage by Stephen H. Provost/public domain image
Back cover image by Stephen H. Provost

Interior images are adapted from photos by Stephen H. Provost and are or are adapted from images in the public domain.

No part of this book may be reproduced, or stored in a retrieval system, or transmitted in any form or by any means, electronic, mechanical, photocopying, recording, or otherwise, without the express written permission of the individual authors.

The contents of this volume and all other works by Stephen H. Provost are entirely the work of the author, with the exception of direct quotations, attributed material used with permission, and items in the public domain. No artificial intelligence ("AI") programs were used to generate content in the creation of this work. No portion of this book, or any of the author's works, may be used to train or provide content for artificial intelligence (AI) programs.

Published by Dragon Crown Books 2023
All rights reserved.

ISBN: 978-1-949971-39-2

Contents

Editor's Introduction	1
Cobbler **by Gavin Black**	3
Out of Nowhere **by Jay Crowley**	9
The Man Who Fell Apart **by Martin A. David**	23
The Shadow's Edge **by Michael K. Falciani**	27
Slipping Through the Devil's Gate **by L.F. Falconer**	65
Murder on the Desert Express **by Tammy L. Grace**	81
Stuck in the Ribs **by Jacqueline M. Green**	111
The Origins of Mr. Cunningham **by Jade Griffin**	129
The Escape **by Kelli Heitstuman-Tomko**	145
Rebecca on the Streets **by Lisa Kirkman**	155
A Christmas Gift for a Ghost **by Sandie La Nae**	163
Of Camels and Fae **by Angela Laverghetta**	167
Ice Cream on Tuesday **by Laura Magee**	177
The Culling **by Richard Moreno**	189
Not My Daughter **by Ashley Hanna Morgan**	209
Friday the 13th **by Marie Navarro**	211
Gold Fish **by Janice Oberding**	225
The Shining Night **by Sharon Marie Provost**	229
Ghostbusted! **by Stephen H. Provost**	243
Selected Poems **by Peggy Rew**	265
Miracle in the Rain **by Abby Rice**	271
SWOOP! **by Ken Sutherland**	277
Bury Me Deep **by Richard Thomas**	297
They Call Me Will **by Kitty Turner**	303
Nevada Sonnet **by Kristina Ulm**	309

The ACES Anthology

"You can make anything by writing."

— C.S. Lewis

Editor's Introduction

Many anthologies are tied together by a theme. This one is united by its origins: the keyboards and minds of Northern Nevada's best writers and poets. It also has a purpose: to introduce you, the reader, to the work of these amazing individuals.

Some of the names that appear on these pages will likely be familiar to you; others may not be. This anthology was not created to be an exclusive repository for the works of renowned authors, but rather to showcase the works of both established and emerging authors across Northern Nevada.

This volume presents short stories and poems from twenty-five such writers. Some have written as many as forty or fifty books, while others are making their debut in the pages ahead. Bestselling and award-winning authors are featured side-by-side with newcomers. Whether traditionally or independently published, what they have in common is a passion for writing and a love of the singular swath of land that stretches from Lake Tahoe west to Ely and Elko: a land of majestic mountains, painted deserts, bustling cities, and ghost towns.

Many have chosen to set their stories here, whether in our own time, the recent past, or in the colorful days of the Old West. In the pages ahead, you'll read stories of faerie creatures, intrepid

The ACES Anthology

ghost hunters, a singing cowboy, aliens, and pioneers. You'll find murder mysteries, touching stories of love and loss, creative poetry, a touch of horror, and a few unexpected twists.

Many of the authors included here are showcased on a website dedicated to displaying and promoting their works: ACES of Northern Nevada. ACES (the Authors' Collective e-Shop) is an online hub set up like a virtual bookstore and designed to introduce local authors to readers from across the region and beyond. As an outgrowth of the ACES initiative, this anthology shares that purpose.

If you find an author in these pages whose work touches, inspires, or motivates you to read more, please visit the ACES site at acesofnorthernnevada.com or by scanning the QR Code below and check out their other works. Or seek them out at your local bookstore.

I'd like to personally thank all the authors who agreed to participate in this project, with special thanks to my wife, Sharon Marie Provost, for her assistance with the editing. It is my privilege to present this exciting collection of stories and poems from your neighbors: an array of talented individuals from Carson City, Reno, Sparks, Fallon, and across the region. I invite you to sit back and enjoy *The ACES Anthology*.

Stephen H. Provost
October 5, 2023

Gavin Black
Cobbler

The Cobbler woke up, ate the last of his porridge and headed downstairs to his shop. He stood behind his work bench and looked over to the small display window. There sat the last completed pair of shoes he had made. Things had been rough since his wife died; she always had taken care of the shop and supplies, leaving him to focus on making shoes.

The Cobbler managed to keep the store going well enough. Then, a man came through town, promising better leather for half the price. Thinking that getting twice the leather at twice the quality would afford him more time to work on making shoes, he paid the man. Unfortunately, the man never returned with the leather, leaving the Cobbler penniless.

He resigned himself to living in the local poor house, where they promised him indentured servitude: a cot and food in return for his work. Before leaving, he glanced down at the last pieces of leather on the work bench, and, finding it fruitless to make another pair, he walked over and picked up the shoes in the display and left.

As the Cobbler walked down the street, head hung low, he

pondered what the future held. Being so lost in thought, he didn't notice the hunched-over vagrant woman begging on the street and ran right into her. Both Cobbler and vagrant toppled over onto the ground in a heap.

"I'm so sorry, ma'am" the Cobbler stammered. As he stood up he looked at the last pair of shoes he would make as a free man; they were now scuffed and covered in muck. Tears streamed down the man's face as he realized they were now a reflection of his life: poor, dirty, and useless.

"Those are the most beautiful shoes I have ever seen," The vagrant woman gushed.

The Cobbler looked down at her twisted bare feet, then held out the shoes.

"Here. I have no more need of these and you can clearly use them more than me," the Cobbler said in a somber tone.

The vagrant took the shoes, pulled out a handkerchief that was only slightly less soiled than the shoes, and started to wipe them off.

"Thank you, kind sir! Is there anything that I can do for you?" The vagrant woman gestured to a nearby alley.

"No, no. Just glad that someone can use them," the Cobbler replied, then turned to go.

"Sir, are you sure that a lady of my state cannot help one such as thee?" The voice was high and flowed through the air like a bird's song. Confused, the Cobbler turned to see a beautiful woman dressed in a green and brown dress resembling a tree. The Cobbler scratched his head and looked past the woman, trying to spot the vagrant.

"Good sir! It is I that was here begging." The woman then held out the shoes the Cobbler had given her. They looked a shabby, poor gift compared to the woman's beauty and stature. An understanding suddenly overcame the Cobbler: He was standing

The ACES Anthology

in front of a lady of the Fae. The Cobbler quickly ran a hand through his hair, dropped to one knee and bowed his head "Your highness, I am at your service," the Cobbler said in a shaky voice, knowing the Fae were a folk not to be trifled with.

"You may rise, and, as a thank-you for your kind offer of these shoes, I grant you one wish," the lady of the Fae proclaimed. The Cobbler started to tremble, for his day had gone from bad to worse. The last thing he wanted was a gift from the Fae. He had heard the story of the princess who stumbled upon the seven kings of the Fae. If he recalled correctly, when given a wish, she asked for eternal beauty, only to be cursed with eternal rest in a glass coffin, now displayed in a prince's castle.

"I thank your highness for such a wonderful gift; however, one such as I who has known so little in life cannot think of anything to ask for," the Cobbler said as reverently as possible as he started to sweat.

"I cannot return knowing that I am in your debt. Ask now before my patience wears thin!" The Fae shrieked. Quaking in the muck, the Cobbler quickly turned over in his mind what to do. How could he trick the Fae? He wished his wife was there; she would know what to do. Suddenly, the answer came to him.

"Marry me as my equal in marriage and reside in my realm," the Cobbler stammered.

"What?! How dare you ask such a thing!" Spittle flew from the Fae lady's lips in rage. As it hit the Cobbler's face, he noticed a smell like spring rain. He cowered further into the muck and noticed that no one walking by took heed of what was happening.

"That is my wish. If you choose not to abide by it, we can nullify it." The words came high-pitched and squeaky from the Cobbler.

"I am bound by the laws of my people and, if that is your wish, it is granted," the lady of the Fae said in disgust.

They were soon married under a willow tree, which wrapped its long vines around the newlyweds' hands to consecrate the marriage. The lady of the Fae then moved into the small living space above the shop, which she felt was far too small for one such as herself.

The next morning, as the Cobbler headed downstairs to craft the shoes with the last strips of leather he still had, he found instead a finely crafted pair of shoes. As he stared down at them, his wife's voice drifted down the stairs: "You wanted to be equals in marriage; that means I get to craft shoes as well."

Glowering at the shoes but having no other choice, the Cobbler placed them in the window. Just as he was about to close for the day, a man walking by stopped and bought the shoes straight away. The Cobbler took the money and hurried over to the tanner's shop to get leather so he could start work the next morning.

The following day, he awoke early, eager to get started on his work; instead, the Cobbler found a dozen finely crafted shoes in place of the leather. Stamping his foot in frustration, he yelled up the stairs to his wife: "Witch." Reluctantly, he placed the shoes out to sell. Just as the day before, the Cobbler sold out of his shoes just before closing. He hurried over to get leather for the following day and bought all that he could afford, confident there was no way his wife could turn all of it into shoes in one night.

That night, as he lay on the floor beside the bed his wife occupied, the Cobbler watched and waited for her to leave, though she did not move once. Confident that he could finally get back to his work, the Cobbler groggily stumbled down the stairs, and found his shop stocked with the finest shoes he had ever seen.

Too tired to care, the Cobbler opened his shop and found a

line of customers eagerly waiting to enter. The shoes sold out before mid-day. Thinking he had time to get to work making shoes that afternoon, he headed back over to the tanner and purchased more materials. Once he got back to his store, the Cobbler sat at his work bench, planning to get to work, but promptly fell asleep.

Awaking the next morning, he found his store once again stocked with shoes. The Cobbler realized that it was a hopeless matter. As he sat there throughout the day, selling the shoes, he pondered how his wife had the time to make them. She did not move all night and stayed upstairs all day sulking. As he thought of the Fae who spun straw into gold a thought struck him: It was said there were small impish creatures that were slaves of the Fae. There was no reason a lady of the Fae would put in effort when she could have someone else do the work for her, the Cobbler surmised.

As the Cobbler was returning home from the tanner, the king came to mind. A few years back, the Fae had tricked him into paying them money for the finest clothes they could make. The Fae sent the imps to do the work, but since they could not wear clothes, they tricked the king into wearing nothing as well.

The Cobbler hurriedly made a stop at the seamstress's before going home, buying several sets of children's clothes. After dinner, the lady of the Fae went straight to bed, just as she had previously done every night, but this time, the Cobbler sneaked down the stairs and laid out the children's clothes, hoping they were the right size.

"You aren't working now, are you?" The Cobbler's wife called out,

"No, dear! Just making sure the leather is all set out for you," he replied

The Cobbler ran upstairs and to bed, sleeping well for the

first time since his wish was granted. He was abruptly awakened in the morning by the screams of his wife.

"How dare you free the imps? Those were my slaves!" The lady of the Fae screamed out, stamping her foot on the floor. "They had been in my family's service for two thousand years! Who is going to work for me now?"

The Cobbler just held out his hands in response.

"Pfft, you think that is going to fix it? I was already the laughing stock of the Fae when I had to marry you, and you go and do this. I wouldn't have been so generous and given you a wish if I had known this would be the outcome."

⚜

A loud knock came from the store's front door. Not knowing what else to do, the Cobbler turned away and headed downstairs. He found the imps had left behind their finest work yet, along with a note that simply said: "Thank you."

At the end of the day, after coming home from the tanner, the Cobbler headed upstairs to find his wife had already gone to bed.

The next morning, the Cobbler awoke to find a willow vine broken in half with a sack of gold on the bed. Cautiously, he crept downstairs to find the stack of leather right where he left it the night before. Smiling, the Cobbler sat down to make a pair of shoes.

⚜

"The Cobbler" is ©2023 by Gavin Black. It appears here for the first time. The author made his debut in 2021 with the publication of "Crop Burner: The Tale Of Fearn & The Deamhon," a fantasy novel on Global Book Publishing in the tradition of C.S. Lewis, Terry Brooks, and Neil Gaiman. His latest novel is "The Friend Exchange."

Jay Crowley

Out of Nowhere

The year was 1952...

Mickey was at the bus depot waiting for a bus to take him to his new job. He could not believe his luck; he finally had found employment. He was a healthy, good-looking, forty-year-old veteran. Mickey had been living on the streets in Las Vegas for over a year. No one wanted to hire him, as he was missing an arm. The VA said there was nothing they could do for him. They gave him counseling and therapy, but his arm was too damaged for a prosthesis.

Mickey received a $150 check from the government each month for the loss of the arm. But it wasn't enough to live on. The cheapest apartment he could find was $100 a month plus the cost of utilities. When the cost of food was added, it was more than he received. So he lived on the street.

A day earlier, he had been eating a 79-cent breakfast at a local casino when a man approached him out of nowhere. "Hi, my name is John," he said. "Are you looking for work? I am looking for laborers. We pay $5 an hour. Are you interested?"

"Yes sir, I am," said Mickey, jumping off the stool. "I have been looking for work for quite a while."

"Well, be at the Greyhound bus station tomorrow at seven and look for bus Number 772. The driver will take you to the job."

"Yes, sir, I will be there."

"Here are some forms for you to fill out and bring with you." He opened his briefcase and handed Mickey the packet of papers.

"Will do. By the way, my name is Mickey."

"Fine, fine." He waved his hand. "Names are not important. I just need people who want to work."

Mickey looked at him and calmly said, "Will I be able to do the work for you with my missing arm?"

"Not a problem. You will also receive room and board. The job is doing paperwork."

"Where is the job?"

"I am not at liberty to say. You will find out tomorrow. The job entails you staying there for fourteen days and then seven days off. Will this be okay? Do you have a family?"

"No family, and that work shift will be fine."

"Great, they will see you tomorrow morning." John turned, threw down a dollar on the table for Mickey's breakfast, and left.

Mickey felt like a weight had been lifted from him.

I have a job with my disability. What more would I want? Wow, $5 an hour! That's a lot of money. His mind was racing. He would be getting $200 a week, plus room and board; he just couldn't believe his luck.

※

The private bus picked up Mickey, nine other men, and two women. He recognized a couple of the men from the street, who were homeless, too. The grey-haired, stocky driver introduced himself as Joe and said, "This is about a two-hour trip." Joe seemed like a happy-go-lucky guy. "Make yourselves comfortable; coffee and donuts are in the back of the bus."

Everyone grabbed a donut and coffee and said, "Thank you."

The driver told them he was taking them to a military base bordered by a dry lakebed called Groom Lake. To the west were mountains. The closest town, Tempiute Village, Nevada, was 25 miles north of the base. (Its name would later be changed to Rachel.) The buildings occupied only a fraction of the more than 90,000-acre base. They would be staying in a big three-story boarding house a mile or so away from the main structures.

Joe liked to talk, so he went on in some detail. "Some people suspect that what you see on the surface of the base is only a tiny part of the actual facility. Some say there are many levels under the base. I do know they use underground railways for the underground bombs. However, I believe, for the most part, what you see is what you get." Joe gave a smirk and laughed.

The trip went quickly; soon, they reached the base. It consisted of a large airplane hangar, guard shack, radar antennas, and housing, along with a mess hall, offices, and a runway.

They drove through to a three-story red brick boarding house, which sat out in the open. A two-car garage-type building sat behind it, but the cars were parked outside. That was it: Nothing else around. No other buildings. Not even any landscaping.

"This is your home for fourteen days; I will see you on the return trip. A van will take you to and from work."

And with that, Joe opened the bus doors, and everyone stepped out into the warm morning.

The ACES Anthology

The house door opened, and an older woman emerged, wiping her hands on her apron. "Welcome. Welcome. Come in, and I will show you your rooms. My name is Martha, and I am the housekeeper and the cook."

Martha took everyone around to their rooms. "Everyone will have to share the one bathroom on each floor," she said, then turned to the ladies and asked, "I hope that's okay." They agreed it would be fine.

She guided six people each to the first and second floors of the three-story building. On the bus, everyone had introduced themselves—first names only: Mickey, Bob, Pete, Kyle, Irene, and Edith would be on the first floor; Tim, Tom, Joe, Rick, Danny, and Eric were on the second.

Everyone was homeless and looking for work. Eric and Danny were also veterans of the Korean War. The two ladies had lost their husbands, one in the war, and the other to a heart attack. Mickey noticed the odd thing about this group was that no one had any family.

As they sat around the dining room table eating lunch, Mickey asked, "So what goes on at this base?"

Martha said in a rehearsed speech (they must have had her practice the speech), "Well, according to the military, this facility's main purpose is *'the testing of technologies for operations critical to the security of the United States. All specifics about the facility and the bombing tests are classified.'* And that is all I know, folks." She smiled.

"It all sounds technical. What do they want with a bunch of homeless people?"

"Eat up. You find that out this afternoon at the briefing." And with that, she left the room.

The ACES Anthology

At 1 p.m. sharp, a small school bus was there to pick them up and take them into town. The driver said, "My name is Ralph. I will pick you up every morning at 7 and drop you off in the evening at 5, so be ready to go. You will eat lunch at your job location."

Ralph didn't leave room for chit-chat. He was a tall, thin, abrupt-speaking man and didn't want to be asked questions. Everyone rode in the bus quietly for the one-mile drive back to the main base.

The bus dropped them off at a building that looked like headquarters. Ralph had told them to go to Room C, which they all did. Inside, it was like a classroom; they each got a seat. No one was there. They waited... and waited. Finally, about 1:30 p.m., a lieutenant came into the room. He looked rushed. "Sorry to have kept you waiting, but I couldn't get away."

Everyone mumbled it was okay.

"My name is Lieutenant James Woods; I will be your supervisor while you are here. Everyone will have a different job, which I will explain individually to each of you. Our work here is highly classified.

"Did you fill out the forms you were given?"

Everyone answered, "Yes." They got up and handed them to him.

"Thank you." He glanced through the paperwork to ensure it was filled out correctly and signed.

"Kyle, I will start with you and then get to the rest of you. Please be patient. I will spend about ten minutes with each of you. Coffee and soft drinks are in the back of the room."

About then, someone came in with a tray of cookies. Mickey thought to himself, *They sure do feed you here*, and grabbed a couple of the chocolate chip cookies and a soft drink.

Finally, it was Mickey's turn. He went in the attached room

with the lieutenant to be interviewed or whatever, as no one said anything when they came out.

"Tell me about yourself, Mickey," asked the lieutenant.

Matt proceeded to talk about his time in the military and his injury. They talked for about five minutes. Finally, Mickey asked, "What will I be doing?"

The lieutenant sighed and said, "Mickey, what we are doing here is testing A-bombs. I will be having you take a reading on the radiation of equipment with a Geiger counter and maintaining records. We have built a city out in the desert, which we will bomb. You will check to see how cars and military equipment survive the bombing blast."

He continued. "As you know, you'll be living here, so you may be here when a bomb goes off underground or above ground. Is that OK?" he said, looking at Mickey as he nodded his head yes. "You will be paid $5 per hour for 24 hours, 14 days, or roughly $1,600 for your time plus room and board. The catch is you can't tell anyone what we are doing. Is all of this OK with you?"

Mickey's mind raced as he thought about the money. "Yes, sir, it is OK with me, and I'll not talk about the job." *Hell. I'll work every day here; I do not need to return to Vegas. I have no family.*

The lieutenant smiled at that, "You folks can talk to each other about your job; I would prefer you don't, but that is up to you."

However, from his tone, Mickey felt he would not be talking about his job.

"I will work as long as you need me," Mickey said, glowing.

"I know you will. Thank you, you may go now." They both got up and walked out.

While Mickey waited for the rest of the people to be interviewed, he thought, *I would earn over $2,000 monthly. That is $24,000 a year; I can buy a car and maybe a house. What a lucky break. I am* *so blessed to have this job.*

That night at dinner, everyone was talking about what a great job this was going to be. Yet no one said what they would be doing. When everyone went to bed, they had visions of their good luck running through their heads. Few people slept.

The next morning, they had new clothes to wear when they woke up. They were all up and dressed, ate breakfast, and waited for the bus. Every person got dropped off at different areas. Life was good, Mickey thought, and his job was a breeze. He could handle it with no problem. He hadn't been this happy for so long.

The days flew by. Lieutenant Woods called them all together on the eighth day and said, "We will drop the A-bomb in three days. On that day, you will stay home until we tell you it is safe, and the base will lock down. Just close the windows in your room and make sure to close the house up. Enjoy your day off. It is a Saturday, so you can watch westerns on the television".

Everyone laughed; the ladies said they would read.

Saturday came; the bomb was to be dropped at 10 a.m. Martha fixed them breakfast and made sandwiches for lunch. At about 9 a.m., she excused herself and said she was going to Las Vegas to go shopping. Mickey thought that was weird, as everyone would be locked down and staying inside the house.

At almost 10, they heard sirens and all kinds of warning sounds—and then they heard the plane. It sounded close. It dropped the bomb. They could hear it when it dropped. A loud whoosh and a whine, then KABOOM!

Shit!

The whole house shook. Windows blew in, with glass flying

everywhere. One of the ladies sitting by the window reading was cut badly and screaming. Mickey heard all the screams and was trying to reason what was going on. He was in the bathroom, apparently a secure part of the house. The bathroom had a small high window, which was opened so no glass flew. The house, however, felt like it was going to collapse.

Finally, the house creaking and cracking stopped. The bathroom was fine; things were knocked down, but he was OK.

He tried to open the door but had to push it as something was leaning against it. Finally, he squeezed out and looked around.

The hall was a mess. Pictures had fallen off the wall. The doors to the rooms were blown open. He crept down the hall and peeked into a bedroom. Kyle was dead, and Mickey knew it. His eyes were bugged out. It looked like he'd had a heart attack; the bomb must have terrified him.

What in the hell is going on?

He walked farther down the hall. Pete was lying by his bedroom door; it looked like his walking stick had gone through him, like a sword. No one was in any of the next three rooms. *They must all be downstairs watching television.*

Mickey walked down the stairs. Debris was everywhere, and all the windows were broken, leaving broken glass all over. It looked like a war zone. Tim, Tom, and Joe had been sitting on the couch in the family room when some of the ceiling beams had landed on them. Mickey couldn't tell if they were dead or badly injured. Bob was in the recliner, dead: The console television had struck him in the head, and blood was everywhere.

Mickey went looking for Eric, Danny, Rick, and the girls. He had heard one of the women screaming when he was in the bathroom, but all was quiet now. In the kitchen, he found Rick. He must have been getting a beer out of the commercial fridge—

which had landed on top of him. Mickey tried to move it but could not do it by himself. He entered the front room; the chandelier had fallen and landed on Irene. She was badly cut and bloodied but looked OK; he ran over and helped her up. Edith had been sitting by the window when it blew out, the glass cutting her throat.

"I can't find Eric and Danny," Mickey told Irene.

They went looking for them, yelling out their names.

The two of them stopped by the kitchen and tried to pull the fridge off Rick, but he was gone. *It must have crushed his chest.* Irene washed herself off in the sink, and Mickey helped her remove the glass from her cuts and hair. She needed first aid badly. He told her to sit down, and he would look for the other two guys.

Mickey looked all over the house, all three floors and the bathrooms; Eric and Danny were not in the house. Where could they be? Mickey heard sirens coming. What had gone wrong with the bombing?

The kitchen door opened with a bang, and several soldiers rushed in. One saw Irene and started helping her out the door to an ambulance. Mickey recognized one of the soldiers and said, "The rest are dead, except I can't find two men, Eric and Danny."

One of the soldiers asked, "Are you OK? You look OK. You were lucky."

"Yes, I am fine. I was in the bathroom when the bomb hit. What went wrong?"

"It is a long story."

"Well, I have time," snapped Mickey.

"Later, come with us. Not sure this house is safe. It could catch fire."

Mickey followed the men out of the house. *Shit*, he had never thought of fire.

The ACES Anthology

The remainder of the 14 days went by. Mickey and Irene stayed on base in one of the housing units. The bus came to pick them up; Joe never asked about the rest of the people. Mickey thought it was odd, seeing only two people were going back, he and Irene. Joe was not as talkative as before. Mickey did not care, as he and Irene were richer than when this adventure had started. On top of what they'd been promised, the military gave them a bonus of $5,000 each.

Mickey never heard what went wrong or why the bomb did so much damage to the house where they were staying. It was a blessing it was a mile or so out of town.

"Will you be picking us up again after seven days?" asked, Mickey.

"You want to go back?" asked Joe.

"Hell yeah, this is good money."

Irene said, "I don't want to go back; I gave Lieutenant Woods my resignation. I can live quite a while on this money I just received, thank you."

Joe took them back to the bus depot and told Mickey, "See you in eight days."

Eric and Danny were at headquarters with Lieutenant Woods back at the base. No one on the base knew that Eric and Danny were alien survivors from Area 51, outside of the Tempiute Village. Even Lieutenant Woods didn't know. The aliens were there seeking world domination.

In the late 40's...

A spaceship wrecked in New Mexico. It was concealed from the government by a military organization. They brought the ship and survivors to Area 51. Aboard the ship were two male aliens. In interrogating the aliens, this group found them to be quite intelligent. The two survivors were not little green men with antennas coming out of their heads. In fact, they looked a lot like most human beings, except they had powers to heal themselves and survive.

Some of Mercury and Area 51 revolved around a shadowy group of organizations dedicated to bringing about a New World Order (NWO). Using UFO stories that Area 51 had captured aliens was one of these organizations' tactics to distract the public from its real goal—world domination. It is the old story: Hide them in plain sight.

The aliens told these organizations they could use their powers to help them with world domination. So, a plan was hatched to breed them with homeless women or prostitutes. So far, they have over one hundred children living in Area 51.

The plans were to bomb small countries first and then send the aliens in to take over the area. It would be a slow process, one area at a time. The A-bombing of a city in any country would help soften the target, and this would help them to accomplish their goal of world domination. The plan was to do all of this within 15 years.

Back at the base. The lieutenant said, "We learned so much about this last bombing, using real people and the damage it can do to a house. That was a great idea, Danny. Did you see the cars out back and how they were totaled? I am surprised anyone got out of the house alive."

"Me, too. However, Mickey said he was in the bathroom, and Irene was just lucky," replied Eric.

Danny and Eric thought to themselves, *Most humans cannot survive the blast unless concrete or a double wall protects them.*

"When we rebuild the boarding house, we have to make sure

that doesn't happen again," said Danny. "Or better yet, maybe the next time, we bomb them when they are working."

※ ※

Later in Time...

Little did the members of NWO know that because of their involvement in these bombings, the exposure to the bomb's radiation limited their time. The same people seeking world domination brought upon themselves diseases, which killed them and many other people in the process.

Nonetheless, Eric and Danny survived with their offspring and are still living to this day. They knew of the effects of radiation. *Humans are so stupid.* The aliens planned to rule the world, as they could live for hundreds of years. Now, there are thousands of them throughout the world. They just keep breeding. They're indestructible, and more aliens from their home planet were already coming.

The aliens have infiltrated different governments throughout the world. They decided not to use the bombs: They had a better plan. They would encourage the humans to kill themselves with greed and war; then, they would step in and take over. Earth was perfect for their needs, and they wanted it all. What humans did survive would become slaves and or breeders.

Their day was coming! Earth was theirs.

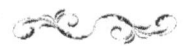

※ ※

"Out of Nowhere" is ©2023 by Jay Crowley. It appears here for the first time. The author lives in Jack's Valley near the base of Lake Tahoe and has written numerous historical novels and short stories, many of which have appeared in anthologies. She was selected to be in "Who's Who of Emerging Writers" in 2020 and 2021. Her books are available on

The ACES Anthology

Amazon and Barnes and Noble, and you can follow her at SweetDreamsBooks.com or Jay Crowley-Sweet Dreams Books-Author on Facebook.

Martin A. David

The Man Who Fell Apart

It was a Wednesday when his hand fell off. It just fell off and landed on the floor with a soft thud. He looked at it for a few seconds and then bent down and picked it up with his other hand.

It felt warm and moist. He studied it, turning it over slowly; a familiar object in an unfamiliar setting. He wasn't frightened, he was just curious.

"Damn," he muttered in amazement.

The hand recoiled slightly. It looked so helpless.

"Disgusting," he said. Then he got mad at it. It had served him well, solidly and firmly attached for almost seven decades. Somehow he overlooked that record of faithful support and got thoroughly pissed at it.

"Fuck you," he said into his open palm. His palm—he still thought of it as his even though it had fallen off.

The hand was defiant, downright sassy. It responded by curling three fingers downward and leaving the middle finger pointed skyward. The thumb remained neutral.

Suddenly he had a bad hand. He was tempted to throw it against the wall. Instead he put it back on. He stuck it in place, and it stayed there.

At first it was a little sensitive. He used it gingerly and with a great deal of circumspection. Then, little by little, he forgot about it—as much as one could forget about such a thing.

He didn't think of it a while later when his ankle went out. It left, took off, vamoosed, went AWOL—and took the whole damned foot with it.

He was laid up in bed for a week until the foot was recovered and the ankle put in place. He limped for a while after that. When people asked him what had happened, he told them, "Oh, my ankle went out, and now I have a bad foot."

He did think of punishing his bad foot for being bad, but couldn't come up with anything appropriate. He eventually let it pass.

The process went on, sporadically, unpredictably. Nothing shocked him anymore, but new episodes always caught him by surprise.

His eyes both went at the same time. He got hold of them before they rolled too far and was able to prevent further escape by always wearing his glasses in front of them.

His back went out one time and started doing all sorts of tricks—behind his back, as it were.

So it went. There always seemed to be something wrong.

Once, when he was downtown, a kidney popped out. He grabbed it before anyone could see it and stuck it in his jacket pocket. He hurried home. When he got there, he took off the jacket and flung it in a corner. He went about his business. Later, something made him think of it, and he rushed back to find the kidney and put it in its place.

"That would have been something," he thought, "if I had lost that somewhere."

He had a sudden vision of his mother. She used to tell him, "You'd lose your head if it weren't attached."

His head was still attached.

Not long after that, his head fell off. It just lay there with a silly expression on its face. A small, unimportant thing made it come loose, but once it started, it went all the way.

He had a feeling he could just take hold of it and put it back on, but he didn't. Somehow it was not an altogether unpleasant experience to be out to lunch, not home, out of his head for a time. He got lots of attention over this one. People came and took care of him, made sure his needs were met, got him up in the morning and made sure his clothing was on right (except for hats—he was not wearing any hats at that point in time.)

He didn't let his head get far away, though. He thought of his mother. He saw her gloating face coming back to haunt him if he really lost it.

"See I told you, you're always losing things."

Gradually he got bored with this game and decided to bring it to an end. He managed to get his head on straight again and move forward.

For a while everything was fine. He held everything together. Even the days seemed to hang together. They connected, one to the other to make up weeks, and just as the neck bone is connected to the back bone, the weeks linked up to make months and the months formed a year.

The man who fell apart had no major losses to speak of. His hair, a few wisps at a time, packed its bags and departed with absolutely no intention of coming back. Sizable chunks of memory either went their own way or hitched a ride with the hair. The eyes didn't wander any further off, but they often seemed to be more on vacation than on duty.

The winter came. The winter went. Sometimes things stayed and sometimes they left. Even when they stayed, the parts became cantankerous and uncooperative. Time and again they just refused to work together at all. The man didn't know what to do. He tried to settle those disputes and disagreements he could and ignore the rest. He coped with the desertions and disappearances the best he knew how.

This business of keeping things together took more and more energy. Finally he just gave up. He stopped holding it all upright like some precariously balanced stack of Chinese acrobats.

Predictably, it all fell apart—hand, arm, back, ankle, kidney, eyes and head—all of it. Each went rattling off in its own direction.

At the funeral, a distant relative who hadn't been around for a long time spoke to another, nearer, relative.

"It's a shame. The last time I saw him, he seemed like such a healthy type."

"He was," answered the second. "He was—but then he just seemed to fall apart."

⚜

"The Man Who Fell Apart" is ©2010 by Martin A. David. The author has lived in such cities as New York, Paris, Rome, Copenhagen, Los Angeles, Oakland, and San Francisco, but now resides with his dear wife, Carol, in Reno. He has published approximately a million words in books, magazine and newspaper articles, columns, and essays. He has also worked as an actor, visual artist, and craftsman. You can find him at www.mardavbooks.com.

Michael K. Falciani
The Shadow's Edge

She opened her ebony-hued fingers; her hand pulsated with power. A nimbus of white magic shot forth, surrounding the crooked and bent body of a creature that stood not ten paces in front of her. The hag-like monstrosity froze in place, captured in a powerful spell of paralysis. Angrily, the creature glared at Adaline, its crimson eyes burning with malevolence.

"This is not the end," the hag croaked, fighting against the magic. "I will find a way. You cannot stop the return of your brethren. This is their realm—they are the rightful rulers here, as am I."

The ebony-skinned witch turned the full lips of her mouth in a measured frown. "You are mistaken, Jaylocke. Your attempt to bring back the Nine has failed. Now tell me, where is your familiar?"

"Long gone from here, wretch!" the old woman screeched. "Search the ends of the Earth for all your days, but you will not find her."

"Perhaps not, but she will not stray far from your side, even unto death," Adaline said.

"Fah! You will not kill me, *Decem*," the creature shot back. "You've not the stomach for it."

In answer, the Witch of the Adirondacks smiled. "You are right, child of the shadow, but there *are* fates worse than death."

Adaline raised her oaken staff sharply and shouted out words steeped in eldritch power.

"Sit umbra tue carcerem!"

The white nimbus pulsing from her hands intensified, illuminating the open field with its light.

Defiant to the end, the nightmarish creature of the fey began to sink into the ground, a frustrated scream of her hatred trailing behind her.

"This is not the end..." the hag promised before Jaylocke's bestial head slipped under the earth. Her words were cut off; leaving the meadow silent, save for the song of katydids chirping in the golden, knee-high grass nearby. The ground healed itself under the strength of Adaline's magic, leaving not a trace of Jaylocke's presence.

Adaline lowered her staff and dropped her hand to her side, panting with effort.

"May you stay imprisoned for all eternity," the witch muttered, wiping a trickle of sweat from her brow. Giving the field one last glance, Adaline strode off, a look of tired satisfaction crossing her beautiful countenance.

At the very moment the ancient Witch of the Adirondacks stepped out of the field, into the forest, a thin tendril of green sprouted from the ground behind her. The tiny plant cast a long shadow in the dying light of the setting sun—and a remnant of Jaylocke's scream wafted on the breeze.

"There's two outs, not three!" the ruddy-faced coach screamed from the dugout on the third-base line.

"You tell him, honey!" barked Thaya's mother, who was sitting next to her daughter on the metal bleachers at Korning's Little League Fields. There was a line of smoke wafting around her head from the Salem menthol sticking out of the side of her mouth.

Thaya rolled her eyes skyward, wondering how her mother could be gullible enough to let her new boyfriend talk them into going out to his son's tee ball game.

"Don't encourage him," sixteen-year-old Thaya admonished, shaking her head.

"Mind your business," her mother replied, giving her daughter a disgusted look. "Steven's family now, or haven't you figured that out yet?"

Thaya sighed, slumping her shoulders. "Steven Mullner is the biggest asshole in town. You've been out with the guy twice, Mom... one of those times was in the dressing room at Pearl's. The owner had to kick you out."

"People in town talk too much," her mother sniffed, turning back to the game.

Thaya frowned, knowing her mother did not have the common decency to acknowledge the truth of the embarrassing situation.

"I was there, Sherry..." Thaya began to argue before her mother whipped her head around and stilled her tongue with a look.

"Don't you *dare* disrespect me in public," she snarled through a row of yellow teeth. "I went through eighteen hours of hard labor bringing you into this world. You shut your mouth, girl, and give me the goddamn respect I deserve!"

Sherry's voice had been loud enough that some of the other spectators glanced over. From the chastising looks aimed at Thaya, it was clear they had heard only the final exchange rather than the conversation that had led to her mother's outburst.

"Kids today," Thaya heard one of the parents mutter, as most of the eyes turned back to the game.

"My Christine told me she causes trouble in school," a diminutive man, Mr. Larcotte, interjected, looking at Thaya with derision from under his battered red cap. "Her father was the same way."

"Don't talk about my father!" Thaya shot back, unable to hold her tongue.

Mr. Larcotte took a drag from his unfiltered Camel, taking in the willowy thin teenager with a pair of beady eyes. "I remember him back in the day. Thought he was better than all of us. He was a punk kid, just like you are."

Thaya could feel the heat of anger building inside her.

"You have my pity, Sherry," Mr. Larcotte continued, turning back to the game where the red-headed Coach Steve was tearing into the umpire.

Thaya brushed her dark bangs out of her eyes and glared at Mr. Larcotte, trying to remember what her father had said about losing her temper. *"You cannot argue with the ignorant,"* he'd offered. *"The best you can hope for is to respectfully disagree."*

It was sound advice, unfortunately, Thaya was about to ignore it.

"Your opinion about my dad means nothing, considering the source!" Thaya spat.

"*What* did you say to me?" Mr. Larcotte snarled, snapping his head back around.

"The whole town knows," she continued. "Will Larcotte, a known drunk and a liar. You are a shit stain on a pair of tighty whities compared to my father."

Mr. Larcotte looked apoplectic. In a fury, he stood from his seat, his face growing to match the color of his hat.

"And another thing," Thaya hissed, undeterred. "Your little angel of a daughter, Christine, is pregnant. Did you know? From what I hear, she's an even bigger whore than her mother was. Maybe that's why she decided to sleep with the entire soccer team!"

"You little *bitch!*" Mr. Larcotte roared, storming down the metal bleachers, the gray hair of his mullet flying behind him.

Thaya shot out of her seat and bolted along the fence that led toward the forest behind the outfield.

"Thaya Elanor Joseph, you apologize this instant," her mother screeched, Sherry's face clouded by a ring of smoke.

"Get back here, you bitch," Thaya heard Mr. Larcotte curse from behind her.

"Come and get me!" Thaya fired back, darting onto a bike trail that ran through the forest.

As a member of the varsity track and cross-country team, Thaya had run these trails on many occasions. Within seconds, she was beyond the range of the Little League field. She had run nearly a mile when she finally slowed her pace to a brisk walk. Panting, she scanned her surroundings.

Thaya knew this path well. The trail would eventually take her to Forsett Drive, and then Yegglestone Street. Thaya shook her head inwardly. She did not want to rejoin civilization, not yet. The thought of dealing with another upstate townie churned her stomach. Instead, Thaya glanced south, seeing an old game trail that was barely visible to the naked eye. Thaya blinked, remembering this was Beldam Woods. A touch of uncertainty crossed over her heart. No one ever came here. Even Thaya's father, the most curious person she had ever known, told her to avoid the place.

Behind Thaya came the dull rattling sound of a small motor. She held her breath and listened carefully. The motor had a distinctive high-pitched whine like all dirt bikes, but underneath it, she could hear a song waft in the breeze.

"I'm just looking at the sky, 'cause it's getting me high..."

"Shit," Talya muttered, glancing down the trail.

She knew that song and she knew that bike.

It belonged to Mr. Larcotte.

Thaya would never have guessed she'd have upset the man enough to where he'd come after her personally. She felt an involuntary shudder run down her back. The thought of being cornered out here in the woods all alone by Will Larcotte was terrifying. Knowing she only had seconds, Thaya sprinted into the forest, praying she ducked out of sight in time.

Ten minutes later, Thaya was still picking her way through the woods as the sun approached its zenith. After more than a mile, the tree line ended and she came to the edge of a wide-open field filled with tall, yellow grass. There was a mysticism to the place; a feeling of undisturbed serenity. A smile came to Thaya's face. She watched in wonder as a gentle breeze swished its way through the grass. In the distance, she could hear the faint sound of katydids chirping together like a symphony.

"It's beautiful here," Thaya murmured, reaching down to stroke one of the long stems of grass that grew up past her hips. She felt an icy shock of pain run along the length of her index finger.

"Shit," she hissed, withdrawing her hand quickly. She looked down to see a line of blood on her finger where the blade of grass had cut into it.

"Figures," she muttered, knowing she should head back and deal with her mother. Thaya lifted her gaze for one final look until she spied something that struck her as out of place. There, in the middle of the field was a huge, solitary tree.

"That's curious," Thaya said under her breath. She felt drawn to the tree, as though it was familiar to her somehow. Without conscious thought, the teenage girl began to walk toward it, like a moth drawn to flame.

As she approached, Thaya saw this tree was taller than all the others she'd seen in the surrounding area. Its bark was thick, and brown, crusted with dull, olive-colored moss that grew in patches on every side. Overhead, the limbs branched outward where tens of thousands of broad leaves blocked out the light of the sun. Thaya came to a halt at the very edge of the shadow the tree cast on the ground and stared straight ahead, looking intently at the tree's base. On the west side of the trunk there was an opening. It started perhaps four feet off the ground and widened gradually on the way down like the entrance to one of her father's tents.

Thaya leaned close, listening under the song of the katydids. She could have sworn she heard something. Dark and hollow, Thaya sensed there was something odd about the hollowed-out portion of the trunk. Without realizing it, she stepped under the tree's shadow.

There! She heard it now. The whisper of a voice, old and sotted, as though fighting its way out from underground. It was saying something, but Thaya could not quite make out what it was.

Thaya made to step forward but came to an abrupt stop as her heart suddenly went cold.

In her efforts to hear the whisper, Thaya had not realized the katydids had gone silent.

"I need to leave," Thaya thought, taking a step backward.

"*No*," hissed a voice, coming from inside the hollow.

Thaya's eyes widened at the sound. "What?" she said aloud, looking into the recesses of the hollow.

"*Stay there, child of the light!*" the voice insisted.

Thaya thought her heart would stop. Not because of the voice, which she'd been expecting. It was due to the red eyes she saw staring at her from the hollow.

"What the fuck...?" Thaya said, taking a step away from the tree, her heart in her throat.

"*Stay out of the light!*" the voice shouted, sounding harsh in Thaya's ears.

Without warning, a creature of nightmare shambled out of the hollow. It was feminine in appearance, with muddy braids of knotted hair hanging loosely about its head. Wrapped in a tattered dress of red and green, the haggard, gray face let out a cry of desperation.

The hag-like creature shuffled its way toward Thaya, who looked on in horror, leaping backward in fear. The panicked girl felt her feet roll over a rough spot on the ground, and she lost her balance, falling heavily. Closing rapidly, the creature sprang forward, barely an inch away from Thaya. The girl held her hands up, knowing there was nothing she could do.

A quintet of terrifying heartbeats went by before Thaya dared to open her eyes. The creature had stopped. It was stuck, clawing at an invisible barrier at the edge of the tree's shadow. Raging, the monster balled one of her taloned hands into a fist and smashed it against the barrier with a force that belied her size. Like an animal imprisoned in a tank, the monstrosity stayed imprisoned inside the darkness.

Furious at her failure, the hag raised a gnarled wooden staff and thrust it toward Thaya. A bolt of red fire shot from the tip and shattered against the barrier, unable to penetrate.

With an anguished cry, the creature began to foam at the

mouth, her blazing red eyes staring at Thaya in loathing.

"What the fuck are you?" Thaya cursed, scrambling to her feet, unable to look away.

The hag did not respond. Instead, she glanced upward with a snarl, her eyes shifting to the sky.

"You can't move past the shadow, can you?" Thaya reasoned, watching as the hag paced the shadow's edge. "You're trapped in there."

The hag howled again in frustration before going silent. Whipping its head around, the hag retreated into the darkness under the tree.

"There you are, bitch," came a voice from woods.

Thaya heard a rush of footsteps in the dry grass behind her. Before she could turn, Thaya felt a powerful hand clamp down on her shoulder. A wave of old nicotine washed over her.

Mr. Larcotte.

"Thought you could get away from me?" he barked, forcing Thaya to her knees.

"Mr. Larcotte," the girl shouted, panic in her voice. "Please stop! There is something under the tree!"

Thaya turned her head to see the leather-faced man sneering at her in longing. "Oh something's gonna be under that tree alright." He slid his hand to his waist and undid the strap holding up his pants. He took the hardened leather belt and looped one end around his fist.

"I'm gonna whip your hide until your ears bleed," he threatened, his hazel eyes filled with the promise of pain.

"Mr. Larcotte, you don't understand..." Thaya tried to say. He stepped forward and casually backhanded her across the face.

"No, *you* don't understand," he spat, easing his way to her left. He bent down close until he was only inches from her face; his eyes narrowed dangerously. "No one insults me like that in public, you little slut—no one."

Hand snaking out, Will Larcotte snatched Thaya by her shirt collar and began to drag her under the tree.

"Mr. Larcotte!" Thaya tried again, trying to pry his grip off.

"This will be a beating you will never for..." he began, pulling her along behind him.

Will Larcotte's words were cut short by a high-pitched scream as he took his first step into the tree's shadow.

There was an explosion of movement from under the tree. Thaya's tormentor did not even have time to turn around.

Mr. Larcotte's grip on Thaya's shirt collar never broke. The white polyester stayed in his hand as he was dragged away and torn to pieces in a wash of teeth and claws.

Thaya looked on in abject terror at the edge of the shadow as Mr. Larcotte was eviscerated in front of her. The hag, drenched from head to toe in hot blood, raised its staff and shouted words Thaya had never heard before.

"*Sumite umbrum, et nucite noctem!*"

The tree, stark still a moment before, began to vibrate in place. Amongst the thousands of leaves that engulfed the branches overhead came an explosion of flowers. A pale white at first, the petals changed to a deep violet, opening themselves to the sunlight above. A gust of wind struck, and several of the leaves and flowers came loose, falling downward, showering Thaya in leaves and blossoms.

Simultaneously, the opening at the base of the tree widened, and a high-pitched cry came from deep within its depths.

The hag spun around and stared malevolently at Thaya, her eyes radiating with power.

"The call has been issued!" she hissed. "Tonight, the Nine will come forth for the first time since the Jessups called upon The Tenth! I will ascend, and the *Decem* will fall!"

The ACES Anthology

The ACES Anthology

Thaya hadn't an inkling as to what the hag was talking about and had no desire to wait around to find out. Instead, Thaya ran for her life, the withered cackle of the hag echoing in her ears from behind her.

⚜

Ten minutes later, Thaya's lithe figure burst onto the trail she'd traversed earlier in the day. She came to a screeching halt, her mind struggling to comprehend what she'd witnessed in the clearing. The same thought kept running through her brain: Mr. Larcotte was dead—murdered by a hag-like beast at the outskirts of Beldam Woods. She needed to tell someone, anyone who would listen.

Unfortunately, her options were limited. Her mother would never believe her, nor did she have any close friends she could confide in. After a moment of consideration, she realized there was no one in Korning that would ever take what she said at face value.

Father, she thought finally. *Yes, my father will believe me... no matter how crazy it all sounds.*

In order to get a hold of him, she'd have to make a phone call, and that meant going home.

No, she shook her head. Her mother would be there, or worse, her new boyfriend, who needed little excuse to be abusive. The Mullners had a horrible reputation for domestic violence, and Steven was the worst of them. *There has to be another...*she began to think when someone yelled, "Look out!" from behind her.

Whirling, she caught of glimpse of a large bike approaching her at speed on the trail. The rider had only just seen Thaya and quickly slammed on the brakes. Thaya raised her hands and managed to grab hold of the handlebars, causing the bicycle to come to an abrupt stop before it ran into her. The rider had not anticipated the sudden halt and was propelled forward, flying past Thaya, where he tumbled to the ground in a heap. Turning her head, Thaya blinked rapidly checking to see if the rider was all right.

"Gosh darn it," a voice said, rising from the dust that had been kicked up. "Are you ok?"

"Perry?" Thaya asked hesitantly. "Is that you?"

"Hi, Thaya," a gangly young man said stepping forward, brushing the dirt off a pair of light blue dungarees. "I'm sorry I almost ran you over, I wasn't expecting to see anyone out near the Beldam Woods today."

The boy was Perry Aires, the politest kid in town. He wore a faded, blue-collared shirt with one of the tails untucked behind him. On his wrist was a digital watch with a calculator. His friendly countenance wore an apologetic grin and his light brown eyes were bespeckled with a thick pair of glasses. On top of his head was a banged-up bicycle helmet, with fresh scratches on the side.

"Oh my God, Perry, am I glad to see you!" Thaya shouted, rushing up to him, and hugging him impulsively.

"I... you are?" he gaped, trying to disentangle himself from Thaya's arms. "I mean it's nice to see you too, but..."

"Perry, do you have a phone at your house?" Thaya asked, releasing him.

"I... a phone?" he questioned, a bit flummoxed at her question. "No... that is, my parents don't believe in phones. They like their privacy. What happened to your shirt?"

Thaya's eyes closed, crestfallen.

"But, once in a while my dad will use the pay phone down at The Grand," Perry offered, speaking of the only grocery store in town. "I can take you there on the Chopper if you want?"

"The Chopper?" Thaya asked.

Perry nodded to his bicycle. "The MK2 Chopper," he beamed proudly. "Got it for a dollar fifty at a garage sale last week at Pastor Lowenstein's house. Used to belong to his youngest son, Andrew."

Thaya looked warily at the rusted bike. "Is that thing safe?" she asked.

Perry beamed at her. "Course it is. Terrance once told me his father blessed all the kids' bikes in order to keep them from harm."

Perry puffed up his chest and continued. "I've made a few modifications to it, as you can see." He pointed to a black basket at the front of the bike, expertly connected with some wire. "Just added this," he crooned, patting the basket fondly. "I can collect all kinds of plants now. I study them when I get home. I'm going to be a botanist someday."

He paused, looking into the woods. "That's why I came out here. No one ever catalogues any of the species that grow in..."

"Perry," she said, cutting him off. "I don't want to be rude, but, do you think we could go to that payphone now? It's kind of urgent."

The boy shrugged and moved past her, tapping the back end of the banana seat with his hand. "Hop on!" He smiled, adjusting his helmet. "I say," he whispered excitedly, pointing to the back of Thaya's head. "What is that?"

"What do you mean?" she asked, confused.

Perry reached behind her and gently plucked something from Thaya's hair. "I've never seen this species before," he muttered, his eyes widening.

In his hand was an object of a deep violet. A flower that had been shaken loose from the tree in the clearing.

"We need to go," Thaya whispered, shying away from the

flower.

"Fascinating," he breathed, wrapping it in a red bandana, before placing the blossom carefully inside his basket. "I'll have to do some research when I get a chance, see if I can find out what species it is."

He grabbed a second helmet from inside the basket and passed it back to Thaya, along with a yellow shirt that had a smiley face on it.

"Best put those on," he said. "As our woodshop teacher always says, safety first!"

Thaya slipped the shirt over her torn garment and placed the helmet on her head, clicking the plastic lock underneath her chin in place.

"Keep your legs away from the chain," Perry warned, grabbing the handlebars. "They will chew you up worse than a bed full of thorns."

⚜

Ten minutes later, they were zooming down the half-mile-long hill on Main Street that led into the "downtown" area. The Business District of Korning was no more than a dozen shops, each struggling to stay open in the Reagan trickle-down economy. Passing through the only stoplight in town at the bottom of the hill, the pair cruised into the parking lot of The Grand, by far the busiest place in town.

Thaya removed her helmet and nearly ran inside, locating the public pay phone near the exit. Digging into her pocket, she found a quarter, lifted the black receiver, and pushed the quarter through the pay slot. Listening closely, she heard the phone go from silent to the dull hum of a tone. Swiftly, she dialed her father's number, praying he was home this Saturday afternoon.

"Take it easy, will ya?" said an annoyed voice from across the way. It came from an old woman dressed all in black who was running register four. She was looking sourly at Thaya, adjusting the button of a black cat she wore on her work vest.

"My apologies Miss Ida," Thaya mumbled, turning her back on the woman, praying her father would pick up.

The phone rang twice, and a sigh of relief filled Thaya as she heard her father's deep baritone on the other end.

"Hello?"

"Dad, it's Thaya," she said, close to tears.

"Hey there, little girl... are you alright?" he questioned, a note of concern in his voice. "You sound upset."

"No, Dad I..." she faltered, realizing what she was about to tell him was ludicrous.

"Honey, what is it?" he asked. "Is it Mom?"

"No, no, Mom is... Mom," she answered, taking a calming breath.

"Well what is...?" he began.

"I went into Beldam Woods," she answered in a rush.

There were several seconds of silence on the other end.

"You saw the tree, didn't you?" he asked, his voice matter-of-fact.

"I... how did you... yes," she blurted, stumbling over herself. "Have you been there? Did you know?"

"What happened?" he asked sharply. "Tell me you did not go near it."

Thaya blinked twice in rapid succession as her breath caught in her throat. "I... I did," she stammered.

"Did you see her?" he demanded. "Is she still trapped by the shadow?"

Thaya's eyes widened in surprise. "You *knew* about the hag?" she asked, her voice stunned.

"Dammit, Thaya, I told you to never go into those woods," he rasped, his anger coming through the receiver. "You could have been killed! Jaylocke is one of the deadliest creatures the Adirondacks have ever known."

"Jaylocke?" she asked. "Is that her...?"

"Please deposit twenty-five cents to continue this call," said an automated voice.

"Shit, I don't have any more money," Thaya growled, feeling in her pockets. "Perry?" she gasped, looking through the window for her chauffeur.

The gangly lad was still outside the store, standing against The Grand's red brick outer wall.

"Oh fuck," Thaya muttered seeing he'd been surrounded by several of the local school bullies.

"Dad, I have to go, what should I do?"

"Don't go back to the woods," he ordered. "I'm on my way from Saranac Lake. Stay somewhere safe until I get there. There is only one person in town you can trust. It's the..."

The call went dead, disconnected in mid-sentence.

"Dammit to hell," Thaya hissed in frustration, slamming the phone down on the hook.

"Take it easy with that," Miss Ida warned, looking at Thaya angrily. "That's the only pay phone in town."

"Sorry," Thaya mumbled, staring at the receiver as if it had betrayed her.

"Miss Ida," came a voice over the intercom. "You have a call at the main office."

"Probably my ninety-seven-year-old witch of a mother," the old woman sighed in annoyance, shuffling from behind the register toward the main office. "Only way the old bat will pass on is if her heart falls out!"

Thaya ignored Ida and raced back outside.

Perry was standing with his back against the wall, arms

outstretched in front of him. Blocking his path were three young men, all with mullets hanging well past their shoulders. Two were juniors in high school, one grade ahead of Thaya: Demerson Bole and Rickard Lake. Demerson was fat, best known for running his mouth. Rickard was lean and tough, with a reputation for picking on anyone he believed weaker than he was.

The leader of the trio was Aaron Bowers. A high school dropout, Aaron would have graduated more than a year ago. Of the three, he was the most dangerous. He was known to carry a switchblade knife in his back pocket at all times. Aaron had been in jail on assault charges over the last six months. Thaya guessed he had just gotten out.

"Where's the weed your old man promised us?" Aaron was saying, pushing Perry hard against the wall.

"I told you, I had to dump it," Perry answered, grimacing in pain.

"Where?" Aaron demanded, reaching for his back pocket.

"In the underbrush out by the old bottle dump," Perry answered, his eyes glancing nervously at the toughs that had boxed him in. "There's an old tree stump there. You know the one? I hid it in the underbrush in a small plastic bag. You can't miss it."

"What the fuck did you leave it there for?" Demerson leered.

"The cops were following me," Perry replied. "I couldn't get caught with it. I figured I'd hide it there and come back for it later."

"Leave him alone," Thaya said, stepping boldly in front of Perry.

The three toughs took a moment to assess the interruption.

"What the fuck is this?" Rickard asked, shaking his head. "You get a bodyguard, plant boy?"

All three laughed.

"I know you," Aaron said. "Thaya Joseph. Tell me, are you as big a slut as that mother of yours?" Aaron continued, sidling up next to Thaya, his dark eyes filled with lust. "I hear she'll fuck anything with a pulse." He reached out, and Thaya felt his hand touch her backside.

Thaya could feel the anger building inside of her. Without thinking, she lashed out, slapping Aaron across the face. The older tough staggered a moment before regaining his senses.

"You little bitch," he swore, reaching into his back pocket.

"Go ahead and pull it out," a new voice said coming around the corner.

All five looked up and saw two tall, athletic-looking black men coming toward them. It was the Tyson brothers, Zane and Kade. Both stood over six feet in height and were renowned athletes in town. The older of the two, Kade had a metal bat resting easily on his shoulder. He was staring at Rickard and Demerson with a venomous look.

The taller of the two, Zane, needed no such weapon. He towered over the rest. An all-state Greco-Roman wrestler, Zane was a mountain of muscle and savage quickness. Both of their parents were teachers at the high school, and the two had a reputation of being upstanding young men.

"Hello, Perry," Kade said nodding at the lanky boy against the wall. "These idiots giving you trouble?"

"Fuck you," Demerson snarled, his hazel eyes narrowing in hate.

"Fuck a paunchy scumbag like you?" Kade asked affably, unlimbering the bat from his shoulder. "I'd rather eat glass."

"This doesn't concern you two," Aaron said, letting his hand fall to his side, leery of them both. "We were just leaving."

"You do that," Zane put in, crossing his arms in front of him.

"It's amazing how quickly the rats run for cover when they lose the upper hand," Kade quipped, staring at the toughs' departure.

"Fuck you, asshole," Aaron retorted, flipping them off as he sidled away.

"So long, Nelson," Zane replied, giving them a wave.

Thaya saw the blood drain from Aaron's face as the trio walked away.

"Nelson?" Thaya asked turning in question to Zane.

Zane shrugged. "Our neighbor called him Nelson once when we were little kids. Aaron went berserk because of it. Hit the neighbor with a rock when his back was turned. Aaron's a sociopath. No idea why, but he hates being called Nelson."

"Your intervention was timely," Perry said, letting out a pent-up breath. "I think they wanted to thrash me again."

"You have any more issues with those asshats, you let us know," Kade said, placing the bat back on his shoulder. "I've been wanting to kick Demerson's ass since he cheap-shotted me in pee wee hockey. Rickard Lake is just as bad, tried to jump me in the boy's room at the Fall Dance last year."

"We have to go," Thaya said, grabbing hold of Perry and dragging him toward the Chopper.

"That was a nice slap you gave Nelson," Zane said, looking at Thaya, impressed. "Watch your back around him. He's not the forgiving type."

Thaya did not answer. She swung her leg over the back of the bicycle seat and grabbed hold of Perry's waist.

"Where to?" Perry asked, craning his neck behind him.

"Someplace safe," Thaya answered.

"The library," Tim nodded thoughtfully. "I need to go there anyway. I've got some research to do."

Thaya leaned in close and whispered in Perry's ear. "Did you really ditch a whole bag of weed out by the bottle dump?"

"Sure did," he confirmed. "I hid it in the underbrush, just like I said."

"Underbrush?" Thaya asked.

She saw the corner of his mouth raise in a smile. "Yes, it's hidden under a patch of poison ivy."

⚜

The Korning Public Library was no more than a two-minute bike ride away. The pair rode the beat-up Chopper across Main Street and down the block to the building adjacent to the public beach. Above the door, painted in dark green lettering, it read, Korning Free Library.

They chained the Chopper to the bike rack and ascended the stairs. Pushing open the door, the pair were greeted with a serene silence, followed immediately by the musty smell of thousands of books.

"Hello?" came a sweet voice from the counter in front of them. "Can I help... oh, Perry, it's you. Come to do more botanical research?"

"Hello, Mrs. Tomie," Perry said sheepishly. "Yes, something like that."

Francine Tomie was the village librarian. She had lived in town longer than most of the books had been there. A small woman, Mrs. Tomie was known for her keen intellect paired with a waspish disposition.

"Well, you know the way to the encyclopedias," she said, her gaze shifting to Thaya. "Let me know if you need anything."

"Yes ma'am," Perry answered, pulling Thaya along behind him.

They made their way to the back of the library in a section

titled, "The World's Plants and Botanicals." Thaya saw dozens of thick, red bound books that filled two shelves, top to bottom.

"Mrs. Tomie knows everything about this town," Perry said to Thaya. "Especially about its history."

Perry eased himself into a chair and happily began digging into the tomes, his eyes searching for clues to the violet flower he unwrapped from his bandana.

After watching Tim for a minute or two, Thaya wandered away, entering a different section of the building. Something had been nagging at her all day. Something she'd heard but could not place. It was something the hag had hissed at her. Thaya had been so stunned by the events in the Beldam Woods, she was having trouble remembering.

What was it Jaylocke said? She thought to herself. *Something about the Nine, and...*

Try as she might, Thaya could not recall what it was. Irritated, the young woman wandered into the history section. There, on a stand was a book written by a Mable Pipken. In bold letting on the front it read, "Korning, New York, from the Jessup Brothers Until Now, a History."

Thaya turned away and froze in place. Looking back, she read the title again and remembered.

"Tonight, the Nine will come for the first time since the Jessups called forth The Tenth! I will ascend, and the Decem will fall!"

"The Jessups," Thaya muttered, running her fingers over the book's cover. "*That's* what she meant."

Thaya reached forward and opened the book and began thumbing through the pages.

The initial chapters were nothing more than what you might find in any non-fiction book. Factual accounts and quotes from the founding fathers of Korning back in the day. Occasionally these accounts were accompanied by a black-and-white sketch depicting the surrounding lands when Korning was still considered the frontier.

Thaya's eyes narrowed as she gazed upon a section labeled, Legends of Korning. Tentatively, she began to read the excerpt.

Upon landing, the Jessup brothers spoke to the Mohawk natives who lived in the area.

It seems there was a legend of an ancient evil that lived in the woods south of the Hudson River. It was alleged that the Jessups brought in a voodoo woman from across the Atlantic who drove the evil away before they decided to settle in the area. However, this was widely believed to be a common folktale used to embellish the Jessups' right to the land and scare off any other claimants. The Jessups named the afflicted area the Beldam Woods and began their logging operations to the north.

"The Beldam Woods," Thaya whispered to herself. "There was a problem even back then."

"Can I help you, dearie?" came the voice of the librarian, startling Thaya.

"Actually, yes," Thaya answered, turning around, recovering quickly.

Mrs. Tomie gave Thaya a sweet smile. "I see you're reading Mable's book. It's one of my favorites."

"Mrs. Tomie," Thaya began, "what can you tell me about this passage here?" she asked, pointing to what she had been reading. "Is there any truth that an ancient evil lived in the Beldam Woods?"

The librarian looked closely at Thaya, her gray eyes studying the young girl's face.

"You have been there, haven't you?" she questioned, her voice quiet. "Don't deny it girl. I can see it in your eyes."

Thaya blinked at her, taken aback.

The librarian's eyes widened in surprise. "Oh my, you *have* been there," she surmised. "Did you see her? Does the magic still hold? Does she remain within the confines of the tree?"

The old woman paused, her voice going still. "Have the flowers bloomed? Has she fed upon the living?"

Thaya felt the hair on the back of her neck rise. "How do you know about that?" was all she could say.

In answer, Mrs. Tomie pointed to the book. "It is right here," she replied, her finger resting under a single word.

Beldam.

"What does it mean?" Thaya asked, her voice breathless.

"The beldam are powerful creatures, steeped in the magic of the fey," the librarian explained. "The old legends are true. There's one trapped in the woods, not far from here. Most avoid the area, as it is located well off the beaten path."

The librarian stopped speaking and took out old newspaper clippings from a shelf under the book.

"As you can see," she explained, laying the clippings flat on the book, "every now and then, someone gets lost, or grows curious, and is never seen again."

Thaya felt a chill run down her spine. There were a half-dozen articles dating back to the early 1900s. Each spoke of someone going missing in the area.

"My father, he knew about the beldam too," Thaya confessed. "He said not to go near it, to stay someplace safe. He's on his way from Saranac Lake to help."

The librarian's face beamed at Thaya. "He was right. A smart man, your father. I remember him. He was clever, even as a young boy."

Thaya looked back up at Mrs. Tomie. "Can... can I stay here with you until my father arrives?"

"Of course, child, there is no need to..." Her voice trailed off as Perry was making his way toward them.

"I can't find any information about this flower anywhere," he complained. "It's almost like no one has ever seen one before."

"Where did you get that?" the librarian hissed, staring in shock at the blossom.

"It was stuck in Thaya's hair out near Beldam Woods," Perry explained.

"It is violet!" Mrs. Tomie hissed, looking at Thaya, anger in her eyes. "You said the flowers were not in bloom!"

"I... I didn't say anything about the flowers... Is that important?" Thaya asked.

"It changes everything," the librarian snapped, shaking her head. "I would have guessed they were white flowers, only."

"What are you talking about?" Perry asked. "You've seen this plant before?"

Mrs. Tomie took a deep breath before answering. "It is called the *Nox Umbra Arboris*; its name in common speech is the Shadow Thorn Tree."

"I've never heard of it before," Perry said, looking at the blossom in wonder.

"That's because it does not grow here, or should not at any rate," the librarian replied. "It is a plant of the fey realm, lost long ago to this world."

"The fey realm?" Thaya asked, a quiver in her voice. "What is that?"

Mrs. Tomie looked at them both, studying the pair closely. "You are part of this now. I cannot shield you from the truth."

"Part of what?" Perry asked. "What is she talking about?"

"Perry," Thaya began, not wanting to explain to him what happened in the woods, "when you found me, I... I saw a hag, a horrible monster that killed Mr. Larcotte."

"What?" Perry said, his eyes wide with amazement. "Why didn't you say anything?"

The ACES Anthology

Thaya raised her chin defensively. "I didn't think you would believe me. I saw it happen, and *I* hardly believe it. This... beldam murdered him, tore him to pieces right in front of me with nothing more than her bare hands."

"The girl speaks the truth," Mrs. Tomie nodded.

"How can you be so sure?" Perry asked, his voice quiet.

"The evidence is in your hands," the librarian explained. "A violet blossom is the final metamorphosis."

Mrs. Tomie looked back at Thaya. "Was there an opening of some kind at the base of the tree?"

"Yes," Thaya answered. "It grew after... what happened to Mr. Larcotte. The beldam said the call had been issued. The Nine would be coming tonight."

"The Nine?" the librarian said, startled. "Tonight?"

"That is what Jaylocke said," Thaya confirmed.

The librarian's face took on a hardened look. "Then we've no time to waste. We must go back to the Shade Thorn tree as soon as we can."

"But my father said to stay away from the tree," Thaya argued.

"Did he know about the violet blossoms?" Mrs. Tomie questioned.

Thaya shook her head.

"I am sorry, dears, but this must be done. It is too important to wait a moment longer."

"Wait a minute," Perry put in. "You are an eighty-year-old librarian, and we're just a couple of kids. Even if I believed you, which I don't, what are we supposed to do? I can't fight some kind of..." Perry began flailing his hands about in front of him, "magical being. I can't even fold my socks right!"

"Perry has a point," Thaya agreed. "I'm not much of a fighter. We need to call the police, or... the National Guard."

The ACES Anthology

"And tell them what?" Mrs. Tomie asked pointedly. "That some magical creature from the fey realm is about to unleash the nine most powerful beings the Earth has ever known? The authorities will commit us to an insane asylum before we can snap our fingers."

Thaya glanced at Perry knowing the old librarian was speaking the truth.

"Can't we at least wait for my father?" Thaya asked.

Mrs. Tomie shook her head. "Would that we could, child, but he's a good two or three hours away. We must act, and it must be now."

"Why can't we wait...?" Perry began.

"The longer we wait, the longer those shadows under the tree are going to get," Mrs. Tomie chided. "Every inch gets the beldam closer to escape. The shield only extends as far as the edge of the woods. Once the shadows reach the border of the forest, she will no longer be trapped."

Perry looked down at the flower in his hand, wrestling with his courage. "What is it you want us to do?" he asked reluctantly.

"Head over to Beldam Woods," she instructed, patting him on the back. "Get to the clearing, but don't go into it. I know of a containment spell that will last through the night. I will gather the things I need and meet you there."

"You're going to cast a spell?" Thaya asked.

"No, *we* are," Mrs. Tomie replied. "I cannot do it alone. Three is the mystical number for enchantments. I will need you both."

"How do you know all this?" Perry asked, his face now a pale green.

The librarian smiled. "I have waited many years for this day. I knew Jaylocke would eventually try and break free. There are old tomes here underneath the library that speak of the fey realm. I have read them all."

She stopped and looked at them both, matter of fact. "Go. I will meet you there in half an hour. Don't stop. Don't tell anyone what you are doing. The fewer that know the better."

Thaya followed Perry out the door to the Chopper, both lost in their own thoughts. They strapped on their helmets and mounted the bicycle. Perry had a troubled look on his face.

"Are you OK?" Thaya asked him.

"No!" Perry answered, his voice an equal mix of fear and frustration. "I am not OK, Thaya. I am not OK at all. Do I look ok to you? This is madness, it's... it's..."

"It's fucked up," she finished for him.

"Yes, well I wasn't going to put it quite like that," he replied. "I'd would have said... messed up, or fouled up, maybe, 'bent...'"

A smile slithered across Thaya's face. "You never swear, do you?"

"Sure, I do," Perry sniffed. "Just last week when I was putting on the basket here, I said the "B" word.

"Bitch?" she offered.

"Heavens, no!" he said, glancing around.

"Bastard?" she guessed again.

"My god, what is wrong with you?" he said, shooting her a frown.

"What "B" word was it then?"

Perry looked around and lowered his voice. "Baloney," he answered, before pushing off the ground, and pedaling up Main.

"Baloney?" she laughed, shaking her head. "*That* was your big swear word?"

"Yes," he admitted, glancing behind her. "I used it in vain when I was vexed. I'm half-surprised this blessed bicycle didn't electrify me after such blasphemy. I said three Hail Marys and confessed my heathen ways to Pastor Lowenstein. He forgave me."

She gave him a long look. "Don't you sell marijuana for your dad?" she asked.

Perry paused a moment before answering.

"Yes," he admitted.

"That's peddling an illegal narcotic," Thaya pointed out.

"Organic herbal medications do not fall under the umbrella of sin," he explained. "I predict one day the sale of marijuana will be legal *and* medicinal. My conscience is clear on that account."

"That's never gonna happen," Thaya disagreed, rolling her eyes to the heavens.

⚜

They reached the edge of the Beldam Woods a good three hours before dusk. Carefully, they made their way through the trees, pushing the Chopper along with them. Perry refused to leave it behind, saying anyone could just come along and take it. Though it took some extra time, they made it to the clearing twenty minutes later. Thaya peered out at the field while a shudder of fear ran through her.

"That's the tree?" Perry asked, staring out at the huge growth standing in the middle of the field.

"Yes," Thaya answered, peering at it closely. The sun was off to their right, casting the tree's shadow to the east. She did not see any movement, nor was there any trace of Mr. Larcotte's murder. The field looked as serene now as it had when Thaya had first ventured here.

"I hope she gets here soon," Perry muttered, casting his gaze back toward the woods they had traversed.

"Listen," Thaya whispered, cocking an ear behind them. "I think she's coming."

There was a rustling in the underbrush behind them, and she

made to greet the librarian. Thaya's heart stopped when she saw who it was.

"You little fuck!" Aaron hissed, switchblade in hand. "You think it's funny hiding our weed in a patch of poison ivy?"

Flanking him were Demerson and Rickard, both with blisters and red sores all over their arms and neck. Aaron was the worst off. He was scratching at the sides of his face, where a rash had broken out, causing his cheeks to swell in irritation.

"Answer me, you shithead!" Aaron continued, spitting off to the side.

"I... I didn't know," Perry argued weakly.

"You knew *exactly* what you were doing, plant nerd," Aaron snarled holding the knife out in front of him.

"No! I... I..."

Aaron pushed a button on his knife and the blade snapped into place. "No one does this shit to me. I'm going to carve my name on your skull."

Thaya could see this was no empty threat. There was murder in Aaron's eyes.

Perry looked at Thaya, who did the only thing she could think of.

"Run!" she barked, grabbing Perry's hand and sprinting toward the tree.

"Get them!" she heard Aaron howl from behind.

Thaya had been running for most of her life. Alone, she knew she could outdistance the pack of bullies behind her. Perry, however, was much slower. She had to drag him behind her, forcing him to move as fast as he could. She chanced a look back and saw Aaron was close, only a few paces behind. The others in his group were staggering along, Demerson lagging farthest behind.

"Almost there," Thaya shouted, seeing the shadow of the tree a few yards in front of them.

"I thought we needed to avoid the shadow!" Perry shouted in a panic.

"Did you want to take your chances with the maniac chasing us?" she howled back.

Perry did not answer. Thaya led them to the edge of the tree's shadow, and plunged under it, turning immediately to the east, racing along the shadow's edge.

Aaron was close now, near enough that Thaya could hear his breathing behind them. Perry, his stamina fading, slowed enough to where Aaron reached out and grabbed the collar of his shirt.

"No!" Perry cried, falling in a heap to the ground, Aaron brandishing the switchblade over his head.

"Get off him!" Thaya screamed. She pivoted and kicked out with her foot. Her toe snapped sharply, catching the unsuspecting Aaron under the chin. Stunned by the blow, his knife went flying out of his hand to fall in the grass at the edge of the sunlight. Richard, who was only a few steps behind, launched himself at Thaya, who spun to the side just enough that he tumbled past her.

"Demerson!" shouted Aaron, reeling from the kick. "Where the fuck are you?"

"Perry, come on!" screamed Thaya, who was staring at a smoldering pair of blood-red eyes glaring at them from the trunk of the tree.

"I can't," the lanky boy blubbered, unable to catch his breath.

At that moment, a bloodcurdling scream erupted from the empty space at the trunk of the tree.

"What the fuck was that?" said Demerson, screeching to a halt in the light of the sun.

"Run!" screamed Thaya, grabbing hold of Perry, forcing him to his feet.

Shooting from the darkness came Jaylocke, hell-bent on slaking her thirst for blood.

"Nelson, get out of there!" Thaya warned, half dragging Perry behind her.

"That's *not* my fucking name!" Aaron snarled, unaware of the danger.

"Look out!" Rickard managed to yell right as Jaylocke's claws tore through Aaron's chest, ripping him apart.

"Rickard, come on!" Demerson gasped, stepping away from the shadow.

"Help me!" Rickard pleaded, racing toward his friend.

"This way!" Thaya bellowed, beckoning for the boy to run toward them.

Ignoring her, Rickard raced toward Demerson and leapt forward into the light.

"Made it." Rickard breathed a sigh of relief.

"Rickard, your leg!" Thaya warned, seeing his left foot was still in the shadow.

Rickard glanced down just as a taloned hand grabbed onto his ankle. He clamped his arms onto Demerson and screamed in abject terror.

"Pull, you fat fuck!" Rickard bellowed, his face twisted in horror.

"Get off me!" Demerson howled, unsuccessfully trying to wrest himself loose. Both were dragged into the darkness.

"Noooo!" Demerson managed to scream, before his voice went silent forever.

Thaya and Perry stood there panting, trying to comprehend what they had just witnessed.

"I... I did not believe you," Perry said, staring at the beldam. "I am so sorry..."

"I told you to wait," came a voice from behind them.

Thaya turned to see Francine Tomie standing behind them, her face in shock.

"We waited for you," Thaya said, "but those assholes came after us with a knife."

"I see," the librarian stated, looking curiously at the beldam. "Look at the way she feeds," the librarian observed, watching Jaylocke devour her prey. "She hasn't lost any of her appetites."

Thaya's blood ran cold. Looking close, she observed the old woman, seeing her with fresh eyes.

"You aren't here to stop her," Thaya accused. "You are in league with her!"

Mrs. Tomie smiled wickedly at Thaya. "Clever child, just like your father."

The old woman walked boldly into the shadows and bowed before the creature in front of her.

"Welcome, *Nota*," Jaylocke said in greeting.

"Mistress," Mrs. Tomie acknowledged with a bow.

"But, what about the spell of containment?" Perry asked, rising to his feet. "Surely you will..."

"I will not," the librarian cut him off. "Even if I wanted to, no spell of mind could hold my mistress for long. She has feasted on three of the most unholy humans I've ever seen. I was going to give the two of you to her, but now, I will feed you to our queen instead."

"*Nota?*" Perry said, recognizing the word. "You are her familiar?"

"Ahh, very good," the librarian congratulated him. "Nice to see some of those Latin words you study have been remembered."

Mrs. Tomie pointed a finger at them both. "Now, enough talk. Come here. It will be much easier if you don't resist."

"The fuck we will," Thaya snarled, grabbing Perry's hand.

"Ahh, well, you had your chance," the librarian said, raising her hand in front of her.

"*Empediendum*," she hissed.

Thaya's feet began to float off the ground.

"You are not going anywhere," Mrs. Tomie cackled.

Thaya was stuck in the air. She tried moving, but all she accomplished was running in place three feet off the ground.

"Let go of me!" Thaya shouted in frustration.

"No, your blood will restore my queen to her glory once..."

"*Corrumpebant!*"

A new voice cut through the air. Thaya and Perry came crashing to the ground.

"It cannot be," Mrs. Tomie shouted, her eyes wide in disbelief.

"It is," came the voice of Thaya's father.

The librarian let out a scream of terror before she changed into a black cat, hissing in fury. A moment later, the explosion of a shotgun echoed throughout the field. Where there had been a cat moments before, was now a small red stain, with tufts of black fur sticking to the grass.

"Dad!" Thaya shouted, running over, embracing her father.

"I'm sorry it took so long," he said, his eyes never leaving Jaylocke.

"Dad, I don't think she can be stopped."

Glancing down at his daughter, Michael Joseph smiled. "I brought some help," he said.

Walking out of the wood behind him was the withered form of Ms. Ida, the checkout clerk from aisle four.

"I'll take it from here," the wrinkled woman said.

Thaya blinked her eyes as the air around Ms. Ida shimmered. One moment she was the wizened old clerk, the next, she had transformed into a young, beautiful woman with skin the color of cinnamon.

The ACES Anthology

"You are the voodoo woman the Jessups hired," Thaya guessed.

The Witch of the Adirondacks gave her a nod. "I am Adaline, the Tenth," she agreed. "Now stand back child. Jaylocke has feasted. Her power is restored by the unholy blood of the fallen."

"Both of you, go," her father stated, recocking his shotgun.

Jaylocke lowered her staff and cast a spell of red fire.

Adaline countered it with a wall of white magic the fire could not pierce.

"She is strong," Adaline whispered, her brow already slick with sweat. "The Nine are coming."

"I will do what I can," Michael shouted, running forward.

"No," Adaline shouted. "The portal cannot be closed with force."

She dropped her eyes and looked at Perry. "Only a holy object can counter the beldam's magic. Something blessed by a holy man."

Perry blanched and glanced at the edge of the clearing. There, gleaming in the sunlight, was the Chopper, magnificent in its rusted chrome.

"I'm on it," he grunted, racing toward the bicycle.

"Go with him," Thaya's father ordered, firing off a shot. "We will keep Jaylocke busy."

"D...dad," Thaya stammered. "I love you."

Michael smiled. "I know, pumpkin. Now go, help your friend."

Thaya nodded and bolted toward the forest, easily catching up to Perry.

"What's the plan?" she hissed, running alongside him.

"I'll pedal like mad and ram the portal." He shrugged. "Simple plans are often the best."

"I like it!" Thaya, agreed, smirking at him madly.

They drew alongside the Chopper, and Perry snapped on his helmet.

"Safety first!" he said with a nervous grin.

Moments later, he was on the Chopper, pedaling for all he was worth. Thaya had grabbed a hold of the back seat and was pushing the bike from behind.

"Jump clear once you get it up to speed," she warned, grunting with effort.

"Don't worry, I'm no hero," Perry yelled over his shoulder.

Faster and faster they went, until Thaya could no longer keep up. As Perry pulled away from her, he entered the shadow. Thaya looked over to see her father blasting away with his shotgun, standing in front of the still form of Adaline. The witch was down, senseless or dead. Jaylocke was at the edge of the shadow, casting bolts of red fire at Adaline's staunch defender. One of the bolts hit Thaya's father a glancing blow to the chest, and she saw him stumble to the ground.

"No!" Thaya yelled, trying to distract the beldam.

Jaylocke turned and glanced over at Thaya. Her eyes widened as she saw that Perry was only a few feet from the trunk of the tree.

The beldam let out a cry of rage and tore after the Chopper.

"Bail, you crazy son-of-a-bitch!" Thaya thundered, willing Perry to jump clear.

A moment before the Chopper hit the opening, Perry leapt from the banana seat and rolled into the sunlight. The blessed bicycle smashed into the portal's opening a split second before Jaylocke could intercept it. A resounding explosion shook the entire field as the holy and unholy forces neutralized one another. The tree, huge and magnificent moments before, split down the middle with a resounding crack, destroying the portal. A high-pitched scream of rage and frustration echoed throughout the field as the gateway to the fey realm imploded upon itself.

Jaylocke, her victory denied, let out a deafening cry of her own. Defeated, she turned her gaze to Thaya, vengeance foremost in her mind.

Thaya glanced over to her father, who was still down. She saw Adaline's eyes flicker open. The witch's finger moved, pointing at something next to Thaya. The fifteen-year-old girl saw what Adaline was pointing at.

Nelson's switchblade knife.

At that moment, with crystalline clarity, she heard Ms. Ida's words from the Grand echo in her mind.

"Probably my ninety-seven-year-old witch of a mother... Only way the old bat will pass on is if her heart falls out!"

Sweeping up the knife, Thaya charged the beldam. The fey creature pointed her staff at Thaya and blasted a bolt at her.

Expecting the attack, Thaya dodged one, then a second shot before leaping straight ahead, bowling the beldam over. Using the knife, Thaya cut open the creature's chest in one swift stroke. Dropping the switchblade, she reached in and ripped out the beldam's heart.

Jaylocke threw back her head and let out a cry of agony. The fey creature fell to the ground convulsing in its death throes. Finally, she came to rest, her body twisted and still.

Thaya stood over the corpse of the monster, blood trickling down the side of her head. One by one, Adaline, her father, and Perry walked over and stood by her side, staring down at the creature of the fey.

"That was some crazy, fucking shit," Perry said at last.

The ACES Anthology

"The Shadow's Edge" is ©2023 by Michael K. Falciani. It appears here for the first time. The Carson City resident is the author of the ongoing fantasy series, "The Raven and the Crow." His novels "The Dwarves of Rahn" and "The Raven and the Crow: The Gray Throne," won Imadjinn Awards for best steampunk novel and best fantasy novel, respectively, at the 2023 Imaginarium Convention. His books are available on Amazon.

L.F. Falconer

Slipping Through the Devil's Gate

I have partaken of the opium before, so paid no heed to Wallace's warning to keep clear of the China camp. He claims that the dead walks among them—a pale, soul-eating ghoul. In his frenzy to paint the Orientals as yellow demons, my brother seems inclined toward metaphors far wilder than those of my own making. My experiences with the Chinese run quite the contrary, for during my short sojourn in San Francisco, I often found the denizens of the opium parlors to be particularly blithesome, most willing to aid me in the perpetuation of my own demise.

A native son of California, I'd begun to make a name for myself writing for the *Herald* in San Francisco after the rush for gold hit its stride, until I squandered my worth romancing Lady Opium. In his hopes to rehabilitate me, my brother, Wallace, lured me away from the coast with an enticing offer of $25 a week to write for the *Territorial Enterprise* in the Nevada Territory city of Virginia. *"Vincit qui se vincit,"* he said. "He conquers who conquers himself." Convinced my brother had my best interests at heart, despite some of his previous behaviors, I headed east.

When I crossed over the Sierra Nevada Mountains, before me stretched a most ungodly blight of land, desolate, untamed, and so forbidding my horse could no longer abide to live. If ever a man were to seek heaven, the Nevada Territory would not be the place to do it. Even as I tracked by foot the final leg of my journey up Gold Canyon and passed though the pillars of the Devil's Gate into a booming town being built upon silver, I knew surely I was treading onto unhallowed ground.

I temporarily settled into the Comstock Hotel, and soon thereafter, my fate was sealed. In the office of the *Territorial Enterprise*, our coffee is served by a young man of Chinese descent. Born in America, this son of a railroad worker speaks fair English, is polite, and efficient with his service. Folks are bound in indifference concerning these foreigners, often dubbing them Joe, or Mary, or Sue. Our coffee server was known simply as Tom.

As we gathered in the newspaper office, I had just lit up my morning cigar. Wallace stood before the printing press, heartily regaling us all with his winning maneuvers at the Faro table in John Piper's Saloon the previous evening when Tom inadvertently sloshed coffee over the brim of my cup while filling it.

"Many apologies, Mistah O'Shea," he mumbled, hurriedly pulling a handkerchief from his pocket to wipe the spill.

The small clink of glass tumbling against the floor plank caught my attention. Tom swiftly bent to retrieve the tiny vial, stowing it back into his pocket, but when his eyes met mine, the secret was shared between us. The yearning for an old euphoria swept over me like Noah's flood. I lost all interest in Wallace's boasts, dreaming instead of my own ethereal pleasance.

When Tom left the office, I stubbed out my cigar and stowed its remains in my inner jacket pocket, silently donned my bowler, and followed him out.

"Boy," I called, once outside. But, with his single long braid swinging like a pendulum across his back, Tom scurried off the boardwalk, hurrying into a street still muddy from a drenching rain, which had accompanied last night's thunder.

"Tom," I shouted. "Stop!"

He came to a halt, albeit a hesitant one, and turned slowly to face me. Our gaze, yet again, shared a secret. I waved him over.

"Tell me your name," I said as he approached.

"Tom."

"No. Tell me your true name. The name you were given at birth."

Nearly as an apology, he answered, "Li Wang."

I pulled a silver dollar from my pocket. "It is a fine name. I will give you this dollar, Li Wang, if you will guide me to the opium parlor."

His eyes lit up, but a dark reluctance shadowed his interest.

I pulled another dollar from my pocket. "Please."

After another moment of thought, he agreed. "Follow me." He turned to hurry back across the street, taking me on a long, downhill trek all the way to "E" Street and beyond. Far from the respectable business district and the homes of Caucasian inhabitants up the hill—one rung lower than the prostitutes' shanties, Chinatown met us, the dusty air laced with sharp spice and fermentation.

Li Wang's black-slippered feet were keen as he led me through the cluster of shacks and canvas, coming to a full stop near the bottommost edge of town. Before us stood a ramshackle domicile, the sickly-sweet odor of joss sticks creeping through the cedar logs.

"The House of the Dead, Mistah O'Shea."

"Thank you." I patted the young man on the back and gave him his reward. "You're a good man, Li Wang."

His eyes did not reflect my own pleasure. "Perhaps not," he mumbled before taking my silver and darting away, vanishing amid the crowded encampment.

Now that I knew where to go, I needed his guidance no more. I turned to depart as well, though found my feet lagging. It was early in the day—I was meant to be at work. I had a deadline to meet. That being said, since I was already here, perhaps it wouldn't hurt to become acquainted with the proprietor. Perhaps test the quality of his offerings. One quick taste. Then back to work. In this wild frontier, news came easily. Wallace would hardly know I was gone.

It is said that in Virginia City, every man has a right to go to hell in his own way. Yet one man's vision of hell is another man's view of heaven. I sought heaven. Even in hell. No liquor, no diluted laudanum for me. A flight once taken, that sweet ethereal opium ascent could never be rivaled. Or forgotten. Or denied.

The House of the Dead, Li Wang had called it. Or, in another man's view, mine for instance, a portal to the divine.

I turned the door knob and stepped inside.

The parlor I frequented in San Francisco had been opulent, with silk brocade draperies and velvet sofas, gilded chandeliers, and a hint of jasmine mingling with the incense and vapors, providing an ambience of mystery and delight. A quiet little flower, or concubine if you will, would accompany me in my ceremonies, for a moist warm mouth upon me thoroughly enhanced the seraphic splendor as I dreamily romanced Lady Opium.

Conversely, the House of the Dead was bereft of all luxury. A single candle lamp provided a dim and ghastly light. No little flowers graced the parlor. The ancient proprietor was long and reedy with a dangling moustache and beard of exaggerated length. The old man led me through a thin calico curtain into a candlelit room festooned with threadbare cushions besmirched with sweat and sundry stains. The air reeked of the heavy incense snaking from numerous joss sticks.

I was left in the care of a silent, graying woman who held charge of the lamp apparatus. Gently, she prepared a bit of opium as I removed my jacket and bowler, laying them aside before settling into the filthy cushions. I loosened my tie and the top two buttons of my shirt at the collar. Across the dim room I spied a small, aged Chinese gentleman reposed in the sweet grip of the heavenly vapors, his eyes half-closed against the light of reality. I envied his languor, impatiently awaiting my own.

The lamp tender's fingers were deft and practiced. With the opium nestled inside a white ceramic bowl delicately marked in blue flowers, the lamp tender held the ivory pipe stem expertly above the oil lamp's flame, turning it precisely so, until the coveted contents within the bowl heated to its ideal state. I received the pipe from the old woman's gnarled hand, breathing in the warm vapors before reclining into the red and gold cushions, anticipating with eagerness the approach of my tranquility. Again, I brought the pipe to my lips and soon my body slowly melted into the cushions below—my mind rising up... up... up....

Romancing Lady Opium is a selfish act, one that cannot truly be shared with another, one greedily kept in the vault of one's own soul. It is a hungry act, one never to be fully sated, no matter how often one tries. Lady Opium is a relentless mistress. She teases with paradisiacal bliss, only to strip it away, leaving you begging for more. I am her willing thrall; loving her, adoring her, needing her for every morsel of celestial serenity she allows. Only in her embrace do I truly feel alive.

This is as close to heaven as a man can get and still be bound to the earth. There are no threats. No worries. No fears. Simply a timeless tranquility. Dreams within dreams within dreams.

A fleeting flight through the cosmos, the bliss is always temporary, and fades swiftly back to an earthbound existence. Lady Opium retreats into the shadows of Eden, leaving me wanting in an insatiable need.

I open my sleep-sticky eyes in the darkened parlor. Across the room, where before an older gentleman had lain, now nestle two others, a man and a woman, both Caucasian, each one giving much more love to Lady Opium than they do to one another.

Forcing myself to sit upright, I nearly gag on the incense-laden air that congests the small room. While adjusting my tie, the flickering candles on the wall catch my eye. A blue damask curtain is pulled back from a door near the rear of the parlor. The lamp tender steps through it, yet a glimpse of the room behind her reveals three men, sitting upright on a narrow bench. Three dead men, their cheeks sunken, eyes wide-open, jaws slack. They are sallow and emaciated and naked.

I rub my eyes as the damask curtain closes, shielding the men from view. I surmise them to be unfortunates who have completely surrendered themselves to subsist upon vapors alone. They are not truly dead. Not yet anyway.

A chilled shudder creeps down my spine as I rise to reclaim my jacket and hat. The proprietor has proven his wares with ease, and I nearly wish it hadn't been so. Wallace could be justified in warning me away from this place. Yet he has never partaken, so cannot fathom the seductive power the lady possesses. Am I strong enough to abstain? Perhaps. Perhaps.

Stumbling my way to the outer door, I bid the proprietor a good day. I shall not return here in the daylight again, but keep my visits nocturnal, therefore ensuring Wallace not lose faith in me. Like our father before him, Wallace keeps in his employ men to help him achieve certain ends, and he has warned me against disobedience. I have no wish to endure another beating or any broken fingers.

Outside, the sweltering sunshine announces it is midday already, all vestiges of last night's rainstorm a mere memory, though clouds gathering distant bespeak a warning of more to come. I spent hours in the opium parlor, lost in my celestial voyage. Bringing my hat down to shield against the temple-pulsing brightness of the sun, I make my way up the hillside, heading for the Comstock Hotel. I need to cleanse myself of any telltale residue, to abolish the sticky reek of incense from my clothing before I dare greet my brother again. But my effort proves to be in vain. Wallace departs the hotel as I approach.

"Robert," he says. "Where have you been all day?" His eyes convey the dreadful knowledge he fails to utter.

I take a short step back, pulling the remnants of this morning's cigar from my inner jacket pocket. "I was investigating a possible story," I tell him, striking a match, puffing the cigar smoke downward so it might cling to my clothing, to obscure the scent of incense.

He cocks his eyebrow and heads down the boardwalk. "Without consulting me first? The only stories worth writing are those worth printing, and none of them involve the Chinese."

I walk slightly behind, trying to keep some distance between us. "If you cannot trust me to judge what is newsworthy and what is not, then why did you hire me?"

He turns and grabs my arm. "Stay out of the China camp, Robert, or it will eat you alive. There's plenty of tomfoolery and swindlers in the upper levels of this god-forsaken town. There's no need to worry about the Chinese. If you know what's good for you, you'll leave them to their own."

From what I observed today, there is a story to be told, but not one that Wallace, or the general populace of this town, would give a damn about. They would prefer to blame opium addiction on a mythical Chinese ghoul.

We reach the intersection, and Wallace rounds the corner to head up the hill toward "A" Street. "Join me tonight at Piper's after supper."

It's not a request. He wants to keep an eye on me.

Our monsters only truly live inside us. We feed them and give them life and strength. We starve them and hear them howl, demanding our attention. John Piper's Saloon provides acceptable, comfortable demons. Wallace's demons. The ones he would prefer I entertain.

"I will see you after supper," I assure him.

"Good." He smiles broadly. "Now go write me a story I can print. One that'll spice up our readers' morning eggs."

After we part ways, a dispute between some Confederate and Union sympathizers produces a free-wheeling brawl in a saloon near The Comstock Hotel. I have little problem finding Wallace a story. Two persons are shot, neither fatally. To please Wallace, I exaggerate the amount of bloodshed and mayhem to add the necessary scintillation to our readers' breakfasts.

I do not take any supper—I have no appetite for food, so at the appropriate hour I walk down to Piper's on "D" Street to join my brother. The bottle of beer I sip while Wallace gets lost in whiskey and Faro is intolerable to my palate, the piano songs grating like a rasp against my sensitivities. To Wallace, my presence is barely noticed. However, there are two men I've seen previously in his company who appear to be taking an unseemly interest in my movements. I make acquaintance with a hurdy gurdy girl to ensure a sense of propriety to my early departure and together, under scrutiny, we disappear to a shanty behind the saloon for a little horizontal refreshment. She's a delight, and I might have asked her to join me further in this subsequent insalubrious journey toward the China camp, but can't be certain she could be trusted to such secrecy if pressed. I wish her to come to no harm.

The wind freshens, and my pocket watch indicates the approach of midnight, my footsteps irresistibly drawn toward the House of the Dead. The night is dark and thunderous, besieged with shadows and gloom. When the opium parlor's dim, amber windows come into view, a silent pall veils the neighborhood. No longer can I hear the distant piano of the saloon, rustlings of feet scuffling across the hardpan street, or tin rattling in the wind. It's as if a shroud has enwrapped the place—becalmed within the eye of the storm.

To my left, a distant whistle, like a long and lonely howl causes my steps to slow. From the rear of the cedar shack whispers a scraping, gravelly grind of what must surely be a garbage-scrapping dog gnawing on a bone. I turn and peer into the dark. A flash of lightning brightens the night. My skin prickles and I petrify at a vision that sucks the breath from my chest, a sight caught only for the briefest of moments. Near the rear of the house stands a woman, her white hair blowing freely in the wind, her pale nightdress clinging to thin and bony legs. Her skin is ashen, powdery, brindled; her lean arms long, fingers like claws. It is not the lamp tender, for this woman is taller, wilder, and appears more dead than the corpse she drags behind her. Bits of gore cling to her cheeks and chin as she gnaws with jagged teeth upon an arm ripped from the body in her possession. Carmine eyes linger after the lightning is swallowed by darkness, then blink out into the black. Immediately, another bolt of lightning shatters the night. The wraith and her prize have vanished from sight.

I flee into the shelter of the House of the Dead.

Soon, I find myself adrift under the silent ministrations of the lamp tender. Despite my fears mellowing beneath the vapors, my gaze refuses to stray from the damask curtain at the rear of the parlor. In this late hour the house is well populated, the lamp tender kept occupied. Though swimming in a calm sea, my curiosity wishes to be happily satisfied, and when the old woman leaves my side, I stumble-crawl from my cushions in the corner toward the rear of the room. Clutching the wall beside the blue curtain, I pull the veil back, the weave of the damask like velvet upon my palm. Two dead men seated upon the bench bring me no sense of horror, yet my assumption of the fate of the one no longer there does. The pupils of the furthest man shift to look straight at me, a palpable fear screaming words he cannot speak, and I stagger back a step.

A gentle hand pulls the curtain from my grip and draws the veil closed once more. I look down upon the lamp tender at my side, her countenance plaintive, yet stern. As if I am a disobedient child, she leads me in silence back to my corner, and helps me settle upon the cushions before offering me the pipe. And though two dead men rise up with me into the ether of my mind, we soon part company, for Lady Opium can only appreciate individual regard. And I fully appease her demands in her den of iniquity.

Continuing to breathe the breath of God, I slip into Eden, alone.

The sun has not yet broken over the hillsides when I stumble home to the hotel. I could use a warm bath, but this morning there is no time. A change of clothes and a harried shave will have to suffice.

Li Wang does not bring us coffee this morning, a younger boy taking his place, a boy who does not speak English as well as Li Wang, and I ponder the abrupt change.

Wallace provides an answer to the question I did not ask. "Tom proved he couldn't be trusted, so I traded him in for Joe."

Why do I not believe he's telling me the truth? Is it the slight glint in his eye? The minuscule downturn in the left corner of his lip? The presumptuous tug on his jacket lapels as he speaks? I long to tell him about last night—that I saw the ghoul he warned me of. Yet to do so would betray my whereabouts of the evening, and he would know I hadn't spent the entire night in the company of a prostitute.

My brother's steely glint sharpens as he continues to speak. "If you really want to write about the Chinese, Robert, go talk to Marshal Newman. Seems one of the devils was hanged last night on a telegraph pole. There's the story you've been itching for. Write it and be done with them."

This command is underscored with broad and threatening strokes, and an unknown urgency drives my footsteps down the block.

Marshal Newman appears a pleasant fellow with a gruff beard and moustache, his unruly waves of bourbon-colored hair liberally laced with silver. He looks a bit dandy, clad in a black silk tie and a black waistcoat bulging at its buttons beneath his jacket. The tin star pinned to his lapel is tarnished around the edges.

"I understand someone lynched a Chinese last night," I begin, taking a seat in the marshal's office.

"I don't think it was a lynching," he tells me, brushing his fingers over his moustache. "Boy was likely dead before he was strung up."

"What makes you think that?"

"There was no noose, O'Shea. The boy was tied on the post by the braid in his hair, wrapped around a railroad spike about four feet off the ground. Poor bastard dangled like a discarded rag doll. No, it wasn't a hanging. Tying him to a telegraph pole like that, seems to me it was more like someone trying to send someone else a message." He winks his left eye.

I go bone cold, as if a San Francisco fog has rolled in and wrapped me up inside it. "Did you identify him?"

"Could be anybody. It's hard to tell one from another. He's over at the undertaker's, waiting for someone to possibly claim him."

"Do you know how he died?"

"From the pitch of his head when we took him down, I reckon it was a broken neck."

The squeeze begins in my stomach working up to my throat, my knees reluctant to support my weight as I rise. "Thank you for your time, Marshal." Sweat sops my forehead as I head for the undertaker's office on the street below.

The short walk seems an eternity. As I stare down at Li Wang in mortem, a drowning sea of remorse floods in. Like a surge of lightning, Wallace's message jolts through. But I never dreamed he'd resort to murder. And how much does the marshal truly know?

"His name is Li Wang," I tell the undertaker once my voice comes back under my command. "He may or may not have been a good man." It's the only epitaph I can offer. I barely knew the lad.

There is a story to be told here. The question is, which story do I tell—the one Wallace will print, or the one that exposes the truth?

Vincit qui se vincit. I may not be a conqueror, but I shall never again become my brother's toady. The time has come to break my chains.

Retreating to my hotel room, I begin to set pen to paper. By late afternoon, two letters are written. One to Wallace, tendering my resignation, complete with every detailed reason why. The other is addressed to James Nye, the Nevada Territorial Governor. Whether either letter will have been worth the effort, I shall never know, for by the time they reach their destinations, I shall be well on my way to another. I choose not to die on this side of the Devil's Gate. I am reluctant to head eastward toward the war. Perhaps I will head north to the Oregon country. Wherever I go, it is my hope that Wallace never finds me, for I sincerely doubt his complicity in the death of Li Wang will ever be pursued. The young man was, after all, merely Chinese.

Though I hadn't performed the deed myself, my own burden of guilt is haunting enough, for it was I who bribed him to lead me back into the grasp of the demon of my choice. For a mere two dollars, I had sold out his life as well as my own.

I post the letters before I proceed back down to the China camp. Armed only with a name, I seek out Li Wang's family. Twilight darkens the world as I try to convey to his father and mother his fate. Unsure if they understand, I draw them a map directing the way to the undertaker. I pray they find their son before it's too late. The boy's remains don't belong in a potter's field, unmarked and alone.

In my retreat, I have no intention of visiting the House of the Dead. I have every intention of returning to the hotel in order to catch the morning stage. Yet my feet lead me here as if of their own accord. Perhaps a farewell to my lady is in order. This scandalous love affair needs to end.

There lingers an eerie silence inside the house tonight. The proprietor's eyes reflect a secret, as if he's borne witness to an unspeakable tragedy, but any second thoughts this might arouse are quelled by the eager anticipation of the courtship of my lady.

"*Baíjiu*," the proprietor quietly speaks to the silent lamp tender. She nods and wordlessly leads me into the parlor. Tonight, it is empty, save for me. A private place to bid my adieu. It is fitting.

I relax upon the cushions and soon receive the pipe, which swiftly ushers me into a hazy, amber dream unlike any other. When the corporeal melds with the ethereal, I am joined by a vision as my mind expands and in this most divine journey, I touch the hand of a goddess. My skin shivers in burgeoning nakedness as she strips me of my clothes. Whispering in my ear, the damnable seductress begs me not to desert her, promising me eternal bliss if I but surrender.

Could I float upon this tide forever? No worries. No fear. No pain. No Wallace. To dream forever enraptured by the wavering amber light in the embrace of Lady Opium. Such a bliss I cannot refuse.

"Yes," I whisper. "Take me away."

She climbs bestride me. Her lips lay upon my own. The stench of death—not a new death or one gone to dust—but a death fetid and ripe, erases the ever-present reek of the incense. With bitter bile rising in my gorge, wakefulness rushes up from my legs, surges through my chest, my arms, my cheeks. My eyes shoot open, my heart pounding in a warm and wicked flush, my toes twitching, unfettered by the shroud of boots.

My lady. The lady. A wraith. A ghoul.

Beguiling me is the woman with hair of white and eyes of flame, skin ashen, mottled in blues and black, flaking and peeling like loose shingles. Her thin pale nightdress clings to her bones.

Captured within my lethargic dream, I clutch at the pillows beneath me, squirming to be free. Her rancid breath sets fire to my lips, my throat, my eyes. Through my tears I spy the lamp tender lurking near the calico curtain at the parlor door and I reach out to her in a silent plea. She makes no move, merely observing. Not as a voyeur, but a watchman.

I struggle to rise, held thoroughly captive by the strength of the ghoul upon me and the buoyant cloud of exquisite joy I am spooled within. Her touch is ice, her thirst without lust, relentlessly keeping her mouth pressed against mine, breathing, sucking the bile from my throat, milking the air from my lungs, sluicing the wretched spirit from my soul. A burn sizzles deep within my bowels, rising up, up, and out. In silence, a cold and empty void settles within and I dwindle, withering into a bleak and wintery desolation.

Wallace was wrong. This is no soul-sucking ghoul, for my soul she leaves to me. Only my soul, to linger in a paralyzed wasteland within a body I no longer control, kept alive merely by the blood which still trickles through my veins.

My life—that which makes living alive—is gone. It now belongs to her. He conquers who conquers himself. That is, unless he romances Lady Opium. Then it is she who conquers. It shall always be she. And I gave her my everything.

Physical sensation has vanished. Only my mind perceives.

The ghoul removes her mouth from mine and dismounts.

I cannot move. There is no pain. Yet there is fear. Dreadful, dreadful fear.

In the wavering, amber light, the ghoul jerks back with a haunting howl and disappears behind the blue damask curtain.

How long I lie on these foul, stained cushions in this insensate and unhappy state, I cannot know.

When the lamp tender and proprietor come, I am helpless against them. They lift and carry me, naked and lifeless, through the blue curtain and sit me upright upon a narrow bench beside two dead men. No, not truly dead. Not yet anyway.

My eyes still see. And I see only terror. I see above me, on the ceiling in the corner, clinging like a cellar spider in wait, the lady. The ghoul. And too soon, she will hunger for my flesh.

<hr>

"Slipping Through the Devil's Gate" is ©2021 by L.F. Falconer. It was originally published in 2021 in the author's short story collection "Beyond the Veil: 13 Tales on the Dark Side." The Nevada-born author currently resides in Fallon. She has published nine novels and two short story collections, available in the ACES bookshop at acesofnorthernnevada.com. In her spare time, Falconer enjoys exploring the roads less traveled and visiting ghost towns and old mining camps. She often collects interesting stones and, not necessarily by choice, dust. You can follow her at www.amazon.com/author/lffalconer.

Tammy L. Grace
Murder on the Desert Express

June 1965

Tilly smoothed her skirt as she slid into her seat aboard the bus. She was the first to board, having arrived early so as not to chance missing the departure. This was her first trip by bus. Her first trip alone since Bert died last year. She deposited her giant tote bag on the seat next to her and hoped she wouldn't have a seatmate for her trip to Salt Lake City. She waved a brochure from the bus depot in front of her in a futile attempt to move the hot summer air.

She looked inside her bag and saw the sandwiches she had made still snug in their waxed paper wrapping. She spied the container of cookies and brownies she had baked and her apple and banana. Her thermos of water was heavy but necessary. It was a long ride from Reno, where Tilly had been dropped at the bus depot. The bus didn't service her small hometown. Her daughter had warned her that the bus stopped several times, but there was no guarantee food would be available at those stops.

After finishing the inventory of her bag, Tilly nodded. She had a few gifts for her grandchildren wedged into the space and a tin full of butterscotch candies. She rummaged on the side of the bag and pulled out a book while she waited for the driver to finish loading the luggage. A young man in uniform stepped onto the bus, and her shoulders relaxed. She always felt better with a military man in the crowd. Her Bert had been in the U.S. Navy and had been such a gentleman.

The young man passed her by with a polite nod and found a seat a few rows behind her. Next to board was a young woman with a little boy. The woman held his hand in a tight grip while she surveyed the available seats. She selected the pair across from Tilly and gave her a hurried smile as she ushered the boy into the seat by the window. He said, "You can have the window, Mommy."

The woman shook her head and smiled. "No, Charlie, this way you can watch everything. It will be more fun."

Tilly was watching the youngster and took her eye off the doorway. She was surprised when a man in the aisle disrupted her view. He was unshaven and wearing tattered clothes. She couldn't resist the instinct to bring her hand to her nose to block the odor that trailed him. She scrutinized him as he passed by and took the last seat on the bus.

The next fourteen hours were going to be longer than she thought. She took to using her book to fan herself. A group of passengers came aboard, and she noticed a middle-aged couple sit in front of her and a lone young woman wearing a bright pink sundress continue down the aisle.

A man followed by two young women stepped into the bus. Tilly saw the dark-haired man look at her tote bag, and she shut her eyes in a silent prayer that he would keep going. When she opened her eyes, he was gone and the two young women, who were dressed in matching plaid dresses, took their seats in front of the mother and young boy.

Tilly checked her watch and saw it was only five minutes before the scheduled departure time. A grim-looking man and a woman wearing a fancy hat were the last to board and slipped into the two seats behind Tilly.

The bus driver introduced himself as David and reminded the passengers they were on a bus to Salt Lake and explained they would be making three stops during the journey. He gave a quick smile and slid into his seat and started the engine.

The bus pulled away with a rumble, and Tilly watched out the window as they traveled to the Lincoln Highway. She opened her book and started to read, but the conversations around her kept her distracted.

She heard the woman with the hat behind her say, "Gerald, I wish our car was in better shape. Driving on our own would be so much nicer than this."

The man muttered something and then, in a quiet voice said, "Carol, just calm down. We don't have a choice. The funeral is the day after tomorrow, and there was no time to deal with the car. It'll be fine. Try to enjoy the trip."

"It's just so tedious. All these strangers." She tsked and sighed.

Tilly saw the young mother across from her retrieve some stubby crayons and a dog-eared coloring book from her bag. She handed them to Charlie and said, "Here, you can color or draw things you see." As he reached for them, one slid from her hand and rolled on the floor where it was stopped by Tilly's shoe.

Tilly bent down and retrieved it. "Here you go," she said, handing it across the aisle. "I'm Tilly. I'm on my way to visit my daughter and her family near Salt Lake. Are you visiting someone?"

The woman nodded. "Thank you. Yes, we're on our way to visit my aunt. She's ill."

Tilly noticed the sheen of sweat on the woman's red face and the long-sleeved sweater she wore over her dress. "It's so hot in here, dear. You ought to take off that sweater."

"Oh, I'm fine. I get cold easily," she said, turning her attention to Charlie.

"What are you coloring, Charlie?" asked Tilly.

Charlie gave his mother a questioning look, and she dipped her head in a tiny nod. He leaned forward and showed Tilly the page in his coloring book. "It's a horse, ma'am."

"You do a terrific job. Maybe you'll see a real horse on our trip." Tilly smiled, and the boy went back to his work. Tilly looked at the mother and added, "What a polite young man. You should be proud. I'm sorry I've forgotten your name."

"It's Diane, and yes, Charlie is a good boy." She moved her hand and tousled her son's hair.

"Enjoy him. Time goes too fast. I remember when my daughter was his age, and now she's grown with her own children. This is my first trip alone. My husband and I always drove, but he died last year."

The two young ladies in front of Diane turned, and the one in the aisle seat said, "This is our first trip by ourselves. We're going to visit our grandparents." She smiled and looked at her sister.

"We're twins," said the one in the window seat. "I'm Missy, and this is Shelly."

"Pleased to meet you, girls," said Tilly. "How exciting for you to be on your first big adventure."

Charlie looked up and saw Missy peering at him over the

seat. "Nice horse," she said. He smiled and went back to his crayons.

The bus motored on, and Tilly focused on the page in her book. She started to read but overheard the couple seated in front of her and tuned into their conversation. "I hope the dress I packed isn't too wrinkled by the time we get there. I don't want to look like country bumpkins at this wedding."

The man leaned closer to her. "It'll be fine, darling. You'll look beautiful, as always."

"I just hated smashing it into that suitcase. Your suit jacket is in there, and it will be rumpled."

"We'll just have to hang them in the bathroom and run the shower. Won't that work?"

She shrugged. "I guess it'll have to do." She paused and said, "I just know how my sister is. She'll like nothing more than to comment about us being hillbillies."

He brought her hand to his lips and kissed it. "You worry too much. It's only for a few hours. We'll manage. Then we'll have the next day to ourselves before we head home."

Tilly read several chapters as the bus rolled down the highway. There wasn't much to see except desert. She cracked the stubborn window to let in some air. All it seemed to do was move the hot air around her a bit. She dug into her tote bag and retrieved a cookie from the container. She saw Charlie look over at her as she took a bite.

She reached back into the bag and offered him one. He raised his eyes to his mother, and she smiled and said, "Go ahead." He plucked one from Tilly's outstretched hand and began to nibble.

Diane turned to Tilly and said, "Thank you. That was kind of you to share."

"You two didn't pack any food to bring with you?"

Diane shook her head. "No. It was a last-minute trip. We just got the news about my aunt and had to rush to make the bus."

"Well, I have plenty, so if you need a sandwich later, let me know. I know the driver said we'd be stopping at a diner close to dinner time."

Diane gave her a nod. "Thanks for the offer. I think we'll be okay until we get there."

Tilly unearthed her thermos and took a sip of cold water. She repacked her tote and alternated between reading and watching out the window. She turned her head and looked behind her to discover a few of the passengers asleep and the others staring ahead or out their own windows.

They traveled through a small farming town, and Charlie was treated to views of cows and horses before the landscape returned to desert surrounded by mountains. Sagebrush dotted the sand-covered terrain for mile after mile.

The bus slowed and turned into a graveled parking lot in front of a rustic building that had a sign above the covered wooden walkway announcing a café. Tilly stowed her book and got ready to disembark.

David parked and stood in the aisle. "We'll have about twenty minutes here, so get something to eat. Restrooms are outside at the rear of the building. Make sure you're back on the bus in less than twenty minutes. There are only a couple of cars in the lot, so it shouldn't be very busy."

The passengers made their way down the aisle, and Tilly wrestled her bag as she shuffled sideways. She felt a tap on her shoulder, and the nice young man in uniform smiled at her. "Ma'am, if you'll allow me, I'll carry your bag."

She beamed with delight and transferred the canvas handle to his hand. "That would be wonderful. What's your name?"

He grabbed the tote with ease and said, "It's Joe Kobel. Pleased to meet you, ma'am."

Tilly introduced herself and told him about this being her first bus trip. She chatted while they walked to the door of the diner. She settled into her seat, smiling at the family seated in the adjacent booth. Joe offered to order her something, and she gave him some coins and asked for a drink.

She reached into her bag and unwrapped one of her sandwiches while the other travelers formed a line at the counter. Joe was back in a few minutes with her drink and his meal. She finished half of her sandwich and offered him a cookie.

"Thank you, ma'am." He took a bite and pronounced it as good as his mother's. They ate and talked as they watched their fellow riders come and go.

Tilly glanced at her watch. "I better visit the restroom. Will you watch my bag?"

Joe agreed, and she hurried out the door and around the back of the building. When she came out of the bathroom, she bumped into the disheveled passenger from the bus. "Oh, my, I'm sorry. I didn't see you." Bushes surrounded the area, and although it was dusk, the lights weren't on, obscuring the walkway.

He grunted and mumbled something unintelligible.

Tilly hurried back to the diner, thankful for the bright lights and the smiling face of Joe. She scooted into the booth. "Whew, I just ran into that man who's sitting in the back of the bus. He startled me when I came out of the restroom."

"Are you hurt?" asked Joe.

She shook her head. "No, no. Just shocked." She gripped her cup and tugged on her tote bag. "I'm going to get back on the bus. We only have a few minutes."

"Here, I'll take that for you. I'll walk you to the bus, and then I need to use the facilities."

He saw Tilly settle back in her seat with her bag. Charlie and his mother were already aboard, as were the twin girls in front of them. Shelly turned around and faced Tilly. "The bus driver said our next stop is in three hours, so he wanted to make sure we used the bathroom."

Tilly smiled and nodded. "He's a wise man." The passengers began to wander onto the bus. She looked out the window and made out Joe talking to the driver and gesturing to the building. The driver and Joe hurried inside the diner and reappeared moments later with the cook. They all ran to the back of the building and disappeared into the bushes surrounding the restrooms.

Tilly's forehead wrinkled as she squinted to see the activity. "I wonder what the devil is going on?"

Diane followed Tilly's gaze. "We need to get moving. It's been twenty minutes."

"Something's happening back there," said Tilly, stretching her neck.

The man in front of Tilly and the one behind her stood and started down the aisle. "You folks stay on the bus," said the man in front of her. "We'll find out what's holding up the driver."

Tilly studied the seats and noticed that in addition to the man with the dirty clothes, the other lone gentleman was missing from the bus. The young woman in the pink dress was not in her seat either. Tilly kept her eye on the sidewalk leading behind the diner.

Soon she spied activity and saw the bus driver motioning the people behind him back into the diner. She saw the dark-haired gentleman and the man who had startled her in the group. Joe and the cook were the last two to emerge, and she saw the driver walking toward the bus.

He clomped up the stairs and said, "I'm afraid there's been an incident. We're all going to have to stay here at the diner until the police arrive."

The ACES Anthology

"The police?" said Tilly. "What's happened?"

His eyes darted sideways as he glanced at the young girls and Charlie. "I'll explain things when we get inside. I'm sorry for the inconvenience, but you'll be more comfortable in the diner."

He ushered them off, urging them to take their things. Tilly was the last to exit, and the driver lugged her tote bag to the diner. She chose the same booth she had sat in when she ate her dinner. She saw Joe at the counter talking with the cook and noticed the young woman in the pink dress seated at a table.

The cook asked Dot, the lone waitress, to take the youngsters in the back and let them pick out some ice cream bars. As soon as they left, the driver cleared his throat. "I didn't want to alarm the children. One of the passengers discovered a dead man in the back of the diner, near the restroom."

A collective gasp went through the room. Tilly put a hand to her throat. She studied the room, ticking off the passengers in her head. They were all in the diner. It wasn't someone from the bus.

She glanced out the window and saw one car in the lot. The same car that had been there when the bus arrived. The other car had belonged to the family in the booth next to hers. She had watched them leave when she was eating.

The driver continued. "To keep the children from getting upset, I'd like us to agree that we are stuck here due to an engine problem with the bus. I'd encourage everyone to remain calm. I want us to keep them occupied until we can get this cleared up with the police. I have to ask you all to stay here in the diner. There is a small staff restroom off the kitchen we can use. You'll need to see Dot or Mel if you need to use it." The cook raised his hand at the mention of his name.

The murmur of chatter and questions surrounded her, but Tilly focused on remembering if she had seen anyone else in the diner when she and Joe arrived. Her interest piqued when she heard the driver say Joe had found the dead body.

The cook announced that the police had been called, but it could take several hours for them to arrive. "There's a good chance they won't be here until morning, and they have asked us to make sure nobody is alone. It's best if we can stay together, but if you need to go back to the bus, you'll need to take someone with you."

The driver added, "I've reported our delay to the main office, and they will alert our destination. If you have loved ones waiting in Salt Lake, they will know there is a delay and that you are all safe."

Groans and grumbles conveyed their dismay. Carol, the woman wearing the hat, did little to hide her irritation. She was barking in her husband's face. "Do you see why we should have never taken this stupid bus? This is your fault, you know. Now we're stuck here with these... these people."

In his attempt to calm her, he put his hands on her shoulders and tried to reason with her, but she was having none of it. She fumed and glared at the group. Tilly considered the rest of the passengers. The smelly man sat at a corner table, alone. The couple who had been sitting in front of her on the bus were huddled together in the booth nearest Tilly. The woman was upset, and the man had his arm around her.

Tilly strained to listen as the woman whispered. "I will never hear the end of it if we miss Eve's wedding. I can't believe this is happening."

Tilly scanned the room and saw Diane stand and make her way to the kitchen door. She peeked in and called to Charlie. A few minutes later, he emerged, licking what remained of his ice cream treat off the stick. She grabbed his hand and led him to the table. The two young girls followed and took their treats to a table next to Charlie.

The ACES Anthology

The cook interrupted Tilly's observations and announced that he would be happy to prepare snacks and Dot would be taking drink orders. "All your meals will be covered by the bus company."

Joe slid into the booth across from Tilly. "How are you doing, ma'am?"

Tilly's eyes sparkled. "Just fine." She lowered her voice and leaned closer. "I noticed all the passengers are accounted for. Do you know who the dead man is?"

He shook his head. "No. The cook said he was a customer, but had never seen him before."

"Hmm. That must be his car out front," she said, pointing out the window.

"Makes sense. The staff parks in the back." Dot approached the table, and they both requested coffee and water.

"This is quite the unexpected adventure. Do you know how he died?"

"I'm no expert, but there was a piece of rusty pipe on the ground next to him. He had an awful gash in his head. Looks like someone hit him."

"Oh, my. That means someone here killed him?"

"I'm afraid so. You mentioned you were startled when you visited the restroom. Did you see anyone in addition to the man from the bus?"

She shook her head. "No, just him. He was sort of lurking there."

Joe scanned the passengers. "I'm trying to piece together when I saw people relative to the time I found the man." Dot delivered their drinks and a couple of slices of pie.

Tilly eyed the pie and took a small bite. "I guess if we have to be stranded, it's best to be at a place with pie." She gave Joe a wink.

"You don't seem upset."

"Nah." She took another bite. "No sense in getting all bothered by something beyond my control." She leaned across the table and whispered. "It's actually exciting. Like one of those murder movies in real life."

She put down her fork and reached for the condiments at the far end of the table. She started lining up the mustard and ketchup and salt shaker. She did a quick count and said, "So, we have fourteen people on the bus, including the driver. The cook and the waitress make sixteen suspects. I'm going to go out on a limb and eliminate the three children along with you."

"If we eliminate you that leaves us with eleven possible suspects." Joe smiled at her and pushed the sugar closer to Tilly. "I'm going to see if the driver will go with me and take a look at that car in the parking lot. We didn't want to disturb the body, but maybe we can look at the registration and get the man's name."

Tilly nodded, removed a tube of colored wafer candies from her purse, and kept arranging the objects on the table. She watched as Joe and the driver approached the car and opened the door with a rag before extracting items from the glove box.

When Joe returned, she had the condiments scattered around the table and the napkin holder on its side with a few colored wafers on top of it. "What did you learn?" she asked.

He took out a small notepad from his pocket. "The car is registered to Stanley Wiley out of Sparks, Nevada."

"That doesn't tell us much." She pointed to the table. "So, the napkin holder is the bus. I'm the licorice wafer. It's my favorite," she said with a smile. "The two young girls were on the bus when I arrived along with Diane and Charlie." She pointed to another wafer. "She's the orange wafer."

"The bus driver was outside the door of the diner when I headed to the restroom," said Joe. Tilly moved the cream to represent his position.

"I remember the outspoken woman and her husband were at the table by the door when I left to get on the bus," said Tilly. She moved the salt and pepper shakers. Then she placed the ketchup and mustard outside between the bus and the diner. "That quiet couple going to the wedding was standing outside when we walked by to get to the bus."

Joe moved the green wafer away from the others. "This is the man who startled you by the restroom. I didn't see him back there when I found the body, but I also didn't see him anywhere else."

"I'm certain Dot was at the cash register when we left the diner. I couldn't swear the cook was there, but would think he was in the kitchen." She moved the chocolate wafer to represent Dot and positioned the sugar shaker in the pretend kitchen.

"What about pink dress and the other guy?" asked Joe.

"I don't recall seeing them one way or the other." She shook her head and stared across the room, willing herself to remember.

"Keep thinking. I'm going to start a group conversation and see if we can learn anything."

Joe stood and meandered around the diner, stopping in the center. "Ladies and gentlemen, since we're going to be here for a few hours, I thought we should introduce ourselves." His eyes circled the room. "I'm Joe Kobel. I'm on my way to Salt Lake City to visit family. I'm on leave from a base outside of Reno."

Joe pointed to Tilly to get the ball rolling. She explained she was from a small town outside of Reno on her way to visit her daughter and grandchildren in Salt Lake City.

Joe pointed to the quiet couple—mustard and ketchup in Tilly's diagram. The man said, "I'm Ed, and this is my wife, Margaret. We have a small farm in Washoe Valley, and we're on our way to a family wedding."

Next came salt and pepper. "I'm Gerald, and my wife, Carol, and I are traveling to Salt Lake City for a funeral. We're from Sparks."

The pink dress turned out to be a young woman from Sparks

named Nancy who was traveling to Salt Lake City for a teaching job interview.

The dark-haired man stood, introducing himself as Mike. He was from Reno, traveling to Wyoming to see his brother, who was ill.

Joe saw Tilly writing on a napkin and approached Diane and Charlie next. She put her hand on her son's shoulder, and he continued to chow down on his burger and fries. "I'm Diane, and this is my son, Charlie. We're from Reno, on our way to see my aunt in Salt Lake City."

Next were the sisters. Shelly and Missy told the group they were from Reno and going to spend the summer with their grandparents in Salt Lake City.

Joe saved the man who had startled Tilly for last. "I'm Kevin. I'm from California." Joe nodded in anticipation of more information, but Kevin remained fixated on the plate of food in front of him.

Dave waved his hand. "Nice to meet all of you. I'm Dave Stevens. I've been driving this route for almost five years now. Like Mel said, the food is compliments of the bus company, so don't be shy."

Joe rejoined Tilly in her booth. "Well, if they're telling the truth, salt and pepper and the pink dress are from Sparks, where Mr. Wiley lived. I'm not sure we can discount anyone since Reno is a stone's throw from Sparks."

"I have a feeling our friend who could use a shower was given a ticket on the first bus headed out of town. I'm not sure we can believe his story."

With the meals eaten and the plates cleared, impatience set in and the passengers became restless. Carol complained about having to stay at the diner, and poor Margaret was pacing and nervous about missing her sister's wedding. Dot and Mel had cleaned the kitchen and took a seat at one of the tables, each nursing a soda.

Nancy, the young teacher, offered to entertain the children at her table. Charlie brought his coloring books, and the girls joined in with their totes that held paper and pencils. She soon had them engrossed in a story and drawing pictures.

Joe and Tilly turned their attention to their makeshift map of the diner. With the children occupied, Joe approached Mel and David. They whispered to each other and then Dave nodded and began interviewing each table with Joe. Tilly heard them ask each of the passengers when they had visited the restroom area relative to their arrival.

Tilly scribbled notes for those she could overhear. By the time Joe had finished asking all of them except Nancy, Shelly and Missy were yawning, as was little Charlie. It was almost dark outside.

Dave stood and said, "If the youngsters want to get on the bus and try to sleep or take a nap, I'm happy to sit with them. I just need another volunteer. Remember our rules, none of us can be alone until this gets sorted."

Diane put up her hand. "I'll go. Charlie won't want to be there without me, and I'd like him to rest."

The youngest passengers gathered their things and hugged Nancy before heading out the door with Diane and David. The group watched as they traversed the parking lot and boarded the bus. David turned the lights on as they settled into seats.

Nancy was cleaning up the table and stacking the drawings the children had done and left with her when Joe approached. He asked her what she could tell him about the timing of her visit to the restroom and nodded his thanks before returning to Tilly's booth.

"Let's compare theories," he said. "I figure you would have

seen our victim had he been there when you visited the restroom, so the killer had to visit it after you. If our fellow passengers are telling the truth, we can eliminate Ed and Margaret and Nancy."

"So, by our loose standards, that leaves Kevin, Diane, and Mike as our most likely suspects. Plus we don't know about Mel, the cook."

Joe nodded. "That's how I see it. I don't suspect Mel, just because he was working to get all the orders done, but he could have slipped out the back door, unnoticed."

Tilly looked at the table and lined up the three colored wafers—orange, green, and yellow. She added the sugar shaker to the group. "Kevin seems the most likely since he was behind the building."

"He's not the most talkative, so it's hard to pinpoint what he was doing." Joe shook his head. "Mike was planning to visit the restroom but saw me heading that way and waited inside the diner. I tend to believe him."

The two sipped on their drinks and observed the others, hoping to notice something that would lead them to the killer. Tilly got up to stretch her legs and noticed a crumpled napkin on the floor. She picked it up and was going to toss it but observed the ruddy streaks across the white paper. She frowned and kept it in her hand while making a loop back to the booth.

She raised her brows at Joe and opened her hand. "This was on the floor over there." She motioned behind her to the row of tables where Kevin and Mike sat alone and where Diane had been sitting with Charlie.

Joe examined the napkin and said, "I don't think it's blood. Looks like rust and dirt more than anything."

"Right. Like someone was trying to clean his hands after using an old rusty pipe to bash someone in the head?"

"Could be." He sat back and studied the two men still seated.

"I shook hands with them and don't remember anything unusual. Kevin is not the cleanest guy, so I can't say I would have noticed anything."

"What about Diane? Did you shake her hand?"

He gave it some thought. "I remember shaking Charlie's hand, but not hers."

"I'll go get the coffee pot and offer to fill cups and see if I notice anything," offered Joe.

He stopped and chatted with Dot, who smiled her thanks and pointed to the coffee pot. Joe grabbed a few clean cups and started making the rounds to offer coffee. He fumbled with the cups at Kevin's table. Kevin helped him keep them from falling, and in the process, Joe inspected his hands.

He finished refilling cups, with Mike declining any with his hand raised. Tilly had a clear view of his spotless hand. Joe returned the pot and settled back across from Tilly.

"Kevin's hands are grimy, so it's hard to tell."

"That leaves us with Kevin and Diane. She's on the bus with the kids, so it won't be easy to get a look at her hands."

The minutes stretched into hours, and Tilly's eyes began to flutter in an attempt to stay open. Joe noticed and said, "Get some rest. I'll keep watch for a couple of hours."

She used her tote bag and scrunched it against the wall to serve as a makeshift pillow. She folded herself into it and shut her eyes. When she woke, it was quiet and all the lights were off, except for a dim one over the counter.

She made out Joe's silhouette and saw him raise his hand. He leaned across the table and said, "All's quiet. I'll grab some shut-eye."

He leaned against the wall and stretched out his legs along the booth seat. Tilly squinted to see if she could see any activity on the bus. It was too dark to see anything. She heard a howling sound and shuddered, but realized it was a coyote.

Her thoughts drifted to the dead man outside. She knew they had covered him with table cloths and towels, but the idea of a wild animal roaming around made her cringe. She whispered to herself, "Stanley Wiley. Someone here knows you well enough to kill you. Who is it?"

⚜

Tilly tried to use the quiet hours to solve the mystery but was no closer to a solution when the first hint of light broke the horizon. Joe stirred and repositioned himself. As the sun continued to climb, the passengers began to rouse.

Dot started brewing coffee, and the aroma proved to be a powerful stimulant. Soon the place was bustling with spoons clinking in cups and traffic to and from the kitchen. The smell of bacon grilling mixed with coffee, and Dot came around to take breakfast orders.

Tilly offered to help Dot and filled water glasses and passed out silverware. When she reached Nancy's table, she noticed the colored drawings spread across the table. "Aren't these cute? The kids wanted to draw the bus, and Charlie added a horse to his."

Tilly nodded as she admired the colorful drawings. She noticed the names on each paper, written in crayon. When she saw Charlie's, her eyes went wide. She looked for Joe and saw him chatting with Mike. He caught her eye and made his way across the diner.

She said, "Nancy was just showing me the pictures the kids drew for her last night. Cute, aren't they?" She spread them out so he could see the names at the upper right of each page.

He looked at Tilly with his brows raised. "Very nice." He looked out the window at the bus. "I'm going to go and check on everyone out on the bus and tell the kids how much I like their drawings."

Tilly asked Nancy if she would finish passing out the water and silverware. She grabbed the drawings and hurried after Joe, saying they wanted to give Dave and Diane a chance to come in and get breakfast.

When they reached the bus door, Joe gave it a gentle tap. Dave was behind the wheel and opened the door for them. "Morning. The kids are still asleep, but I think they'll be up soon."

"We thought we'd relieve you. Dot has coffee going and Mel's cooking breakfast."

"That would be great. I could use the walk and the coffee." He waved to Diane, who had Charlie's head slumped against her.

She was seated two rows behind the sleeping twin girls. Joe and Tilly tiptoed down the aisle. Tilly took a seat in front of Diane, and Joe remained standing. "I'll just wait for Charlie to wake up. I don't want to disturb him," she said.

"Diane, do you know Stanley Wiley?" asked Joe.

Her eyes widened, and she swallowed with a gulp. She looked at Tilly and then at Joe. "I can explain."

"Please do," said Tilly.

She slipped her arm out of her cardigan, and Tilly gasped when she saw the black and blue marks covering it. "The other arm is the same way, as is my back." She let out a long breath. "Stan told me he was going to kill me." A tear leaked down her cheek. "I didn't know what to do. I panicked, and the only thing I could think to do was to run. I'd been stashing money here and there, and when he went to work, I got a ride from a neighbor. I had enough money to get us tickets to Salt Lake and took the first bus."

"Do you have an aunt there?" asked Tilly.

"No, ma'am. It was just a story. I told Charlie we were

playing pretend." She lowered her voice to a whisper. "We were in the diner when I saw the car drive up. I took Charlie in the back and hid in the bushes. It didn't work. Stan came back there right after he parked, and Charlie called out to him."

"Stan told me to take Charlie and get in the car. I refused and told Charlie to use the restroom. When he was in there, Stan told me he was going to kill me and leave me out in the desert. I was so scared and worried for Charlie. I saw that old pipe leaning against the post and grabbed it and swung it. I wasn't even sure I could reach him, but then he just collapsed."

She picked up the sleeve of the sweater and brushed it under her eyes. "I didn't know what to do, so I just went to the restroom and tried to clean my hands and got Charlie situated. I told him Daddy changed his mind and said we could take a little trip and that we had to hurry and get on the bus."

"Did Charlie see his dad?"

She shook her head. "No, I stood between them and told him we had to go the other way, so we went around the other side of the building and got back on the bus. Charlie wanted to finish his drink, but I told him the bus would leave and we didn't have time."

"So you got on right before I helped Tilly board?" asked Joe.

"Yeah, we had just taken our seats when you came out of the diner with Tilly."

"And then I found Stanley," said Joe.

She nodded but said nothing. Charlie opened his eyes and smiled. When she bent to him, her hair slid away from her neck. Joe and Tilly saw the red and blue streaks on the back of her neck. They could make out the precise imprints of two sets of fingers.

Joe and Tilly gave each other a knowing look and turned their attention to Charlie. He started talking and asking about Shelly and Missy, and before long they were awake and anxious to get back inside the diner. Joe offered to take them inside for breakfast, and they all clapped and grinned as they followed him off the bus.

As soon as they left the bus, Tilly asked, "Do you have any identification with you?"

Diane rummaged in the seat and pulled out her handbag. "Yes, it's right here."

"I can't imagine the horror you're going through, dear. I would suggest that you give me your license. I'll hide it in my tote bag. The police will be here soon and will be asking all kinds of questions. It's best we keep the children, especially Charlie, away from them. He might slip and say something. Give them a different last name when they ask for yours and tell them you lost your license."

"What do you mean? You're not going to turn me in?"

"No, dear, I'm not. I believe you, and I can't see what good will come from Charlie being without a father and a mother. I know you didn't plan on killing Stan, and I know you were scared for your life. The police and the lawyers will come to the same conclusion, but it will take them a lot longer. Nobody knows Stanley, so I suspect they'll take our statements and let us move on. You can go to Salt Lake and start a new life."

"I don't have any money or a job or anything." Tears cascaded down her cheeks. "I don't know what to do."

"Do you have family somewhere?"

"Pennsylvania. I didn't have enough money to get that far."

"My daughter has lots of friends and connections in Salt Lake. We'll find you a safe place to stay until we can get you back to your family."

"What if the police come looking for me?"

"If they show up in Pennsylvania, just tell them you were traveling and didn't know a thing about it." She paused,

"Something tells me they won't be looking for you anyway."

"I don't know what to say," Diane's lips trembled. "I honestly didn't know what I was going to do. I just kept hoping we could leave here."

Tilly patted her shoulder. "Don't fret now. Let's get your face washed and get you some breakfast. Just keep pretending, like you told Charlie."

They made their way to the diner and found Charlie and the twins at a table. Their plates were piled high with pancakes. The three of them were covered in sticky syrup. Tilly slipped Diane's license into her tote bag.

As Diane made her way through the kitchen, Tilly spied a lighter on the counter. She palmed it and wandered outside to the far edge of the parking lot in the back of the café. Tilly crumpled the drawings the children had drawn into balls and lit them on fire, watching the flames engulf the cheap paper and turn it into black wisps. She stomped her shoe on the remaining ash to make sure it was out and hurried back to the diner.

She found Joe at their booth, and he gave her a questioning look. "I told Diane we're not going to say a word. She's going to continue to Salt Lake, and from there I'll help her get to her family in Pennsylvania. There's no reason to separate that little boy from the only mother he knows. She's a good person, I can tell."

Joe sipped his coffee and smiled over the rim. "I was thinking the same thing. I think Stan got what he deserved and she and Charlie can start over somewhere new."

Tilly leaned closer and whispered. "Now, here's what we're going to tell the police." She outlined her plan and sat back against the worn vinyl booth.

"You surprise me, Tilly," said Joe, with a grin.

The two of them started a conversation loud enough to make sure they were overheard by the other passengers. In the midst of

The ACES Anthology

the chatter and breakfast orders, a police car arrived. A man in a tan uniform and brown hat stepped from the car and took a look at Stan's vehicle parked in the lot. While he made notes, Tilly swept candy wafers from the top of the table and deposited them on her used breakfast plate. She repositioned the condiments and took a long drink of water.

Joe and the driver went outside and introduced themselves to the deputy. They led him past the entrance to the diner and down the sidewalk to the location of the body. After enough time had passed for Tilly to consume two cups of coffee, the officer returned.

"Morning, folks. I'm Deputy Brown. I apologize for the delay, but we had to make sure town was covered with this being forty miles away. I need to collect statements from everyone, and then we can get you on your way."

Mel offered the officer his small office off the kitchen that also served as a food storage area. Joe went first, followed by Dave. Tilly volunteered to go next and after she was done joined Joe in their booth and ordered breakfast.

They both watched when Diane was called for her interview. "Well, do you think this will work?" she asked.

Joe nodded. "I hope so. I told the deputy that I remembered seeing a dark sedan speed away from the side of the café. It will be interesting to see if the power of suggestion makes anyone else remember it."

Tilly smiled. "I said something similar, though I said I thought the car was green or blue."

They ate their breakfast and took note of Diane's return to the table with Charlie. Soon all the passengers had been interviewed, and Deputy Brown emerged. "Thank you all for your cooperation. We have your contact information and appreciate your cooperation with the statements. It doesn't appear any of

The ACES Anthology

you knew the deceased, and several of you reported seeing a car leaving the side of the diner right before Mr. Kobel found the body. If you remember anything further about the car, please get in touch. You all have my cards."

He tipped his hat and started out the door to meet what looked like an old ambulance. A man struggled to get a gurney from the back and wheel it over the bumpy ground past the entrance to the diner.

Dave stood and said, "Okay, let's get moving. Everyone use the facilities off the kitchen and get on the bus. We'll need to stop as little as possible on the rest of the trip to make up some time."

The passengers gathered their belongings and soon boarded the bus. They all took their same seats. Tilly glanced at Diane. The woman was wound tight, her hands trembling as she helped Charlie into his seat and dug out his coloring book.

Tilly saw the driver speaking with the deputy, nodding and then shaking his hand. Dave hurried to the bus and slipped behind the wheel. "Here we go, folks. I hope the rest of our trip is less eventful."

The bus pulled away, leaving a swirl of dust blowing across the parking lot and covering the body bag with a fine grit as the gurney bounced over the gravel lot toward the old ambulance. Tilly watched Diane staring at the site until the diner disappeared from view.

Dave did his best to make up some time, and the passengers cooperated by hurrying off and back on the bus when they did make stops to refuel. They arrived in Salt Lake City almost twelve hours late. The two couples visiting for a funeral and a wedding rushed through the bus station and hurried to find taxis.

Shelly and Missy ran to an older couple who engulfed them in hugs. Mike made his way to the window to inquire about his connection to Wyoming. Nancy waved to a young woman who motioned her to an exit door.

Joe helped Tilly with her tote bag, and Diane and Charlie followed. A young woman and two children hurried to Tilly as soon as she entered the station. She bent and gave them hugs and kissed the young woman on the cheek. "Julie, I'd like you to meet a friend of mine. This is Diane and her son, Charlie." She tousled Charlie's hair. "This is my daughter, Julie and my grandchildren, Matthew and Sarah."

Tilly turned to retrieve her tote from Joe. "This young man is Joe Kobel. We've become fast friends on the trip."

Joe extended his hand to Julie, "Ma'am." He turned his attention to Tilly. "It's been a real pleasure, Tilly. I hope we meet again." He shook Charlie's hand and nodded a farewell to Diane before joining his friends waiting near the exit.

Julie greeted Diane with a warm smile and a hug. She noticed Charlie's coloring book. "Looks like you and Sarah will get along well. She loves to color."

"Diane and Charlie are in need of a little help and a place to stay for a few days."

"We've got plenty of room. Come on, then. I've got leftovers from yesterday when I thought you'd be here."

Charlie smiled and said, "The bus broke something, and we had to stay the night at the diner. We got free burgers and milkshakes." His eyes sparkled with delight.

Julie said, "That sounds like quite the adventure. You can tell us about it when we get home. We also baked some fresh cookies. You look like a boy who would enjoy a cookie."

Charlie looked at his mother and grinned. "Yes, ma'am. Next to horses, cookies are my favorite."

Tilly slipped her arm in Diane's. "It's all going to be okay now. We'll get you back to Pennsylvania as soon as we can."

The ACES Anthology

Tears began to fall from Diane's eyes. "I can't believe you and Joe were so kind to me. I had no idea what we were going to do. I just knew Charlie and I couldn't live like that any longer. I never dreamed any of this would happen."

Tilly patted her hand. "It's all over now. You and Charlie are free and can put all of this behind you." They continued following Julie and the children to her station wagon. "Now tell me all about your family in Pennsylvania, dear."

By the time Julie drove to her house, Tilly had gathered enough information to piece together Diane's background. Over the next few days, Tilly and her daughter worked with the congregation at the church and collected enough donations to buy bus tickets to a small town outside of Philadelphia for Diane and Charlie.

Julie drove them back to the bus station, and Tilly gave Charlie a hug, plus a bag she had stuffed with sandwiches and cookies. "You be a good boy."

She embraced Diane and said, "Oh, I almost forgot." She slipped her hand into her tote and retrieved Diane's license. "Here you go, dear. Now you forget everything that happened. Your family is happy you're coming, and it sounds like they have plenty of room for you and Charlie."

A tear trickled down Diane's face. "I can't thank you enough. We'll never forget you." The driver urged them to board, and Diane hugged Tilly once more.

Julie and Tilly stood and waved at the pair. They continued to wave until the bus became too small to see as it motored down the highway, heading east to the promise of a better life.

Tilly stayed with her daughter until the week before school started. She enjoyed playing with her grandchildren and letting Julie pamper her. She bought her ticket for the bus back to Reno. When she boarded, the driver, Dave, recognized her with a wink. "Ma'am," he said. "Welcome back."

"Hello, Dave. I'm hoping for a smooth ride," said Tilly, hefting her tote bag up the stairs.

"Not any more than I am." He offered to take the bag and followed her to her seat. She settled in, taking stock of the passengers around her and those boarding. She nodded to an older gentleman seated behind her. She scanned each of the newcomers, hoping Joe would be among them. As the door shut, her shoulders slumped. No men in uniform on this ride.

She doubled checked her stash of snacks and made sure her thermos of water hadn't spilled. She smiled at the drawings the children had done and made sure they were safe in between the cardboard she had packed around them and slid into the side of her bag. She had promised to hang them in her house when she got home.

A lone young woman slid into the seat across the aisle from Tilly. The woman gave a weak smile.

Tilly reached her hand across and said, "I'm Tilly. I just visited my grandchildren and am heading back to Reno. Do you live there?"

The woman relaxed and introduced herself as Sally. She was on her way to Reno to get a divorce. Tilly and Sally chatted as the bus lurched from the station and made its way to the highway. The bus retraced its path to Nevada, stopping at the same diner where Stanley had met his death. Tilly shuddered a bit when she made the trek to the restrooms and remembered the ordeal.

This time the stop was uneventful. Tilly splurged and ordered a milkshake to go with the sandwich her daughter had packed. When Dave made the announcement to board, she was the first one back on the bus. She grinned as she climbed the steps, "Better than last time, Dave."

He tipped his cap and said, "Much better, ma'am. We're almost home now."

She never saw Joe or Diane again, but when she returned home and went through her stack of mail, there was a postcard with a photo of the Liberty Bell on the front. On the back, Diane reported she had found a job, and things were going well. Following Diane's brief message was a drawing of a horse and the words "Love, Charlie" in blue crayon.

⚜

"Murder on the Desert Express" is ©2018 by Tammy L. Grace. It appears in print here for the first time. All rights reserved. No portion of this story may be reproduced or transmitted in any form or by any means, electronic or mechanical including photocopying, recording, or by any information storage and retrieval system without the written permission of the author,

The ACES Anthology

except for the use of brief quotations in a book review. For permissions, contact the author directly via electronic mail: tammy@tammylgrace.com.

"Murder on the Desert Express" is a work of fiction. Names, characters, places, and incidents either are products of the author's imagination or are used fictitiously. Any resemblance to actual events, locales, entities, or persons, living or dead, is entirely coincidental.

Tammy L. Grace is a USA Today bestselling author and a resident of Fallon. She has published more than 35 works, including her bestselling "Hometown Harbor" series and her award-winning Cooper Harrington Detective Novels, which are available in the ACES bookshop at acesofnorthernnevada.com. When Tammy isn't working on ideas for a novel, she's walking her spoiled golden retriever or supporting her addiction to books, tea, and chocolate. You can follow her at www.tammylgrace.com.

Jacqueline M. Green

Stuck in the Ribs

A short story in the "Second Chance Reno" cozy mystery series

Molly McGuire wiped sweat from her flushed chin with a gloved hand. She stared at the customer on the other side of the Sierra Hot Ribs counter.

"I thought this booth would be cheaper because it's a local restaurant," the woman said.

"No, ma'am, everyone sells the ribs for the same price." Molly gestured toward the other twenty-plus booths at the annual Nevada Ribfest celebration in downtown Reno.

Molly raised her eyebrows expectantly while also listening to her sister, Melanie, next to her in the booth.

"Take this sample lotion," Melanie told a customer. "It will clear your face in no time. Here's my card for when you run out."

"Pushing drugs with your ribs?" Molly muttered as she raised her eyebrows in expectation.

Melanie chuckled but didn't stop moving. "No mystery here, Mrs. Bartleson. Do you see all the grease being slathered around

The ACES Anthology

this place? We'll see more breakouts than *Hogan's Heroes*."

Molly smiled at the "Mrs. Bartleson" comment, a reference to the main character in their mother's mystery novels. She and her sister had grown up hearing about the fictional detective's adventures.

The woman before Molly sighed in dejection. "All right then. I'll take the sampler."

With an eye on the growing line behind the woman, Molly quickly took her money and snagged the order. She held it out to the woman and pointed toward the napkin holder even as her eyes sought out the next customer.

"Good job, ladies," a voice boomed behind them. "Way to move those ribs."

The owner of the stand, the rib master himself, Bobby Johnson, called out to the people in line. "Best ribs in Nevada!"

"How about a quick selfie?" Melanie asked next to Molly. In response, Bobby put his arm around the sisters, then paused.

"Get in here, you guys!"

Bobby's son, Cal, and Bobby's business partner, Jason, ducked around the side of the booth and jumped laughing into the picture, the five of them in matching red Sierra Hot Ribs T-shirts. Melanie pressed the button, then they all returned to their respective tasks. Cal and Jason worked the grill.

The Nevada Ribfest took over downtown Reno for nearly a week each summer, drawing rib lovers from the West Coast and beyond and raising a small cloud of grill smoke over the city. An army of craft booths sprang up next to the rib cookers, but the pork ribs were the main draw, along with hot corn on the cob dripping with butter, corn bread, macaroni and cheese, lemonade, and soft-serve ice cream. It was a summertime food fest under the relentless Northern Nevada sun.

This was Molly's first time working at the Ribfest. She'd

recently moved to Reno from the Bay Area after discovering her now-soon-to-be-ex-husband was cheating on her.

Melanie had talked Molly into joining her manning Bobby's booth this year to get to know more people in Reno. Bobby was one of Melanie's skin-care customers. The two had become friends, so Melanie helped out in his booth each year. As sweat poured down her back, Molly began to regret her decision.

She started to lick some rib sauce off her gloved hand and instead rubbed her hand on her T-shirt, joining all the other sauce stains she had managed to spread across her shirt that day.

As the night air cooled, the crowds began to thin. Melanie and Molly took a few minutes to sit on stools with their own samplers. The ribs were meaty and delicate, the sauce smoky and sweet but not cloying. It was all Molly could do not to groan in pleasure. She licked the sauce from her fingers and wiped the remainder on her paper napkin.

"This is not the first time you've tasted our ribs, is it, Molly?" Bobby peered into the grill, a hefty flashlight in one hand.

"I tried the ribs this morning so I would be able to describe them to customers," Molly said, taking a rib from her mouth to speak. "But they taste even better after a long day."

"Is your flashlight big enough?" Melanie teased.

Bobby laughed. "You gotta use the ones with six batteries. Those double-A weenies won't do the job." He used his spatula to knock out a couple of rib bones, then turned off the light and looked toward the two women.

Bobby smiled at Molly. "It's my own recipe, you know. Years and years of trial and error. I think we have a good product now." He leaned in close to the two women. "I think we even have a shot at the big prize this year, People's Choice for the Best Ribs."

Jason made a face as he slammed down a freshly scrubbed pan. "Don't get ahead of yourself, Bob. Let's just take it a step at a time."

Bobby waved Jason away with a rib. "Nope. This is our time, brother. If we win, we're going to start franchising. If we don't do it right after the win, we won't be able to do it. We've got to ride that wave."

Jason snapped Bobby with his towel, and the two laughed. Jason then folded the towel and set it carefully on the counter. "I'm outta here. Big Dog and I are hitting the poker tables."

He shoved something into his pocket, then turned back to Melanie, showing her his hands. "Thanks for the lotion. It's already helping."

"You're welcome, sweetie. Just keep applying it."

"You're buying Melanie's lotions now?" Bobby sounded incredulous. "You always make fun of me for it."

Jason laughed and threw him a wave, then set off into the fading light to the Big Dog Ribs booth across the way.

"You guys wash your hands all the time." Melanie reached under the counter and grabbed her purse. "My new line really helps hydrate the hands, and the smell is not too feminine."

"Don't I know it?" Bobby stood up, tossing a rib into the trash can. He shoved the big flashlight under a table by the door and straightened the condiments on top. "You ladies can head on out," he said. "I'll finish closing tonight."

He winked at Molly, who blushed and smiled back even as Melanie pulled her by the arm out of the booth.

"Okay, sis," Melanie giggled, "So what do you think?"

"What do you mean?" Molly protested, pulling free from her sister.

Melanie rolled her eyes and took her sister's arm again. "What do you think about Bobby?"

Molly sighed. "I don't know, why? Wait, are you trying to set us up? Nate and I aren't even divorced yet."

She shook her head in dismay, then followed her sister toward the brewery on the far side of the plaza, where a band performed.

Sitting in their chairs on the deck, Melanie ordered a glass of wine and Molly a root beer. Molly wasn't much of a drinker in the best of times, and tonight she felt dead on her feet. She stretched out her legs, tapping her toes to the beat.

Cal stopped at their table. "Mind if I join you?"

Melanie slid back the chair next to her and motioned to Cal.

The lanky young man sat down awkwardly and leaned back in his chair. He lifted his beer in a silent salute, then took a long drink. "Busy day," he finally said.

Molly agreed. "Busy but fun. There were so many people, and your dad's ribs are delicious!"

Cal laughed shortly. "They are. He spent enough time on them while I was growing up."

Molly looked at him expectantly, so he shrugged and continued. "Bobby was always at the restaurant. That's why Mom finally gave up and got divorced. He was never around."

"How old were you when they split?" Molly asked.

"Molly, that's not your business," Melanie hissed at her sister.

Cal waved a hand. "Nah, that's fair. I brought it up." He paused to sip his beer. "I was 12. I went to live with my mom out of state and hardly ever saw my dad until about three years ago. Then I came to Reno for college, and he hired me to work in the business."

"That must have been hard," Molly said.

He nodded slowly. "It was. I was really angry for a long time." He took a deep breath and sat up a little straighter. "But that was three years ago, and now we get along great."

Molly reached for her purse to pay the bill, her hand finding only empty air where her purse should be. She sat up quickly and looked around, then clapped a hand to her forehead.

"I left my purse in the booth." She stood up. "I'll be right back."

Melanie and Cal kept talking as Molly exited the restaurant and trotted down the path back toward the booth. The streets were still filled with people, but the sounds became more distant as Molly neared the edge of the Ribfest. She was glad to see the lights were still on at the booth. Bobby must still be fussing over some detail, she thought.

She walked around the front but couldn't see Bobby through the closed rafters, so she stepped quickly in the dim light to the back, where a small shed with supplies connected to the booth. Molly tapped lightly on the door.

"Bobby?"

Only silence greeted her from within the booth. She tapped again, then pushed through the door, calling a little louder, "Bobby, are you here?"

Molly gasped. Lying on his stomach on the dirt floor was Bobby. She rushed to him, picking up a bloodied knife that lay on his back and tossing it aside. She wrestled him over to his back. Even as her shaking hands dialed 9-1-1, tears began to river down her face as she told the dispatcher her boss was dead.

Molly tried to call Melanie, who didn't pick up, so she left a message telling her to hurry back to the booth. She knew the shakiness of her voice would send Melanie racing back to the tents.

"What the hell is this?" A loud voice shook Molly. A rough hand threw her to the ground. "What did you do?"

Molly looked up from the floor of the shed to see Jason standing over her.

"I didn't do anything," she sputtered. "I found him like that."

Jason scoffed, then wheeled around as a uniformed officer burst through the door. Jason pointed at her. "She did this. I found her here."

Molly protested. "I didn't!"

Other officers started to push into the shed, but the first one held them out, instructing them to call the medics.

A tall man in a brown suit bent his head to enter. Molly had seen him earlier when he stopped by their booth. "What cha got, Jameson?" he asked the officer as his eyes scanned the shed, pausing on Molly and then Jason.

The first officer stood up from the body, taking in the scene around him. He looked closely at Molly. "Ma'am, whose blood is that?"

Molly looked where the officer was looking and saw blood smeared across her shirt and hands. "It's his, Bobby's. I-I-I turned him over when I found him."

The officers talked with her and Jason as other officers poured in, looking at Bobby's body and checking the crime scene. Finally, Jason stood up. "It's been a long day. I need to go home and clean up."

The police officer gave him a card and told him he would be in touch.

"What about me?" asked Molly.

The officer stared at her a long moment. Then he pulled cuffs from his back pocket and reached for her. "Ma'am, you'll need to come with us."

That night felt like the longest of Molly's life. Time after time, to officers and detectives, she told her story. They kept asking her why she had killed him. She asked for a lawyer.

Finally, the room was empty. Molly laid her head on the table in exhaustion. The door opened. The tall man in the brown suit walked in. "Mind if I sit?" he asked.

She shrugged. "Like I have a choice. Any word on my lawyer?"

"That's not really my area." He pulled out a metal chair and sat down. "I'm Paul O'Neill, casino security."

She looked at him through weary eyes. "And?"

"I work with the police on occasion. They sent me in to break you."

"What?" Molly sat up straight, alarm filling her widening eyes.

O'Neill chuckled. "Just kidding. They're waiting on fingerprints, evidence and stuff to see if they should hold you or not." He shrugged as he settled into the chair across from her, the metal scraping on the concrete floor. "But if you wanted to confess, that'd be awesome."

Molly leaned back in the hard metal seat and eyed O'Neill. "You're hilarious. I didn't kill Bobby. I only just met him this morning, well, yesterday morning. Aren't the police looking at any other suspects?"

He ticked them off on his hands. "Jason and Big Dog were at the Big Dog booth. They vouched for each other plus," he said as he waved away her protests, "they're on the security camera. Bobby's son was with you and your sister most of the time. But we can't say where they were before that, so they're all still in the picture." He spread his hands, palms up, and shrugged. "Nobody has a perfect alibi, but you're the one found with the body and blood all over you."

Molly sighed deeply. "Wow. It really does look like it's me. I wonder why I did it."

Paul crossed his arms and stood up, frowning. "You know I don't really think you killed Bobby, right?"

"Thank you for that, but the police sure think I did."

"From what I understand, the cash box was gone." He pointed toward her. "It wasn't found on you, so I'd say it's unlikely you did the deed. Did you notice anything else unusual?"

Molly thought a moment. "It smelled like lotion, but that was probably just because Bobby used it."

Just then, the door burst open. The officer from earlier stepped inside and closed the door. "Ms. McGuire, we are releasing you for now."

"Oh, thank g—"

"But don't leave town." He opened the door and motioned Molly through it.

Melanie sat in a chair in the lobby, her feet tapping as she watched the door. She leaped to her feet as Molly came through. They hugged tightly and filled each other in.

Finally, Melanie stepped back and wiped a hand across her tear-stained face. "Mol, what are we going to do?"

Molly breathed deeply, then lifted her head. "We're going to find out who killed Bobby and clear my name."

Late the next morning, Molly and Melanie warily approached the booth. Jason and Cal stopped what they were doing. Jason wiped his hands on a towel.

"I wasn't sure you'd show up today," he said.

"I wasn't sure you'd let me," Molly said.

Jason nodded. "I'm sorry I yelled those things last night. I don't really think you killed Bobby." He reached a hand across the counter and Molly shook it. He looked up, his eyes surveying the Ribfest crowds. "The police need to find out who did. They're out there."

Molly nodded. "Can you think of anyone who might have wanted to kill Bobby?"

Jason blew out air as he shook his head. "No. ... Yes. ... I mean, no one who knew him well would want to kill him. The police said it looked like a robbery."

"What about other rib masters?" Molly ventured.

Jason hesitated. "I don't want to throw anybody under the bus, but yeah." He turned and looked at a booth kitty-corner to theirs, Big Dog Ribs. "Bobby was making some of the bigger cookers nervous. He was ambitious for us."

He turned back toward the grill, and Molly eyed the Big Dog booth from the corner of her eye.

When there was a lull in the line, Molly slipped out of the booth and over to Big Dog. She ordered a three-rib plate and leaned on the counter to wait. A burly man with a beard walked toward her, pointing at her T-shirt emblazoned with Bobby's logo. "You work there?"

She looked down and realized she had forgotten she was wearing the Sierra Hot Ribs shirt. Not much of a detective, she thought.

"I'm Big Dog. Sorry about your boss. He was a good guy. Ironic he was stabbed in the ribs." He leaned on the counter. "I kind of thought this was going to be his year. He deserved it. He should've won last year, but something got into the last batch and made a bunch of people sick."

The counter worker handed her the rib plate. "You weren't worried he would win?" she asked.

The man smiled. "Naw, it's a friendly competition."

"But isn't there a big cash prize at the end?" Molly asked, her eyes narrowed.

Big Dog stood, suddenly awkward. "Yeah, but who would kill over that?"

He turned away, clearly dismissing Molly. She left the booth, nibbling on the ribs. She bit into one, then wiped rib sauce off her lips and tossed the ribs into a garbage bin. Bobby's ribs definitely were better than Big Dog's. He should have been worried. She slid back into the booth.

"You have Big Dog sauce on your face, sis," Melanie said, handing her a napkin. "What were you doing over there?"

Molly scrubbed at her cheek. "I was trying to find out who killed Bobby. It could have been Big Dog. He thought Bobby was going to win this year."

"So he has motive." Melanie punched the air, then apologized to the customer she nearly hit.

"But I don't think he did it."

"How can you tell?"

Molly shrugged. "He just didn't seem like a killer."

Melanie turned to the next customer. "Molly, killers don't wear T-shirts that advertise it."

Maybe Melanie was right.

"Then what are we going to do?" Molly stared at her sister in frustration.

"Right now, we're going to sell ribs," Melanie said, a catlike smile playing at her lips. "But I have an idea."

That night, Molly waited at home while Melanie got on the phone.

When she reached her client Cynthia Sanders, she hit pay dirt. Cynthia knew Bobby and Jason from high school in Carson Valley and was willing to spill. She called Molly in triumph.

"Bobby and Jason got in some trouble back in the day."

"In high school?" Molly wasn't too surprised. Kids get into

trouble, no matter what generation they're from.

"Not police trouble, but they were fighting over a girl along with that other guy they hung out with, what was his name?" Molly listened patiently to Melanie. "Bobby ended up marrying her, but I heard they got divorced quite some time ago. And there was another boy they hung out with. It was Paul. Paul O'Neill. I think he was a cop or something."

Molly's mouth fell open. What were the odds that the Paul O'Neill who hung out with Bobby and Jason as kids was the same as the security officer from the casino?

She sat down hard in her chair as her sister rambled on.

"Mol, are you there?" It didn't sound like the first time Melanie had said her name.

"Yeah, I need to think about this. I'll talk to you tomorrow." With that, Molly clicked off.

Paul O'Neill had opportunity and apparently motive and an "in" with the police so he could steer them toward her. It was the perfect crime—unless she figured out a way to stop him.

The next day, Molly barely made it to the booth on time. She threw on a clean Sierra Hot Ribs T-shirt and joined Melanie at the counter.

"I know who killed Bobby," she hissed to Melanie, who looked at her with wide eyes.

"Who is it?"

Molly shook her head as they opened the counter. "I'll tell you later. I have to figure out how to trap him first."

Melanie looked alarmed but turned to wait on the first customer.

The day passed quickly. Paul O'Neill sauntered past several

times, always stopping to watch Molly or the booth, she wasn't sure which. The first time their eyes met, Paul smiled and nodded. Molly stared coldly at him. She was not flirting with a killer.

When the shift was over and booths were closing down, Melanie and Cal left to take leftovers into a casino freezer for distribution to the homeless. Molly and Jason worked in companionable silence, scrubbing the counters and grills.

"I hear you and Melanie have some mutual friends," Molly said, wrinkling her nose as she scraped at barbecue sauce that had cooked into the counter. "Cynthia Sanders remembers you from high school."

"Were you checking up on me?" Jason paused mid-scrub and peered at Molly.

"She and Melanie were just talking. You know how Reno is. Everyone is in everyone else's pocket."

Jason snorted. "What did old Cynthia have to say?"

"She said you and Bobby and Paul O'Neill used to hang together and that you fought over a girl," Molly said with a shrug. "Interesting how Paul keeps showing up this week and then Bobby dies, isn't it?"

Jason grunted in response. Molly heard him scrubbing on a pan behind her as her phone dinged. She stripped off her plastic gloves as a message from Melanie popped up, sharing the picture they had taken in the booth the previous day. Molly smiled sadly, then turned and showed the selfie to Jason.

"Happier times, I guess," she murmured.

Jason stared at the picture, so Molly peered more closely. "Yep, that's sauce all over my shirt," Molly said in dismay. "I guess I wore it like that all day. How is it that your shirt is clean?"

Jason laughed as he tipped over a pan to dry. "It's my super power, the one thing I always did better than Bobby. I can work a whole shift without a spot." He opened his arms and looked at his gray T-shirt. "See? We used to joke about that, Bobby and me."

Molly continued to stare at the photo. "But that's not the T-shirt you were wearing when you talked to the police." She looked up at him, puzzled. "You were wearing the red one earlier, same as Bobby and me. Why did you change, I mean, if you have your super power and all?"

He stared at her. "Even superheroes spill sauce some time."

"But you told the police you needed to leave so you could clean up. Clearly, you already had."

Molly opened her mouth in an "o" as she felt fear tingle up her spine. She swiped, then set down her phone and leaned into her work, clearing her throat to cover the awkwardness she felt.

The silence behind her became palpable. Sponge in hand, she turned around.

Jason stood before her with a small gun in his hand. "You talk too much."

Molly crossed her arms over her chest as if they would stop a bullet. "It wasn't Paul O'Neill. You changed your shirt because you killed Bobby, didn't you? Because you got Bobby's blood all over it."

"I didn't mean to. It just happened." Jason shrugged, waving the gun slightly in his hand. "He wanted to expand the business. That would mean bringing in auditors."

"And then he would know that you have been stealing from the business to pay for your gambling and your girlfriend."

Jason's eyes flashed. "That big-mouth Cynthia Sanders."

"This is Reno, Jason. Cynthia knows. Everybody knows. At some point, the police will put it together, too."

He shook his head violently. "Not if I get rid of you, too. They already think you did it."

Molly held both hands up in a question. "Why would I kill him? I barely knew him."

Jason considered her for a moment. "I watched the way you two made googly eyes at each other. You propositioned him and he turned you down. So you stabbed him. And tonight you became despondent and killed yourself."

He smirked, satisfied with his fiction.

Molly's face scrunched up in horror "No one who knows me would ever believe that, and I was not making googly eyes at him. I'm still married."

"Not for long," Jason said, tilting his head to look at her. "I heard what your husband did. We all know. Your life has basically fallen apart, and let's face it, lady, you're no spring chicken."

Molly's mouth fell open. "That's what you think of me? Old and dried out?"

"You said it, not me."

As his words sank in, Molly's shoulders slumped and she sagged against the counter. "Well, life has been a bit more challenging since I moved to Reno. There have been days that I didn't want to get out of bed."

Jason frowned at her, then motioned with the gun. "I'll be sure to tell that to the police when I show them your body." He laughed. "I can't believe you thought it was Paul O'Neill. Let's go."

Jason grabbed Molly's purse and shoved it at her, nearly knocking her over. She clutched the purse, then stumbled ahead of him toward the back door. Just before the exit, Molly tumbled to her knees, dropping her purse and grabbing the hefty flashlight from under the rack by the door. She swung it as hard as she could into Jason's ankle, hearing a satisfying and resounding crack. Before he could react, she kicked with her feet into his knees so that he fell backwards with a crash, firing the gun as the drying pans fell on top of him.

Paul O'Neill appeared in the doorway, pushing her aside as he ran toward Jason, practically jumping onto the arm that held the gun.

"Molly, are you all right?" Melanie raced in, throwing her arms around Molly's shoulders. Molly breathed hard, the flashlight dangling from her hand.

As Paul pulled out handcuffs, Molly walked to Jason and looked him in the eye. "And that, my friend, is what old and dried out looks like."

Paul bit back a smile as she dropped the flashlight in front of Jason. "Molly the police will be here momentarily and will want to take a statement. Fortunately, Melanie and I heard every word."

Jason's eyes widened. "H-h-how?" he said.

Molly smiled. "When I realized I was talking to a killer, I speed-dialed Melanie and left the phone on."

"Once I figured out what was going on, I grabbed Paul and we came to find you." Melanie finished the story.

Police officers hurried into the room. Paul caught them up on what was going on. Molly and Melanie stepped outside.

"Molly," Melanie said quietly, her arm around her sister. "Did you mean what you said about not wanting to get out of bed some days?"

Molly started to shake her head, then paused and turned to look squarely at her sister. "Some days, I've felt a bit at loose ends, but I never felt like I couldn't face the world. And I just took out a killer with a flashlight." She shook her raised fist. "Bring it!"

The two laughed, and Melanie put her head on her sister's shoulder. "Promise me if you do start to feel down, you'll call?"

"Deal."

The ACES Anthology

Molly and Melanie were still finishing their statements when Paul approached. He stopped next to Molly. "You thought I killed Bobby?"

"It seemed like a good idea at the time." Molly felt herself blush as she held up three fingers, ticking them off as she explained. "You knew the victim, you were around all the time, and you had motive."

Paul frowned. "What motive? I moved to the Bay Area after high school and hadn't seen Bobby and Jason in decades."

"Didn't you three fight over a girl?"

Puzzlement settled on Paul's face, then he broke into laughter. "Good grief, in *high school*." He peered closer at Molly and lowered his voice. "Did it ever occur to you that I was hanging around this week because I was interested in *you*?"

Molly backed up in surprise. "Me? Jason just called me old and dried out."

"And you took him down like a boss."

They both laughed. Melanie grinned as she looked back and forth between the two.

"So, Molly, if I am no longer at the top of your suspect's list, can I take you to dinner tomorrow night?" Paul asked.

Molly hesitated. "I'd like that, but technically, I'm still married. That could be awkward."

Paul nodded, then turned to Melanie. "How about we make it a foursome?"

Melanie nodded in agreement. Molly blushed. "Where shall we go?"

Paul's gray eyes smiled back at hers. "I know a place. It has great ribs."

The ACES Anthology

"Stuck in the Ribs" is ©2023 by Jacqueline M. Green. The author grew up in Alaska and has been a resident of Reno/Sparks for the past 20 years. A former newspaper copy editor, Jacqueline has published 10 cozy mysteries and six short stories in the cozy mystery genre. Her books are available on Amazon.

Jade Griffin
The Origins of Mr. Cunningham

January 1923

"Mr. Cunningham, have a seat." President Doud of the Paisley Foundation indicated the chair before his desk with a gesture as curt as his words. It was unpleasant business, learning of subterfuge and even more difficult dealing with it when you'd always been sure of the character of the accused.

The sandy-haired young man turned briefly, shut President Doud's door, and remained standing. He gripped his ledger tightly, fidgeted with his tie, and adopted a look of nervous if silent determination.

Mr. Doud eyed the anxious Paisley Foundation Treasurer with suspicion. "You know I'm going to ask about the Dream Well incantation, and why it was misplaced in the open in Acquisitions."

The ACES Anthology

Even under such scrutiny, the Treasurer held his tongue and his place. When he nodded unabashedly, Doud decided to press harder. "Mr. Cunningham, as one of the four Corners of the Paisley Foundation, I expect you to hold yourself to the same standards as your peers." He paused, again allowing young Mr. Cunningham the opportunity to say something in his defense. As one of the four controlling members of an organization which dealt in secreting and dispensing knowledge of all types, including otherworldly and arcane knowledge, it was imperative that each of them trust the others.

Mr. Cunningham said nothing.

Doud ground his jaw, and his voice rose angrily. "You let our newest and greenest assets find a powerful and potentially harmful spell we know sorely little about, without ever consulting any one of us. Do you have anything to say in explaining this breech?"

"It w-w-ww-was-sn't m-m-mm-mis-p-p-placed."

Mr. Doud blinked his shock.

Ira Cunningham had always stuttered, especially so as a child.

The Paisley Foundation president remembered the first time he met Ira. The boy was only seven, but Tricia had been able to prove without a doubt that her oddly quiet son did have a tremendous gift. Certain allowances were made, at Tricia's insistence. When she began bringing her son into the Paisley Foundation with her, the stuttering lessened. It had all but vanished by the time he replaced her as acting Treasurer. Had they been abusing Mr. Cunningham's ability lately and accidentally broken the man? And could he be fixed before Tricia found out?

Mr. Cunningham stepped forward, opened his ledger, and presented it to Mr. Doud.

The ACES Anthology

There were words on the page.

President Doud,

You will be upset with me for allowing Ms. Clark access to the Dream Well incantation, but I had no time to explain before doing what I must. When you handed me the parchment containing the spell, I did as you asked and focused my psychometry on it. I garnered no hint of its origin or past and thought my ability had failed me, but then my entire body seized and my sight went elsewhere, elsewhen. I saw our newest assets find the incantation. I saw Ms. Clark leading the others in casting Dream Well. I know this was a vision of the future, Mr. Doud, because their new companion, Minerva, was in my vision as well and we have only just met, directly after my vision. I saw that you would call me in for this very moment in time, and that I would have physical difficulty explaining, so I took the effort to write it out.

I do not know who the focus of their incantation was, nor do I understand why I saw a version of the future and why it has affected my speech, but I was strongly provoked to act in favor of bringing about these events. That is all I have seen and all of the impetus I have on the matter. Do you believe I was compelled by nefarious forces? Or that some force of good has granted me a look at the future? What is our next step?

He eyed Mr. Cunningham a moment, took the delay to think up a good response. "For now, we wait. I'm inclined to see where your inclination leads. Keep me apprised if any further visions strike you, Mr. Cunningham."

The young man nodded eagerly, clearly relieved that his explanation was acceptable. He executed a crisp turn and went back to his own office in the south corner.

Mr. Doud watched him go, recalling briefly the first time they met.

The ACES Anthology

Winter 1907

"Mr. Doud, I'd like to bring my son here, to be evaluated."

He frowned at Ms. Cunningham. Yes, everyone at the Paisley Foundation knew their Treasurer had a son, but she was not the type of mother to talk of him. Given her family background, that wasn't a surprise. The source of his confusion stemmed from what she was asking. She knew what went into evaluating someone by Paisley Foundation standards. One didn't request such a thing out of the blue. So he asked, "Can you explain why?"

"He's a good boy, shy; shies away from physical contact. I've tried to find any sign he's being abused or neglected by his nanny, but she similarly reports this behavior, and more. She told me this week that he has been crying by himself for unexplainable reasons and looks scared when she asks what's the matter. He won't tell her a thing—or me." She fidgeted with her hands while she spoke, a nervous gesture he was quite familiar with but hadn't seen her do in some time.

"Mr. Doud, he's only seven. He should be playing with his toys, laughing and running about. He does none of these things. Even an attempt at practical jokes would be welcome. He is terrified of everything, despite my best efforts to make him feel safe and loved, and I don't know what else to do but ask for help in determining the cause, internal or external, and help me eliminate it."

Doud took in a breath and let it out slowly. "Ms. Cunningham, we will of course do what we can, but this is likely a matter for a psychiatrist. You can make that appointment yourself."

Her sharp gaze never faltered, nor did her stalwart tone. "I do not believe this is in his head, Mr. Doud... I tried to test him myself, and he had a most peculiar reaction."

"Oh?"

"Yes. As I said, I tried. His behavior has gotten increasingly jumpy of late. I decided to do something about it. But as I gathered the components for a ritual to determine his malady, he came to me and said that he knew I did magic and that he didn't want me to because it makes him see scary things. He was terribly upset, and I spent the rest of the night trying to console him. He has always been timid, but this is frightening me. I need to know if my family has been or is actively harming my child." Her vehemence and motherly fortitude bent her forward, ready to act on whatever Mr. Doud decided.

"I see. And you'd prefer we do it here, so that you can put your efforts to comforting him and consoling him if it's upsetting; and because your family has no access to this place. I understand, Ms. Cunningham. I'll talk to Mr. Midsommer, and we'll arrange something for..." He glanced at the calendar on the wall of his office. It had the month's listing of the days but also astrological paths and notices. "Tomorrow night."

She knew it could be no sooner, given the celestial paths, so she nodded and returned to her own corner office to the south.

Mr. Doud let loose a deep sigh and reclined in his leather office chair. Not the mood he wanted in his northerly corner to begin the day, but Ms. Cunningham was correct to bring the matter to their attention. It wouldn't be the first time her powerful cultist family tried to bother their "little white sheep." He'd heard of the last time and knew what it cost her, and the Paisley Foundation. Just a few months ago, they'd found their own President Vince Young had been corrupted by a cult following the de Lorraine family. It had shaken the Foundation to its core, but it ultimately made them stronger. It also proved her fears were justified. He hoped for everyone's sake that the boy had neither been touched nor corrupted by the de Lorraines.

The ACES Anthology

Ms. Cunningham was a very sincere and likeable person. Always had been, even before Doud started out sweeping the Paisley Foundation's halls just four years ago. Though still in his early twenties, he'd always felt at home in the role of one of the Paisley Foundation Corners, endeavored to do his utmost for his fellows, and would take Ms. Cunningham's request as seriously as any other matter that came across his desk.

Doud eyed the perfect sphere of compact carbon on his desk, which he knew used to be the previous head of the de Lorraine family. He wasn't around when that incident happened, but he'd heard rumors. None of them seemed likely, but all of them imparted how miraculous it was to manage such a thing against a powerful arcane family like the de Lorraines. Mr. Doud sincerely hoped they weren't behind whatever was wrong with Tricia's son. For once, could the troubles at their door be more mundane and less magical?

Tricia Cunningham and her son arrived after 9 p.m. President Doud sat at the couch closest to Mr. Smith's desk so he could see the boy's long walk up the immense and empty lobby. It was also so that the mysterious and charismatic Mr. Smith would have an opportunity to gauge the situation as well.

The intriguing front desk man appeared to be the same age as himself, but Doud knew Mr. Smith Who Worked The Front Desk hid a lot more than his true age from everyone in an organization bent on discovering and cataloguing all secrets. He was clever, worldly, and not fooled by anything, including Doud's early attempts to glean more of the enigmatic man's past. It was all for naught, as it had been Mr. Paisley's wish to keep Mr. Smith as mysterious as he chose to be. No one had yet to go against their dead founder's order.

As for young Mr. Cunningham, he stayed exactly behind his mother the entire stretch. Mr. Doud couldn't even get a look at the boy until Tricia stopped in front of the President. She then stepped aside quickly and swiveled to position herself behind her son, leaving no chance to hide.

His initial assessment? The kid was terrified. His whole body, from his sandy-haired head to his pristine shoes, trembled. His eyes darted about the huge room and between the two strangers in it.

Settling her hands gently on his tense, little shoulders, she said, "Ira, this is Mr. Doud, and this is Mr. Smith."

Mr. Smith smiled in his usual amiable manner and nodded in greeting. He of course stayed in his seat behind his absurdly large desk, a solid twelve feet across. Mr. Smith had a thing about proximity and never got close to anyone, for good reason. Doud had worked very hard to pry even some of that reason out of the front desk man and still felt great pride at being one of a very few in the know.

To his credit, Mr. Smith was an expert in dodging the curious and levied the required distance with an outward good nature and friendly greeting. "Good evening, Ira."

Mr. Doud also smiled at the boy and said, "Pleasure to meet you, Ira." With only a few feet separating him and the tremulous boy held in place by his mother, Doud leaned forward instead of standing, so as not to appear threatening while offering a hand to shake.

Ira shoved himself backward hard enough to force Tricia off-balance. All to get away from an outstretched hand...

Mr. Doud glanced at Mr. Smith, who smirked and was no doubt thinking this reminded the both of them of the front desk man's own situation. God, let it not be that!

The Paisley Foundation President stood. "Your mother tells

me you like to draw. When we go upstairs, I have some lovely paper and coloring crayons. Have you used those before?"

It was easy to see the boy's interest at the mention of drawing, his eyes widening at the prospect of crayons instead of pencils or chalk. Ira shook his head in answer, just slightly.

Mr. Doud led the way to the elevator. When he glanced back and saw Ira willingly follow along with his mother, Doud silently cheered at such success.

Once inside the elevator, Mr. Doud worked the switches but continued to monitor the boy. Still very nervous about his surroundings. So he told Ira, "The Paisley Foundation is where your mother works. You can go in her office and draw."

Ira looked from Doud to his mother, unsure.

"This is a big building, but I promise this is a very safe place," she admonished.

The elevator stopped. Three of the four typists had gone home by this time, so only the erratic, noisy clacking of a single slow typist assaulted them when the doors parted. Doud waited for them to exit before he, too, stepped out. He caught the typist casting a quick glance their way before busily continuing at his work.

Doud had taken only one step when the boy pointed to the office closest on their right—the south corner office—and looked to his mother.

"Yes. That one is mine. You can go in."

But he didn't. He shrank inward and balled his hands to fists before tucking them into his pockets. Not in a petulant way. His eyes wide with fear, the boy was anything but calcitrant. It was odd.

"Go on, Ira," Tricia encouraged.

The boy moved closer to the door but did not reach for the knob to open it. He looked pleadingly at his mother.

She walked over to him, placed a hand on his back. "It is just an office. Nothing scary inside." She gave him a little nudge.

He resisted but must've realized he couldn't get out of it.

Doud watched, curious, as Ira slowly reached for the doorknob. He made contact with it for a brief moment, then yanked his hand away with a yelp. Tears, then sobs, folded the boy into his confused mother's embrace.

As Tricia tried to calm Ira, Doud hurried to his office. He grabbed a few sheets of untouched paper and the box of crayons, then jogged back to the crying boy. Tricia held him in her lap, both of them seated on the floor. She turned imploring eyes to Doud.

With a free hand, Mr. Doud freed his handkerchief from his suit pocket and handed it to Ms. Cunningham. She dabbed at her boy's face as he tried to pull away from her and just use the sleeve of his coat. She cleaned him up anyway.

The boy was trying hard to stop crying. Doud held out the box of crayons, hoping that would help.

It did. Ira stared longingly at the box with its promise of eight different colors inside. He reached for it but paused halfway: His eager hand froze.

"No one else has touched these," he told the boy. "And I bought them just this morning."

Willing to trust, Ira accepted the crayons. His tense little shoulders relaxed, and he picked up each colorful stick of wax, felt it over, and put it back in the box. A timid smile poked up from the edges of his mouth as he looked at Mr. Doud. "Th-th-thh-thank y-yy-yo-you."

Tricia informed them that her son had a stutter, which was why he assumed the boy hadn't been speaking all this time. To have him open up enough to express gratitude made Doud feel like a king. "You're most welcome. The paper is also fresh." He handed the sheets over.

Ira took them and laid each one out on the floor in front of him. He stared at the vast blankness of the paper. Admiring it, Mr. Doud guessed. If his other guess was correct, there was great appeal for the boy in seeing completely blank paper.

"What I'd like, Ira, is for you to draw what scared you just now. Will you do that? After, you can draw anything else you like."

Tricia's son did not like that idea and bit his lip, tossing a look his mother's way as if to ask if he really had to do it.

She gave him a nod. "Ira, please do as he says."

Ira stared into his box of crayons, selected a few colors, and looked in regret at the crisp, white paper before beginning his artwork.

Doud backed away and went to the western corner office, as Mr. Midsommer had been quietly observing and waiting patiently to see whether he should come out and be introduced to the nervous boy. The Vice President was a tall, sandy-haired man, reserved most of the time but outspoken when need be. He'd been the Secretary for the Paisley Foundation since the beginning, working alongside Tricia and the original President and Vice President, until her family's continued attacks killed several of their number. Vice President Grummond was replaced by one of their agents—Mr. Conrad Turner. Mr. Turner was not done in by Tricia's family but one of the other many cosmic horrors the Paisley Foundation dealt with on a daily basis. As the Corners were still in need of a new Vice President, Mr. Midsommer had stepped in for the time being.

"Approach casually," Doud advised in brief.

Mr. Midsommer nodded while both observed the boy hand Tricia his picture.

When her mouth fell open, Doud quickened his pace to meet her. She threw a startled look his way and handed the drawing to him. On the paper was an undeniable likeness of a portly gentleman in a gray suit, angry fists raised high—the last client to enter Tricia's office.

President Marshall Doud waved Vice President Harold Midsommer over to join him in studying the picture just crayoned by the child of Treasurer Tricia Cunningham.

Ira collected his new gifted box of crayons and the remaining crisp, white paper and walked halfway between his mother's office door and one of the empty typewriters. There, he lay once more on the floor, spread out the paper and crayons, and started a new picture.

All three Corners crowded around the finished drawing. Doud did not miss a slight pause in the typing, flicked a glance over at the single typist also trying to catch a look at the picture.

"That's..."

"Mr. McGillis, yes," Mr. Doud finished for Mr. Midsommer.

Mr. Midsommer looked up from the paper. His eyes lingered on the boy.

Ever cognizant of his peers, Doud followed his gaze. No one spoke of it, but they all suspected that Midsommer was the boy's father. Ms. Cunningham's husband had died eight years before the child was born. She kept to herself on personal matters outside of the Paisley Foundation, but she knew their job was to know everything about everyone. Would it surprise her to know that they'd all agreed not to poke at her affairs? However, given what he'd just seen, it was time to bring the matter forward.

"It's psychometry, isn't it." Not even a question, Ms. Cunningham spoke her suspicion.

They shared a look, Doud and Midsommer. She said what they were all thinking: confirmation of what was already suspected.

Cunningham knelt beside her son, who drew grass with his green crayon while lying on his belly on the cool tile floor. Doud and Midsommer followed.

"Ira, why don't you sit at a desk? It makes drawing easier. I'll even open the door for you."

He shook his sandy-haired head at his mother's suggestion.

Midsommer squatted down but kept his distance. "Is the desk too loud?"

Ira stopped meticulously drawing green blades of grass. He sat up, looked at Midsommer with a curious frown—as if he could not believe someone might understand. Then he nodded.

"But the floor isn't?" Midsommer queried.

The ACES Anthology

"I-i-it-it's qu-quieter. Hum-Hum-mum-m-ming." The boy patted the floor with his left hand.

"Do you understand what it is that you see, feel, and hear when you touch something?"

Doud let Midsommer handle the questions. Midsommer knew more about psychometry than anyone else in the Paisley Foundation. It had been the first incantation the then-Secretary mastered, learning it from Mrs. Paisley, their founder's wife.

Ira nodded. "H-h-how-how d-dyou you s-st-stop it?" His lower lip quivered, but he clenched his jaw to stop himself from crying again.

Midsommer sighed. "I'm sorry, Ira. I truly am. It's called psychometry—to touch something and sense the past of an object. I can do it, but I need to focus to activate it. Your psychometry appears to be an ability that is active all the time. I can try to teach you ways to control it, but I have no easy method. I truly am sorry."

Given the hurting look Ms. Cunningham shot Midsommer, sharing the defeat echoed on her son's face, Doud felt for all three of them. It never occurred to any of them that Cunningham's latent familial talent for magic would pair with Midsommer's learned arcane abilities. Perhaps that isn't exactly what happened to produce a boy with uncontrolled powers, but that is what she ended up with.

The room held a dark aura sensed by all. Ira could no longer hold back tears but, to mitigate his own emotions, he lay flat on the ground again, his head resting sideways on his left arm whilst he selected a black crayon and started furiously coloring the sky of his green grass picture. His tears trailed down his arm but not onto the precious paper.

The room remained silent but for the scribbling. Odd. There had prior been the off-time clacking of the single typist at one of the desks. Doud knew the man to work late, on request, and he'd been busily typing this whole time. He also knew the man had a knack for blending into social scenes, an asset in some ways, but it tended to slow his typing rate proportionate to his propensity to chat. Doud also knew that typing wasn't the reason he'd brought Mr. Johnathan Raine up into the typist's pool. Untapped skills in that man, just as there were in this boy.

As Raine wasn't one to keep so quiet, Doud look up from studying Ira's work.

Raine wasn't paused watching them, nor listening in. He wasn't in his seat at all.

Doud double-checked the other three open corner offices. Empty as well. He began to wonder when exactly Raine had slipped away when the elevator doors opened. Johnathan Raine stepped out, grinning like a cat with a mouse. He had a small, flat box in one big hand and proudly walked it over to the Cunninghams.

"It seems to me, young man, you could try these." Raine squatted down between mother and son and slid the box along the floor toward the boy.

Ira's head righted. He wiped at his tears, sat up, and eyed the box. It was within reach. He looked once at his mother, who nodded, before using the black crayon to flip the lid off the flat rectangular box. Inside lay a pair of small, cream-colored gloves. They were for a woman, but Ira didn't care as he lay one palm atop the silky handwear. He did not pull away. He took out the gloves, eagerly jamming each small hand into them. Then, biting his lower lip, he stared at the doorknob of his mother's office. He stood, went over to it, and gingerly wrapped his gloved hand around the thing. He did not yank back as before but immediately threw a grin his mother's way.

The ACES Anthology

Ms. Cunningham, in uncharacteristic fashion, stood and hugged Raine. "Thank you."

Taken aback by the affection, he muttered a modest, "It was nothing. Just a theory."

"A brilliant one that made the most sense when we momentarily lost our senses," Doud amended, relaxing shoulders, which had gone so tense the last few days. All that build-up melted away. And he grinned at Mr. Johnathan Raine, knowing that it would only be a short time before he was ready for agent status. Perhaps a shorter span after that, the position of Vice President could be properly filled, and Mr. Midsommer could go back to his previous desired position of Secretary. Things, for now, looked like they were falling into place; both for the future of the Paisley Foundation, for Ira Cunningham, and perhaps the world in general. Just had to keep doing what the Paisley Foundation always did: maintaining the political cover of influential people, handling evil cultists, performing the appropriate rites, making sacrifices to ensure the great sleepers slumbered, and hiding it all from the populace. All part of the job.

"The Origins of Mr. Cunningham" is © 2023 by Jade Griffin. The author, a Reno resident, has published a horror story series "The Journals of Lacy Moore: Monster Hunter of the 1800s" and the Call of Cthulhu tabletop RPG series "Amor Fati," with the upcoming "Ebon Roots" finishing the first set and introducing her expanded cosmic mythos which includes the Paisley Foundation. For more on the Paisley Foundation and stories like it, look for the Solo TTPRG "A Lone

The ACES Anthology

Collection" and the upcoming novel "Mr. Smith Who Works The Front Desk," available in the ACES bookshop at acesofnorthernnevada.com and her website. When not releasing her creative firestorm, she enjoys her kids, cats, dinosaurs, and the outdoors. You can find all of her publications at http://jadegriffinauthor.com.

Kelli Heitstuman-Tomko
The Escape

When she looked out through the open door, the buzzards were still eating Jasper, pulling strips of flesh off his body and fighting over his innards. The low cackle of their squabbling echoed off the stable in the waning light, but Jasper had been a big man, and there was enough for all of them.

She closed the door and looked around the shack. Only then did she whisper the names she had been afraid to forget in her imprisonment. The names felt distantly familiar on her lips. She dropped to her knees, and then to the floor and wept.

When she finally pushed herself up into a sitting position, she gasped at the pain in her back and arms, waiting for the blow that would punish her for emitting a sound without permission. She held her breath for a moment before she remembered the dead man in the yard.

She stood and stumbled around the shack until she found the matches. The moon was full and gave her a little light until she had the lantern on the table lit. Afraid of the remaining shadows, she lit the other two lanterns in the single room and shuddered. The filth of her prison was somehow more oppressive in the poor lighting. She stood on the bear-hide rug in the middle of the room, taking deep breaths to slow her heartbeat and fight her rising despair.

It was almost one in the morning if the clock on the chair was correct. It was her clock, a wedding gift from her father, a remembrance to grace the mantle of a home. Instead, it sat on a battered chair, pulled from her husband's Conestoga by a murderer.

It was later than she thought, and she felt she should sleep to rest her body and mind so she could see to her survival, but she couldn't bear returning to the bed where she'd been chained for months while her captor beat her and raped her and so completely traumatized her than she could not remember her own name. It wasn't *Bitch* or *Whore*, the two words used to address her over the past year. Her name was engraved on the back of the clock, but she wasn't ready to read it yet. She only held to the names she didn't want to lose.

She moved to the corner near the woodstove and picked up the burlap bag. Jasper had just come back with supplies two days ago, leaving her chained so she couldn't run while he was gone. But run where? She had no idea where she was or where she would go, and he knew it. But he knew where they were, and if he'd returned to find her gone, he would have no trouble finding her. She was chained only because he did not want to bother looking.

She dropped tins of food into the sack. Her movement was automatic, motivated by memory. She had done this before, far away in Missouri, shifting stock in the Conestoga as they prepared to leave in the morning. How far away was Missouri from where she was now?

He had been excited about the trip to the goldfields. *Matthew.*

It was one of the names she often whispered when she was alone in the darkness in an attempt to save her sanity. Matthew was a cleric, not a man born for grueling work, but he hadn't planned to mine. Where there were miners and mines there was a need for supplies. Matthew would open a dry goods store, and she would bake. There had been so much hope then, so much expectation.

She needed to breathe something besides the stale air in the shack. She opened the door and then stared at the threshold. It was Jasper's line crossing into the forbidden, his invisible line she would never cross, though she'd tried once. He had tattooed her infractions on her naked back with a length of knotted rope, breaking her down with beatings and rape until, even now, when she knew he wasn't coming back, she was afraid to step out.

Maybe just to the stoop, she thought. Maybe she could just get to the stoop tonight. She inhaled the cold air rushing into the shack through the open door and moved her foot toward the threshold, but when she looked up, the owl was there. She froze where she stood.

It was a barn owl, resting just inside the tattered canvas of the Conestoga wagon that sat in the shadow of a tree and the hastily erected stable.

She backed up into the house and slammed the door, breathing hard and trying desperately to make no sound. She tried to remind herself that she was a Christian woman, and she was not superstitious. She'd heard talk, though, from the men when the wagons were circled for the night, about the Indians on the other side of the mountains. The *Mewuk*, one man had called them, believed that when an honorable man died, he became a Great Horned Owl, but when an evil man died, he became a barn owl. She peered through the window at the owl sitting in the wagon watching the house, and memory of the nights camped with the wagons seeped through her being and ran free down her face.

Jasper was an evil man.

Jasper had first shown up on the trail on foot. Indians had killed his saddle partner, he said, had stolen their horses. The trail master had taken Jasper in and allowed him to stay with the train as long as he helped out. Matthew, the memory of his face lost, had whispered low to her as she sat in the wagon feeding the baby.

"Do not have anything to do with that man," he told her. "I don't believe his story. I remember him alone in Missouri, and he watched us all leave. Johnson, the scout, thinks we've been followed by a white man, and we think it's Jasper."

The women of the train took turns feeding Jasper, but Matthew never allowed her to deliver the food when her turn came to donate a meal. He, Matthew, took the food to Jasper. And Jasper always asked after "the little wife."

"Matthew." She spoke the name aloud for the first time since her nightmare began. "Thomas."

She had her own problems on the train, and she had given little thought to the interloper and the feeling of unease he brought to everyone. Baby Thomas, born during the wait in Missouri, became ill. He was unable to keep food down, and his tiny body burned with fever. The day they had buried the baby, she looked up to find Jasper standing ten feet from the wagon, watching, smug, like there was something he knew.

It wasn't a week past the baby's death that the wagon train was hit by white men poorly disguised as Indians. She lay protected in the back of the wagon, but, as she lifted her head to see what was happening, she saw Jasper shoot Matthew through the chest with a rifle, calling to his fellow marauders that he'd captured a wife.

Life became a hell of rape and whippings, and she gave up hope that anyone was searching for her when they arrived at the meager shack in the desert that Jasper called home. She witnessed the changing of seasons, and she lost a child after a bad beating for accidentally burning a chunk of meat. No one came looking for her. Why would they? No one knew she ended up miserable in a desert with a man who was not her husband, that she spent every moment she could whispering the names of her lost husband and son so she would remember this hadn't been the only life she'd known.

Matthew. Thomas.

The owl had moved to the tailgate of the Conestoga. Of course, the owl wasn't Jasper. Jasper was down near the river, lying exposed to the elements just as he'd left Matthew, birds and vermin and wild animals eating his body. Had anyone in the train been left alive to bury the dead? Or was Matthew picked clean like Jasper would be when the birds and the beasts were done with him?

She scraped a little flour and made biscuits to eat with fried bacon and grease. She did not sit as she ate but moved around the shack and considered her situation. She could flee. Could she? There were supplies in the wagon Jasper had never touched, cookware and tools, and clothing.

But she needed rest first, so she slept, but not in the bed. She sat in the rocking chair Jasper would let her touch, her own rocking chair from the wagon. She covered herself with the bear rug. She was almost asleep when the owl flew past the window and into the night.

Despite her late night, she woke with the sun. She bathed, a luxury Jasper rarely gave her, washing her hair twice to rid it of grime. She pulled her hair back and tied it with packing string. She stared into the piece of mirror Jasper used for shaving at an unrecognizable face of mottled bruises, one eye swollen where Jasper's fist had landed the previous morning. It was a face she didn't know to go with the name she couldn't remember.

Matthew. Thomas.

She opened the door and peered toward the river. There were already vultures feasting in the early morning, and more were coming. She looked down at the stoop. Had she not slept in the forbidden rocking chair, eaten food of her own free will, and let the fire go out? Had she suffered for it? She held her breath and put out a bare foot, shoes having been forbidden from the first night Jasper had taken her to keep her from running, and she stepped onto the stoop. She stood for the count of twenty and breathed in the chilly morning air. She took another step, and then another.

Her steps took her to the wagon where her trunk of clothing had been sitting for months. She didn't have the strength to drag it, so she opened it on the tailgate of the wagon and pulled out clean clothes before turning and deliberately returning to the cabin.

She felt exhausted and, yet, somehow, invigorated. She draped her clothes over the rocking chair, then relit the fire and made coffee to have with the rest of the biscuits and a tin of peaches. When she finished eating, she changed into the clean clothes, pulling on stockings and shoes as well.

The clothes gave her new confidence. She returned to the trunk on the tailgate of the wagon. As she did, she looked back toward the river and saw the Indian women had returned with the child. They had been digging near the river yesterday when Jasper had gone to chase them away. In his anger, he had kicked the child, and the older of the two women had stabbed him with her knife. Jasper staggered toward the house, falling only fourteen steps from the river. Less than an hour later, the vultures were there.

Making several trips, she took the rest of her clothing inside. She was under no illusion that she could escape with them. But Matthew had counted on any bandits seeing only clothing in the trunk. Jasper had taken the strong box when he looted the wagon. When she found it, the money was almost gone, but she had expected that. Jasper hadn't known about the paper money sewn into pockets in each of her dresses. She would not have been able to lie to him if he'd demanded more money, but his imagination had not taken him beyond the strongbox, and she was never put to the question.

She worked steadily, not sparing more than two of her dresses as she cut the money from them. She tied it up in a small bag she made from one of the pockets of her dress, keeping it separate from the money in the strongbox.

She put two changes of clothing and the food into the saddlebags that hung on a hook behind the rocking chair and once again walked out to the stoop. She knew that one of the oxen that had pulled the wagon had been butchered, and she had no idea where the other one was. It didn't matter. She would never have been able to yoke it. But Matthew's horse was in the barn, and Shadow would remember her.

Matthew. Thomas.

She carried the saddlebags out to the wagon and set them on the tailgate. She jerked her head around to stare at the stable. Two horses. There were two horses: Shadow and the horse Jasper had waiting here for him when he attacked the train close to the desert crossing. That changed things a little. Should she take more with her? She shook her head, and then shook it again as she second-guessed herself. She climbed into the back of the wagon and prepared a small pack of blankets, matches, a coffee pot, and a pan for cooking. She didn't want to live off the land, but she had no idea where she was, though Jasper was never gone more than a day when he went for supplies.

When she was ready, she returned to the stable. She called for Shadow, and he heard her voice, and nickered, moving toward her followed by Jasper's buckskin. Shadow bumped her hand with his nose. She petted him a moment, before wrapping her arms around his neck and weeping. This was Matthew's horse... Matthew, who she would never see again... her Matthew.

"Oh, Matthew, I need you!" she sobbed. "Thomas, I am so sorry!" The horse stood patiently while she broke down, but she shook herself, and a moment later stood tall.

"Matthew," she said. "Thomas."

She put harnesses on both horses. She'd been riding most of

her life, and she knew how to saddle a horse, but she still struggled as she saddled Shadow first, and then the buckskin. She fastened the saddlebags behind Shadow's saddle, but before she tied the pack to the buckskin's saddle, she went into the shack one more time. She retrieved the clock her father had given her. From behind the door, she grabbed Jasper's rifle, the one that had killed her husband, and boxes of ammunition.

Returning to the horses, she slid the rifle into the boot of Shadow's saddle and put the ammunition into one of the saddle bags. Moving toward the buckskin, she looked back toward the river where the women continued to work cutting reeds. Between her and the women, vultures continued to strip Jasper to the bone, stopping occasionally to squawk at a lone coyote hoping to score something for breakfast.

She made room in the pack she would tie to the buckskin's saddle for the clock her father had given her, but before she settled it into the bag, she turned it over to read the inscription and the name that had eluded her for months. And there, next to Matthew's name was her own.

Julianne Beckett.

It was time to go. She would follow the river and would fill a canteen there before going on. Perhaps she would find help in Gold Hill or Virginia City. Jasper had spoken as if they were close. There had to be someone decent there who would help a widow of the California Trail.

She pulled herself onto Shadow's back and sat tall in the saddle. "My name is Julianne Beckett," she said, loudly. "I am Julianne Beckett."

She started the horses down the path Jasper always took when he rode off. Turning one last time, she looked back at her prison. The barn owl sat on the tailgate of the wagon. It blinked, then flew down the river in the opposite direction.

The ACES Anthology

"The Escape" is ©2020 by Kelli Heitsuman-Tomko. The author is a resident of Fallon and has published eight works, including the Johnny Lister mystery series, which are available in the ACES bookshop at acesofnorthernnevada.com. Kelli is a former cops and courts journalist, an amateur photographer, and a crafter. You can follow her at www.facebook.com/khtwrites.

Lisa Kirkman
Rebecca on the Streets

The Barrett family is on Day 20 of a punishing day-and-night search for their feral rescue cat in Tahoe's rugged Upper Kingsbury neighborhood. Their struggle to search for the cat is a very real demonstration of the family's inability to connect with each other. Rebecca, the mom, has just spectacularly screwed up a late-night attempt to lure the cat into the garage as a trap.

Rebecca stood in the shower. In the dark. Bryan was downstairs with a drink. No more apologies could be given, no further insight could be gained by asking "why?"

The footage of the cat scrambling out of the garage played over and over in her mind. She stood, as wet as she had ever been, as wet as she was ever going to get, with her hands against the wall, head down, arrested by the effort they'd been making to get this cat back.

If only we understood her motivations, we could just go to her and explain, she thought.

Rebecca was a practical person. If she were lost outside, it was obvious the right thing to do would be to simply follow the food and walk through the door to the welcoming bosom of her family.

The value of being safe and inside was vastly better than being outside. Alone.

"She has to want to come home," an uninvited voice offered.

Her eyelids sagged, lulled by the shower's heat and the Sisyphean task of trying and failing to connect with someone who refused to be practical.

Thirty years earlier...

She didn't want the long night ahead of her.

Rebecca didn't want to go to the riverbank at the edge of their neighborhood. But that's where her sister was, so she had to. At dusk. Because her sister was alone. Rebecca's instincts told her to stay home. Home was safer.

Rebecca and her sister grew up in a rolling Sacramento suburb, a community of three- and four-bedroom ranch homes whose color palate ranged from taupe to peach. The curves of streets were determined by the American River bending widely around their subdivision, carrying snowmelt from the Sierra Nevada to the farms of Central California.

Her sister, age 17, ran away, and stayed lost, by walking down their street until the houses petered out and the brush took over at the riverbank, less than a mile away.

The American River's excuse for a beach there is a dark sandy spit of dirt on the river's north shore. With its scrawny trees, the beach was pulled unrelentingly underwater until drowned. The upper portion, which resisted the eternal downward pull of the water, was rugged with an unwelcoming forest of willow whips and spikey chaparral bushes. People rode bikes along lumpy trails that washed out in wet years. Some walked their dogs off-leash. Most drove on the interstate forty feet above, never knowing it ever existed.

Rebecca's sister walked until her feet were wet, which somehow suffocated the noises in her head that had become so overbearing. Sissy sat on the riverbank that first night and listened to the water flow past her. The water lulled her until she tilted over and slept. She stayed close to the river's sharp pebbly sand, tangled in the brush for several weeks.

Sacramento, with circles of suburbs orbiting around Downtown, is disorientingly hot and humid during its improbably long summer. The vast cubic acre-feet of airborne moisture from the convergence of the American, Sacramento, and San Joaquin rivers feeds agriculture, but poaches its human residents. As summer's humidity evaporates, a vagrant heat loiters through autumn. By then, the heat devolves to become criminally dry and itchy. Winter's grey rain deluges the valley in sheets, washing away fall's colors, soaking through skin, and chilling bones.

But three little weeks in April redeem the River City with blooming trees and perfectly heavenly temperatures.

This secret, fleeting spring made it possible for a girl on the cusp of womanhood, overwhelmed by her commitments, and betrayed by misfiring synapses that corroded her mind with a toxic cocktail of neurotransmitters, to lose herself in the weather's reprieve.

When the girls were preschoolers, as a young father whose house payment was greater than his supply of spending cash, he'd held his daughters' hands and walked down to the sandbar to fish or play in the mud and run off their little-kid energy. By elementary school, the gritty sandbar had lost its charms. He hadn't been down there in more than a decade.

Sissy and Rebecca's parents ranged over their neighborhood day and night looking for their eldest daughter, hanging up posters on poles, beating bushes, poking into garden sheds, bursting through unlocked doors, rattling neighbors. It took their father days to piece together Sissy's simple route.

When her sister left, Rebecca assigned herself house duty, making dinner and doing dishes. She was actively "being there" in case her sister returned home.

On the nights her parents could find her, they couldn't convince her to come home so they offered Sissy blankets and sandwiches. She walked away. They offered fruit, candy, baked goods. Clothes. Sleeping bags. Music. A brand-new car. All were ignored.

Sissy's school friends were pressed into service. When Sissy didn't simply walk away from them, she babbled incoherently about threats they couldn't see and accused them of crimes they weren't planning to commit. Her odd affect caused confusion and distress. Some cried. All left the mudflat before making any impression on her.

In their fretful exploration of the riverbank, her parents came across a young reverend from an area church offering food and showers to those made homeless by choice or circumstance. "The Lord doesn't judge why people need help," Father Jamie assured them knowingly. He was the first to suggest mental illness to the family and offered them a deceptively simple solution: attract her with something, or someone, that Sissy wanted.

Rebecca crocheted mittens for her sister in teal blue and lined them with a fluffy fleece: a simple design with high function, just like Rebecca. She asked her parents to give them to Sissy on their next visit. Her mom implored Rebecca to take them to Sissy herself.

"There's so much to do here at the house if everyone else is out running around," Rebecca said. "I can't... I can't leave," gesturing to the empty house.

"But you're so important to your sister," her mom pleaded. They were sure Rebecca could break through whatever was keeping Sissy apart from them.

Rebecca missed her sister desperately. But just as desperately, she did not want to go to the riverbank. She did not want to talk to the people who lived down there. Rebecca was certain that with enough time, Sissy could become one of those people. Dirty. Unrecognizable.

Her dad identified an abandoned horse stable at the western side of the sandbar, and based their rescue operation there: Rebecca would go find her sister, give her the mittens, and walk with her over to the old shed. They'd take her to a hospital from there. Simple.

The do-it-yourselfer rescue squad of parents, priest—and a neighbor who had taken an oddly keen interest—would all wait inside the shed to talk to Sissy. "It was an intervention," they said.

Rebecca saw it for the trap it was, and understood she and her mittens were the bait.

Rebecca was briefed on the priest's improbable way to talk to Sissy. Rebecca was to "L.E.A.P."

"You have to Listen, Empathize, Agree, and Partner with your sister," he'd said, knitting his fingers together solemnly to demonstrate their partnership, "to help her accept the treatment she needs."

"I can't be listening very well if I have to remember this stupid L.E.A.P. script," she snapped.

Rebecca found her sister that night after a frustrating game of telephone with several homeless people who overwhelmed Rebecca with their disinterest or their derangement.

Sissy stood barefoot in her nightgown at the water's edge, looking not quite at the water but at something only she could see in the middle distance, engaged in a conversation with that something. Her wavy golden cheerleader's hair was flat and grimy and brownish. Sissy was gaunt after three weeks outside. Rebecca was scandalized to realize her sister actually had been sleeping in dirt all this time. Deep scratches from the bushes were visible on her legs.

Rebecca estimated they must be a quarter-mile downstream of the old horse shed, and Sissy was not playing her part in the L.E.A.P.ing dialog. They were way off-script. Rebecca had to improvise.

She crept closer to Sissy, used her gentle voice, and strained to talk about the sorts of things they always talked about. Like any other day. She told her sister about kids at school doing dumb things... about an old green dress she'd hemmed for a friend to wear on a date... that her locker jammed up today... about her Chemistry test yesterday.

Usually, Sissy was a vivacious conversational partner. She wanted to talk to anyone about anything. Sissy read widely and remembered everything: facts, dates, names, faces, favorite foods, funny anecdotes. She used the motion of talking at dinner to chew her food because not even having your mouth full should slow down a good story.

Rebecca staggered under the weight of contributing so much material to a conversation. She fidgeted with the mittens and felt light-headed and zipped her windbreaker up to her throat and kicked the dirt.

"I know you're poisoning me," Sissy said in a dead-flat voice. She never broke eye contact with her invisible fixation. "I hear you thinking. You want to kill me. With that poison."

Rebecca boggled. Is she talking to me now? she thought. Are the mittens the poison? Was Sissy poisoned? Is that what happened to her? Was this one of those weird predictions from the oracles that never made sense in Greek Lit class?

Rebecca found herself clutched in a desperate paradox: She could only think of things she wasn't supposed to tell her sister. Shuddering from awkwardness, but driven forward by necessity, Rebecca reached out and touched her sister's arm to comfort her. She was about to say, "No, I made you these mittens. I love you, and we all want you to come home."

At the touch, Sissy jumped straight up like she had been electrocuted. Her face stretched in terror and animal-like fear. "Don't you hurt me anymore!"

Rebecca would never tell anyone about that version of her sister's face, though she would see it in her dreams for the rest of her life. Any memory of that face was always accompanied by a screech that probably wasn't there originally. Her own horror added the sound effect.

With no regard for rocks or glass or danger, Sissy ran like the track star she had been into a dark grove of spindly trees fenced in by waist-high scrubs and curtains of willows. She ran and ran and ran southwest along the river.

Dumbfounded, mouth agape, arm reaching, feet stuck, voice mute, Rebecca couldn't see her sister beyond the trees in the post-twilight gloom.

"That was my chance," Rebecca said. "And she's running away from us! We lost her."

Rebecca pulled up short and corrected herself.

The ACES Anthology

"No. I lost her."

Sissy never came home.

※ ※

"Rebecca on the Streets" is ©2022 by Lisa Kirkman. An excerpt from Lisa's first full-length novel, "Black Cat Walks in the Moonlight." It appears here for the first time. Lisa spent her career in advertising and is excited to roll out a new and improved fiction product because it was a story she really wanted to read about family and connections that never truly break. She lives on Lake Tahoe's rugged Nevada shore with her husband and daughter.

The ACES Anthology

Sandie La Nae

A Christmas Gift for a Ghost

Once upon a time
(Christmas of twenty-o-eight)
A spirit girl,
with a golden curl
Was living at my place.

She emerged as phantom mist
Then in a few more ways:
Presenting her feet,
then all, complete...
Is how I first met this waif.

She was a girl of six
Who died in the ending year
Of her time,
(1889)...
By the flu! The illness severe!

The ACES Anthology

Buried in the desert,
Her parents carried on.
She was left behind
(un-resigned)
And started a search for her mom.

But, asking to rest a while
In my home, I said, "Alright."
A holiday
came our way
And an idea flashed to my mind.

Off to the store I ran
Wanting to find the most
Cutest rag doll,
something I'd call
"A Christmas Gift for a Ghost."

The Eve was upon us now,
A fun festivity.
The spirit was
excited because
Her toy sat under the tree.

The doll was nestled in
A linen towel of red.
With a tag,
Wrapped 'round the bag,
"For the little ghost girl," it said.

The ACES Anthology

Morning time brought joy
To the anxious, phantom miss.
And to me!
This so unique
Of celebration. The bliss!

Then, when came the nights
The dolly sat in a chair.
I'd find it laying,
(from the girl's playing)
On the floor, in morning's air.

It is such delight
To know my house ghost is glad
Of the present –
seemingly pleasant! –
The poppet, dressed in plaid.

Soon though, the specter was gone.
(In search of her absent mother?)
I was pained,
but knew I gained
A memory like no other!

Now sitting on a shelf
The rag doll waits for when,
A ghost, alone,
wants a home
And also a toy to befriend.

The ACES Anthology

The poem: "A Christmas Gift For A Ghost" is ©2015 by Sandie La Nae. The author is a resident of Carson City and has published 31 works, including history and "Weird" series which are available in the ACES bookshop at <u>acesofnorthernnevada.com</u>. Sandie is an author of different genres, host of community TV and radio shows, and Intuitive first and foremost. You can follow the author at <u>www.sandiespsychicstones.com.</u>

Angela Laverghetta

Of Camels and Fae

"Shoo! Out of my garden you menace!"

The woman snapped her bandana back and forth as she clambered over the downed pole fence.

The camel blinked its heavily lashed eyes and ignored her as it ripped up another mouthful of lettuce. It chewed, mouth swinging exaggeratedly from one side to the other, while its feet trampled more of her pea plants.

She wouldn't have known the creature was a camel if she hadn't once seen a picture through a stereoscope. Davy loved the exotic pictures the most. He would have been buzzing with excitement to actually see one.

The woman couldn't muster any emotion besides irritation.

The fence that she'd meticulously cut and set around her precious garden had been pushed completely over on one whole side. A few of the rails were snapped, and most of the posts leaned. It would take days for her to fix it.

For a brief moment, she agreed with all her socialite friends she'd left behind in San Francisco—maybe she was mad to think she could make it on her own. But she shuddered when she imagined being back in gowns and corsets. Besides, this had been the plan, the life she and Davy had wanted.

The camel crunched through more of the lettuce and, almost in slow motion, it lifted its long neck to stare off toward the Sierra Nevada mountains in the distance. Probably wishing it had never seen the American West and was still roaming the desert of its native land. The woman wished that too. Then maybe she wouldn't be looking at a large bill at Mason Huff & Co. come winter with half her harvest consumed by dromedary. In the current situation, her fury at the traitor Davis for even thinking up the idea of importing camels almost neared her rage over the Confederation.

Just beyond the mountaintop, dark clouds congregated. It was hard to know if they'd boil into a squall or scatter away. She certainly didn't want to be out in a storm still trying to protect whatever vegetables were salvageable.

She ripped off her wide-brimmed hat and stepped closer, yelling louder and waving both it and the bandana more frantically.

Finally acknowledging her presence, the camel swung its neck toward her and grumbled low in its throat, mimicking the thunder in the distance.

The woman took a step closer. "Get out!"

The camel grumbled again and charged a few steps forward, using its own head and neck like a swinging bludgeon. The woman jumped away, mindful of the aggressive-looking bony protrusion on the animal's chest—right at the level of her neck. This could all end very badly.

But so would starving to death!

The camel returned to ignoring her and moved from munching lettuce to eating beans.

She slammed her hat on her head and stuffed the bandana into the pocket of her blue pants. She stomped back through her trampled plants, over the downed fence, and bent to grab up the largest rock she could immediately find from the desert ground. Just as she raised her arm to let it fly, a hand grabbed her wrist.

"Aaaahhh," she yelped, ripping her arm free.

She stumbled sideways away from the camel and whoever had grabbed her, yelling, "Who the hell do you think you are?" But when she got a glimpse of the person, her next words barely left her mouth in a whisper. "This is private property."

The man? Was he a man? He seemed too beautiful. Nothing like the miners or other homesteaders or even the suit-wearing banker in town. Definitely didn't smell like them either. This man clearly had access to a bath. He didn't even remind her of the well-bathed, rich, young men she'd met while living in San Francisco. And despite the leather he wore; he physically looked nothing like the Indians that often traded her skins for the doilies she crocheted in the evening.

He was wholly different from any of them. The skin on his face, and what was peeking out from the opening of his shirt, curved pale and smooth like a ceramic doll. His long, chestnut-colored hair hung in one long braid, but curls had escaped and swirled around his ears. Ears that seemed like they almost came to a point.

What an unusual birth defect.

Before the woman could ask him again what he was doing on her land, the strange man made his way into the garden and confronted the camel. He scratched its neck affectionately, murmuring low enough that she couldn't hear. "Is this your camel?" she demanded.

The stranger leaned and pointed to the brand on the camel's haunch. "From the look of that brand, it would seem the owner is the U.S. government." The woman had heard many accents while living in a port city, but this man's was strange, almost Irish but not quite.

He was still suspiciously confident as he made clicking sounds with his tongue, trailing his hand over the coarse brown fur. He moved along the animal's body until he disappeared behind the hump, only his legs visible beneath the belly.

The camel groaned and then stepped away, moving off and out of the garden, like magic. The strange man followed, tapping him lightly on the haunches. The camel gingerly stepped over the downed fence as if it was not responsible for its destruction in the first place. Back on desert footing, it stopped, and the stranger gave the animal another hearty scratch. It dropped its head for him to reach behind the ears. "I know what it's like to never go home, my friend. You must accept it and learn the rules." The man leaned close to the camel's ear and said in a stage whisper as he looked at the woman—were his eyes sparkling?—"We never steal food from children or beautiful women."

She crossed her arms and tilted her head. She didn't trust men who tried to charm her. They always wanted something she wasn't willing to give.

From the direction of the accumulated clouds in the distance, a brisk wind rushed over, swirling the loose sand into the air and peppering the back of her legs with tiny rough-angled pebbles. With it came the smell of rain. The clouds were starting to make up their minds. She plopped a hand on the top of her head to keep her hat on as the wind continued to whip. The stranger clicked with his tongue again and tapped the camel to get it moving. Through the dust, the woman watched it trot off, its body rocking side to side.

The stranger turned and walked toward her. He wasn't altogether tall, but he had an imposing air that lengthened his stature. The wind dipped in velocity for a moment and appeared to pull playfully at his hair. He reached up to push the escaped curls back away from his face, drawing her gaze to his eyes again. As chestnut as his hair, they gleamed with intensity. A flutter, the woman had thought long dead, quickened in her chest.

Only Davy had caused such sensations.

But she wasn't ready to explore where those thoughts led.

She quickly looked away from the stranger, avoiding his direct gaze. "I thank you kindly, mister, but I'll ask you to be on your way now," she said firmly.

Out of the corner of her eye, she saw the stranger reach out a hand, but the woman held her arms tightly to her side. With a smile, he pulled his hand back to his forehead and gave a slight bow. "Good afternoon, ma'am. It was a pleasure to be of service to one such as yourself."

One such as myself? What in the Sam Hill did that mean? She shook her head and took a step toward her cabin. "Yes, well, good day," she called over her shoulder, waving as she walked.

Behind her, the scratching sound of leather soles against the dirt followed her. The flutters in her stomach turned cold and heavy. Where had the man even come from? She lived miles from another homestead.

And why wasn't he leaving?

She spun around, riding a wave of fearful energy. The stranger stumbled to a halt. "Sir," she snapped. "I have thanked you for your help, and now I would see you on your way."

The wind gusted harder, and she squinted as grit clung to her eyelashes. The stranger didn't seem bothered by the rising storm. He stood tall, eyes open.

The woman contemplated how far away her rifle was, resting up against the back wall inside the cabin. Would she be able to dash to it fast enough before the man caught her? Not likely. Above, the dark clouds seemed to finally come to a decision, and now they roiled in their direction, a stampede of atmospheric chaos.

"I'll be off then," the stranger said, acting as if leaving had always been his idea. And from one moment to the next, he disappeared.

Wind battered against her, howling across her ears, as she stood frozen, unable to understand what had just happened. Her family had never been church people, but they'd gone enough times for her to be familiar with the devil. She'd thought it pure nonsense, but...

People do not disappear.

Maybe the stranger really was the devil.

Or maybe she'd truly gone mad out here by herself.

And then he was there again in front of her. "If you would be so kind though, I do have one question," he said loudly to be heard over the oncoming storm.

The woman slammed her back up against the closed door of her cabin and screamed. The hand closest to the latch fumbled frantically, trying to release it.

The stranger scrunched up his face as his shoulders tried to overtake his neck. He patted the air in front of her, "Apologies, ma'am, apologies. If you would allow me to explain. It's just my curiosity you see."

Why wouldn't the damn door open?

"I promise, I mean you no harm. I've watched you for days. You intrigue me."

Her screaming trailed off in disbelief. This man, this whatever he was, spoke as if admitting he'd watched her for days wasn't worse. He'd disappeared and reappeared. People didn't do that sort of thing. Not living ones. "Are you a ghost?" She managed to get out.

"No, not a ghost, ma'am." He set his right fist above his heart and dipped his head. "I'm Fae. A faerie. One of the Wee Folk."

"Wee Folk?" She eyed him up and down.

The stranger dropped his fist. "We didn't pick that last one. Highly inaccurate." He winked.

Was he implying something libidinous? She quickly looked down toward the door and found the latch just as thunder rumbled, building slowly until it boomed, shaking what felt like the entire valley. Both she and the stranger looked skyward as lightning snapped. For a moment, the world was made only of light. The clouds let loose in a deluge of drops so large mud rained upward when they hit the ground.

Situated just within the recess of the doorway, the woman remained relatively dry, but the stranger was immediately soaked. His leather shirt and trousers had darkened to nearly black. "You did thank me, so you'd be owning me a bit o' shelter."

"Owe you?" Outrage colored her words.

"I not be making the rules, but you no doubt can feel the truth of it." He pointed to his chest.

She opened her mouth to disagree and clicked it shut again. She could feel it. It was by all rights completely mad, but she felt the debt sitting within her, requiring fulfillment. "I don't trust you," the woman responded with the only words she could find.

He pointed into the interior as water streamed down his face, plastering the curls to his neck. "Grab your rifle!" he yelled above the downpour. "I promise I mean you no harm, but should you feel threatened, you'll be armed."

She took only a second to decide before she opened the door. Dashing inside, she snatched up the rifle and turned around. Through the open door, the stranger hadn't moved. He raised his hand only to wipe rain from his eyes. Aware she couldn't speak loud enough for him to hear, she waved her rifle to urge him inside.

He didn't run, but walked briskly into her one-room cabin.

Rifle held out for easy use; she circled around him and her single chair to close the door, blocking out much of the noise of the storm. She stayed by the tiny cabin's only egress, comforted by the thought of an easy escape. Now she was alone with the stranger, an experience not even she and Davy had been granted. But this stranger wasn't a person. He was something else entirely. Was that better or worse?

The stranger turned in her direction, again wiping the water that dripped onto his face from his hair. Even in the shadow of the cabin, his eyes seemed to find the light and glow. He pulled at his wet shirt and let it flop back down against him with a soggy slap.

"Shall I start a fire?" she asked. She wasn't as wet as the stranger, but the storm had brought in the chill.

"Allow me," he said. He pointed to the gun. "That way you can keep that ready. In the event I do something you aren't liking."

"You mean like watching me for days, without my knowledge?"

He tipped his head and gave a guilty smirk. "Ahhh that." The stranger moved toward her fireplace. He crouched down, grabbing up the tinder from the nearby basket.

"Well, what do you have to say for yourself?"

He picked up her striker and flint. "Simple. I was lonely."

He said the words with complete sincerity, and the woman found her anger fading. The last two years of her life had been immensely difficult. Hard work, determination: These things had kept her alive. But they hadn't made her any less alone.

A spark caught and began to smoke.

The stranger looked over his shoulder, and they gazed at each other in silence. Only the sound of droplets hitting the ground and roof—lighter now—and the beginning crackle of flames filled the space around them.

As the seconds passed, tension crept over her limbs. To halt the quiet, she asked, "Before, you said you had a question."

"Oh, aye." The stranger reached for more kindling, breaking eye contact, and the woman let out a shuddering breath. Finally, he asked, "Why do you live out here, all alone?"

The rifle had dipped in the woman's hands, the muzzle pointing down. She raised it again. She *was* alone. And she'd let a stranger in. Her heart pounded, but she answered truthfully. "I thought it would bring me closer to someone I once loved."

The stranger nodded. He grabbed a small log and situated it in the hearth. The fire seemed to engulf it immediately. He stared into the flames, silent.

Curiosity started to overtake her fear. She tilted her head. "Why are you lonely?"

"I left all I've known behind to be of service."

She looked at his clothes and thought of the missionaries who were trying to convert the native people. "Like a priest?"

He put another log on the fire. "No. The People have been good to us. But their memories are long. They provide food and clothing; they withhold friendship."

The woman remembered being surrounded by people and always feeling alone. Her sister, Linette, thrived in society, but she'd also been young when their father had struck silver and moved the family to San Francisco. The woman, however, remembered her life before money, and she never felt comfortable in all the lace and pearls and crowded parlor rooms. Her mother had continued to say prosperity had opened the world to them. Instead, it only felt like her world had gotten smaller, tighter.

Davy had understood. He'd promised a life amongst the wide-open vistas of the West. Far from crowded streets, where they could huddle together by a fire and read their favorite adventure stories aloud. After the war, they would have it all. He'd promised.

The war gave no quarter to promises.

"Look at us, a pair of friendless, lonely beings," the stranger said, slapping the sawdust off his hands and standing.

"Shall we be friends?" The woman couldn't believe she'd said the words, but once they were spoken, she found she didn't want to take them back.

The stranger appeared startled; his expression bemused. "Friends? I've never been friends with a human before. How do you go about it?"

The woman laughed and set the gun up against the stone fireplace. A good amount of heat was making its way into the room now. "Maybe we should start simple. An introduction."

"Aye, an introduction." The stranger bowed deeply, nearly clocking his head on the lone wooden chair between them. "Prince Cathal, First son of King Oberon and Lady Aurnia of the Seelie, Duke of Tuatha, and Lord Protector of Danu."

The woman blinked in surprise. A smile bloomed, and she dipped into a curtsy. "Cassandra Wylde of the San Fransico Wyldes. Daughter of Duncan and Maria. Owner of Sinclair Ranch."

"Wonderful, we're friends now," the stranger, Prince Cathal, stated.

Cassandra lifted a finger to explain that there was more to it than that, but the prince was already squeezing around her and grabbing at the latch. Cassandra moved away, but not before his arm brushed against her own, sending a tingle up through her.

The ACES Anthology

"I must go. With the rain over, I'll be needed, but I shall visit again, my friend Cassandra." He opened the door and stepped out into the fading storm.

Cassandra rushed forward, but he was gone. Vanished.

Friends with one of the faerie. Maybe Linette would send her a few books from father's library about faeries. She could discuss it with Prince Cathal when he returned. If he returned.

She caught sight of the destroyed garden and sighed. Maybe if he returned, she could convince him to help her fix it. Do faeries even know how to mend fences? She chuckled at the absurdity. Who would have guessed her day would hold both camels and fae? One thing she was completely certain of—Davy would have loved it.

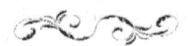

"Of Camels and Fae" is ©2023 by Angela Laverghetta. It appears here for the first time. The author is a resident of Reno and her first novel, "The Buried Knight," was recently published. Angela is a graduate of Western Nevada College, where she honed her craft under the late, great Marilee Swirczek. You can join her newsletter for updates at www.angelalaverghettabooks.com.

Laura Magee
Ice Cream on Tuesday

The two took a seat at a table in the back of the Scoups ice cream shop, just as they had every Tuesday evening that fall. It was late, but the sun was still up, and it was just warm enough to justify eating their frozen treats. Brooklyn had worked hard at her soccer practice, as she always had, so Liz didn't mind the double-scoop sundae with mint chip ice cream that her daughter had ordered. With extra whip, mind you. She was proud of the hard work, grit, and diligence of the girl who sat across from her—no, not a girl. The young woman, she reminded herself. After all, at almost 18, her baby was growing up.

For a moment they sat silently, Liz studying Brooklyn's face, as though trying to memorize every curve and line. Brooklyn, oblivious of her mother's attention (or perhaps not caring), dug into the ice cream with eager abandon. It was no wonder why. Her practice uniform was still wet in several places from sweat, and strands of hair that had pulled free during practice hung loosely around her face. She still had the dirt streak across her forehead where she had wiped away dirty sweat during the suicide drills.

Liz smiled, half hoping Brookie wouldn't notice so she could watch her just a little longer. There never seemed to be enough time, and she wanted to soak in as much as she could.

A minute or so passed in silence, each woman absorbed in their own personal moments.

"I met someone." Brooklyn broke the silence abruptly. Liz could tell she was nervous in the way she tended to be when she had something to say and didn't know how to say it. She paused for a long moment, allowing the news to sink in and determining what to say next.

"Really? When did this happen?" Liz's hand, holding a spoonful of dripping ice cream, stopped halfway to her mouth. She was inquisitive and excited despite her surprise and confusion. A strange pang of pain hit her chest.

"We met in Chemistry of all places." She was always one to play with words. "Ironic, huh?" She giggled.

Liz giggled too, despite the twenty-three years she had on Brooklyn. "Who is he? Tell me all about him!"

"She's really great," Brooklyn answered as though her mother had not made the slip.

She. Oh! Liz thought, suddenly feeling silly for being so presumptuous. "She," she repeated out loud, "Sorry, I just assumed—"

"I know you are probably surprised." Brooklyn looked at her mom pensively. Liz could see that there was something in her eyes. Concern, perhaps, or a desire to be validated and accepted. "I mean, the last time I dated anyone was, ugh, what, like over a year ago, and he was, well... a he—"

"No, well, yes, you surprised me but it's okay! I just feel bad I—" Now they were talking over each other, but that was something both were accustomed to. Liz could see her daughter's nervousness and excitement and knew it was better just to let her talk.

"I really like her, and I think you will too." There was a huge, nervous smile on her face, and she didn't quite meet her mom's eyes. As open as their relationship was, Liz assumed it was still hard for her to talk about this kind of stuff. "She's very smart. She takes honors classes and is even taking dual college credit classes." She brushed back strands of her messy black hair that had fallen in front of her eyes, carelessly tucking them behind her ear.

Liz listened as Brooklyn prattled on about her new love interest. Liz knew exactly what Brooklyn was feeling; any conversation about romance is hard for a young girl... and Brooklyn was still so young! So young. A strange cocktail of feelings and thoughts swirled around in her mind. There was another pang of pain. Tears came to her eyes, but she held them back, smiling as her daughter spoke.

She took a bite of her ice cream to help cover any indications of the feelings that had bubbled up. Spumoni had always been her favorite. The complexity of each flavor and how well they worked together gave her something to focus her attention on, just long enough to let the wave pass.

Brooklyn told Liz how they had met, a serendipitous pairing for a chemistry project. She described how Ann looked: messy brown curls, dark freckles, and glasses. Ann was shorter than Brooklyn, but that wasn't surprising. Then she moved on to what she liked: art, fashion, and anime. She wanted to be an animator, but she also enjoyed sewing her own anime cosplay.

"She wants to be a serious influencer. Her TikTok has over a hundred and fifty thousand subs, and her Insta is over six-hundred K! She's so talented, Mom! I know mine is kinda cool or whatever, but I have like, what, thirteen thousand-ish subs and she's over a hundred thousand already!" Brooklyn grew quiet. She took another bite of her ice cream, which she had been swirling around in its cup as she spoke. Liz cleared her throat and smiled warmly.

Liz remembered how silly she had thought Brooklyn was when she first said she wanted to make content with her showing off various tricks and drills with her ball. Sure, some people make it, but most don't. She remembered the agreement they'd made: As long as you don't fall behind on your schoolwork, I will support you doing your social media thing. Liz felt like she was getting too old, losing touch.

"She sounds wonderful. What's her name?"

"Oh! I forgot to tell you! Her name is Ann. Well, Analise, but everyone calls her Ann. She hates it, but I think it is beautiful!" She looked down at her ice cream, blushing. She really liked this girl, Liz could tell. Brooklyn sat quietly for a while, picking up a spoonful of what was now brownish gloppy goop, all the ingredients having been thoroughly mixed as she talked. The thick liquid ran slowly off the edge of her spoon like snail slime.

Liz considered that one small thing for a moment. Her daughter had always done that, ever since she was little. She mixed her ice cream before eating. She mixed her chicken in with her peas and mashed potatoes. Hell, she even put her chips on her sandwich or crumbled them over her hot dog. She was so different from Liz, who preferred all her food separated. The girl was her own person. Unique. She always did things her own way. Liz loved that about her. She took in a deep breath as spumoni turned in her stomach.

"I'm so happy for you, Brookie. Thank you for telling me about her." Liz's smile was warm and sincere. She wanted to say more. She wanted to ask when she would get to meet this girl. But something stopped her. Don't push it, she thought to herself, just let it be what it is.

"Mom, I— I just wanted to tell you all about her!" Brooklyn was excited now, as though her mom had given her something she had been waiting for, something she had needed. Encouragement. Acknowledgment. Validation. The smile on the younger woman's face was unabashed. Sentimental tears rimmed her eyes. Liz's heart swelled.

"Aww, sweetie! I love when you tell me these things! You can always tell me anything," Her face mirrored her daughter's, not just in sincerity and sentimentality, but in physical features. She remembered how people used to call Brooklyn her "mini-me."

They spent the next few minutes talking. Well, Brooklyn continued to talk, with Liz interjecting a comment or question now and again. Often, Brooklyn ignored the question, pressing on with her line of thought, but Liz was okay with that. She knew that all would become clear eventually. She was just happy to have this connection. They didn't happen much these days. Seldom, in fact. Sometimes it seemed like their Tuesday evening ice cream dates were all they had. Sure there were other conversations, but these seemed the most significant. There was something about the consistency, location, and atmosphere that both women valued greatly.

The dialog lasted a while, although whether it was an hour or less or more, Liz couldn't tell. Nor did she care. The light dimmed through the shop windows as the sun began to set. That told her something of the passage of time, but she ignored it, soaking in every word from her daughter. She continued to study Brooklyn's expressions: all the smiles, the way she looked down at (and played with) her ice cream, the way she met her mom's eyes at exactly the right moments with her own big, beautiful brown eyes that seemed to sparkle with youthful energy.

There was an ebb and flow to the conversation. Sometimes there would be pauses. Each would use that time to make progress on their own goopy, ridiculously sweet, frozen treats. But it would always pick up again. It was interesting to Liz, their cadence. Brooklyn had her own mind and her own ideas of what she wanted to say and when. Liz loved that about her. So strong and independent!

"Hey, Mom?" Brooklyn interjected after a particularly long pause. Her tone had changed noticeably. Her voice cracked.

"Yes, beautiful daughter of mine?" Liz said with sarcastic formality, swinging her spoon around like a scepter. She was trying to bring jollity to the moment to alleviate the sudden tension in Brooklyn's voice. She knew where this was going, and although she could do nothing about it, she fought it back with the flourish of the spoon.

"I love you." Her voice shook. There was so much sweetness in the casual comment. "I know you know that, but I just— I guess I just want to—" she trailed off, unsure how to continue.

"I love you too, baby." Liz felt emotion stab at her heart with a sudden intensity. Those three simple words acknowledged what had remained unspoken between them, that which both knew yet neither wanted to admit.

"I know this sounds silly, but I just really want you to be proud of me. Dorky, right?" Her voice caught, as though tears edged her voice as they now moistened her eyes.

"I am so proud of you! I will always be proud of you. I want you to know that." Liz's heart swelled again. Always. No matter what! The pang in her heart stung, and she felt the same tears welling up in her own eyes. She took a deep breath and smiled, adding, "and it is dorky and that's one of the many things I love about you." She giggled to dissipate what was building up under the surface.

"I've got to leave soon." Brooklyn wasn't looking at her now. She was stirring what was left of her ice cream again. She kept her eyes downcast on her handiwork.

Liz wanted to reach across the table, to grab her daughter's hand, or lift her chin—anything to reassure her baby girl. She wanted to jump up and pull her into a big, tight hug. She did neither. She knew that truthfully, the one she would be reassuring was herself.

"I know you do, sweetheart," was all she could manage at the moment. No matter how often they sat and talked, this part always seemed to be the hardest for both of them.

"I wish I could stay longer." The words hit Liz in a way that was sentimental yet painful. Brooklyn was looking at her now with compassionate eyes. Liz felt the first tear fall. "But I'll come back soon. I promise."

Liz knew she was telling the truth. She would come back. She always did. Yet she still didn't want this time to end. The ice cream was nearly gone, and what was left in each cup was just a drab puddle of melted milk products. Delicious, but nearly at its end. The perfect metaphor, Liz thought with despair. But she held back any more tears. More would come later. For now, she wanted to embrace the moment and enjoy what was left of her time with her beloved daughter.

"I still have a few minutes," Brooklyn said hopefully, "but I don't know what else to say. I feel like I am all talked out. I think I am just going to sit here with you for a few more minutes."

"Of course! You don't have to say anything. I'm happy just to be here with you. I love you, Brookie." She reached across the table toward her daughter. She felt pressure on her hand as Brooklyn took it in her own and held it. The daughter reassures the mother. Liz smiled. Isn't it supposed to happen the other way around?

They held hands for several minutes, neither talking. She both dreaded the inevitable moment and cherished the current one. Her eyes were locked on Brooklyn's as both sat, the atmosphere between them both peaceful and melancholy. The next time Brooklyn broke the silence, Liz knew their time would be over.

Finally, the moment came. Brooklyn squeezed her hand with compassion and love that was almost... motherly.

"I have to go now. I'll be back soon, okay? I love you, Mom!" Her voice was shaky but resolute. She lifted her mother's hand and kissed it softly. Liz felt the coolness of her lips from the ice cream.

"I love you too, baby girl." Liz hadn't taken her eyes off Brooklyn's the entire time they had been quiet, but she did now. She hated this part. She couldn't bear it. She looked down at her ice cream cup. And now the tears came. She watched them fall into the ice cream. Like drops of rain in the mud, she thought. She laughed at the observation, which only made her cry more.

When she felt brave enough, she looked up. Brooklyn was gone, as she knew she would be. The ice cream that Brooklyn had played with so casually and eaten so messily was gone too, as though it had never been. The knowledge that she would be back brought no comfort. Not when she knew the truth. She is gone. She is really gone. Not just now; not just this time. She is gone.

Her arm was still outstretched, reaching for the hand that wasn't there to hold it. She snatched it back, wrapping it around herself protectively, and closed her eyes. She used to sob uncontrollably, but that had changed over time. Tears still came and her heart still hurt, but her emotional tank was empty and she had next to nothing left. Maybe one day she would stop crying altogether. She hoped not. The pain hurt, but it was all she had left.

As silent tears fell, she heard two voices, coming from a few feet away. They were talking in hushed tones, but she heard the conversation clearly. They were talking about her. She glanced out of the corner of her eye to see two women at the ice cream counter. The older of the two worked behind the counter and was leaning with her elbows on the counter, toward the other. Liz knew her well. The other she didn't recognize. A customer, most likely. She was younger, much younger, perhaps in her early twenties. Liz returned her gaze to her ice cream cup, the sugar and dairy suddenly turning sour in her stomach.

"Oh, I see. What happened?" The younger asked. The curiosity struck Liz as intrusive. Was what happened any of her business?

"Such a heartbreaking story. It was a car accident, oh, let's see... it would be nearly five months ago now. She and her daughter were on their way home." She spoke matter-of-factly, but Liz could detect some emotion. Whether it was pity or compassion she couldn't tell. And she didn't care. She hated that they were talking about her, but she felt powerless to stop them. People talked. Let them fucking talk.

The older woman continued. "They had gone out to ice cream after her daughter's soccer practice. Did you know she was one of the top players?" Liz heard no audible response, so she imagined the other woman shaking her head 'no.' "Yeah, she was working toward a sports scholarship. So much potential, the poor thing. It was a drunk driver. The driver died. The mom and daughter, well, you can see." Liz imagined the woman, gesturing at her as she left the last bit unsaid. Pathetic. The woman who can't let go of her daughter. So sad.

Anger began to take the place of sorrow. Who were they to talk about her as though she couldn't hear? Who were they to gossip about other people's business? Yet she felt powerless to speak up and stop them.

The ACES Anthology

"How often does she talk to her?" The younger voice again.

"Oh, I don't know. I imagine as often as possible. But I am always on shift at this time, and she is here every Tuesday, like clockwork. Hasn't missed a day since she recovered from the accident herself."

Liz wanted to lock the voices out, to just get up and leave, but she just couldn't bring herself to move. She'd have to eventually. She had a life to get back to. Responsibilities. The moment had ended, but she wanted it to last just a bit longer and here it was, becoming tainted by the women's conversation. She tried to focus on anything but the voices. There were others in the shop, their babbling incoherent to Liz, and then the faint, whooshing sound of traffic outside with something like the occasional 'beep' of a utility vehicle. She tried to focus on the intrusive beep instead, but it was sporadic and unreliable.

"It's hard on her, I am sure. She's so loving and dedicated. I can't help but feel bad for her." Liz could hear the sadness in her voice, but it brought her little comfort.

Jean, put a comforting hand on Brookyln's shoulder as she passed by. Brooklyn brought both her hands up to Jean's, accepting her comfort. Brooklyn spent so much time here nowadays that the elderly nurse had become somewhat of a surrogate grandmother to her. The new nurse intern, Kylie, smiled uncomfortably. Jean handed Kylie the clipboard she had been holding and turned to Brooklyn. The two left the room, connected by Jean's arm, Kylie following close behind and scratching occasional notes on a chart. At the door, Jean patted Brooklyn and led the student over to the nurse's station.

Brooklyn grabbed the door frame for support as she passed through. Across the white and blueish-grey, sterile hallway, Ann leaned against the wall, staring at her phone. As she saw Brooklyn leave the room, she stood up straight and put her phone in her pocket. Brooklyn wiped a tear away, put on a flimsy smile that barely passed, and walked toward the girl.

"Hey," Brooklyn said weakly.

Ann put her arms around Brooklyn in a tight hug. Not a romantic hug, but one of those tender yet suffocating, emotional, "I got you" hugs. When she pulled away, she kissed her lightly.

"How did it go?" Ann looked concerned. She had never accompanied Brooklyn before, and she wasn't sure how to feel or what to say.

Brooklyn sighed heavily. "As good as expected," she answered vaguely yet truthfully. "I told her about you."

"You did?" Ann's demeanor was still quiet, but it perked up noticeably and she smiled. She hugged Brooklyn again, this time a bit lighter and out of happiness rather than emotional support. "What do you think she would think?" She was sheepishly girlie about it, which Brooklyn adored. Brooklyn took Ann's hand and led her to the door of the room and smiled as she looked in.

"I think she will love you. Maybe next time you can come in with me and she can meet you. They said she can probably hear what you say. I like to think she can." As she spoke, she looked away from Ann, to the woman lying on the hospital bed, tubes and wires protruding from various locations around her body.

She looked peaceful, as though asleep. The cuts and bruises had healed. The only sign that she had even been in the accident was the fact that she just would not wake up. The tubes and wires, paired with the occasional beep of the automatic monitors were ever-present reminders that the woman was not just sleeping, she was fighting for her life.

"I would really love that," Ann said, laying her head on Brooklyn's shoulder. When she spoke, her voice was caring and supportive. "You ready? If you need a few more minutes—"

"No, I am ready. Let's get going." Brooklyn pulled away from the door and wiped a couple of more residual tears from her eyes. Like Liz, she used to break down into long fits of crying. Then shouting and anger. Now the sadness, while always there, had dampened into something she could manage. She would still break down now and again, in moments of vulnerability, but not right now. Right now she felt strong and resolute. She was carrying the residual happiness of having told her mom about Ann with her and she hung on to that.

Hand in hand, the two young women walked down the well-lit hallway, passed under a sign that said "visitors check in here" and through a set of open double doors. They disappeared around a corner in the direction of the visitor's parking lot.

―⁂―

Finally, Liz worked up the motivation to get up and leave. As she pulled open one of the double doors of the ice cream shop, she swore she heard Brooklyn's voice once again, but it was far off in the distance. "Maybe next time you can come in with me and she can meet you. They said she can probably hear what you say. I like to think she can." But she couldn't quite make out all the words. She paused, holding the handle.

―⁂―

Ice Cream on Tuesday is ©2023 by Laura Magee. It appears here for the first time. The author is a resident of Gardnerville who is working on her debut novel, the urban fantasy romance "Untangled." Laura is a deeply inquisitive soul with a relentless passion for learning, living, and expressing herself. She has a bachelor's degree in cultural anthropology, and she built and operates The Next Chapter, a dynamic and inclusive social media platform catering to both aspiring and established writers. You can follow her on Vocal.media under the name Laura Elizabeth.

Richard Moreno

The Culling

Bill Morrow leaned forward and lightly rapped his knuckles against the plaster wall. He took a few steps and repeated the action, listening intently.

"Pipe seems to run along here, Charlie," he mumbled. He slowly moved along the wall, stopping every couple of feet to knock softly, until it ended at a corner.

"We gonna have to punch through that brick wall?" the other man asked.

Morrow nodded and pulled a pair of worn, brown, leather gloves from his back pocket. He slipped on the gloves and picked up a heavy sledgehammer that was lying on the floor. Morrow grunted as he began striking the wall again and again. Soon, the brick face started to chip and fleck away.

"They sure knew how to build 'em, didn't they?" Charlie Whittacker remarked.

After about fifteen minutes, Morrow stopped to rest and handed the hammer to his partner, who continued attacking the wall. Whittacker was thinner, a little taller, and about a decade younger than Bill Morrow. The two plumbers had worked together for nearly fifteen years. After a few more minutes, Whittacker broke through the wall and began making an opening wide enough for Morrow to climb through.

"Let's have a look," Morrow said when Whittacker stopped. He carefully knocked away a few loose bricks, then, flashlight in hand, poked his upper body into the dark hole.

"Holy Shit!—Charlie, go get the sheriff!" Morrow yelled.

⚜

For more than 30 years, Sheriff Ray Quilici had worn his neatly-pressed, khaki-colored uniform, driven a black-and-white Ford Bronco, and arrested an assortment of jaywalkers, cattle-rustlers, wife-beaters, small-time drug dealers, speeders, bar-fighters, and loud drunks. He'd been involved in five murder cases, all of which had been crimes of passion or disputes over money, and an equal number of robberies, all committed by thrill-seeking juveniles. Once, he'd been involved in the pursuit of a Reno bank robber but rolled his Bronco over an embankment during the chase. The state highway patrol apprehended the man in Ely, and the tall, thin lawman gained a permanent limp.

Despite the fact he'd never arrested anyone featured on "America's Most Wanted," Ray Quilici enjoyed his job and his town. He'd grown up in a small town in southern Oregon and appreciated the slow pace in Prosperity. His wife belonged to the local Soroptimists club and sang in the church choir. Recently, he'd been thinking about retiring.

He was smoking a cigarette and sipping his morning cup of coffee at the Night Owl Cafe when Charlie Whittacker rushed through the door.

"Sheriff, come quick!" Whittacker sputtered.

"Hold on, Charlie, what's going on?" the sheriff said.

"Bill and I were searching for a broken water pipe in the basement of the Masonic Lodge, and Bill found something he needs you to see," Whittacker said.

"Is it something serious?" the sheriff asked as he stood up, stubbed out his cigarette, and quickly finished his coffee.

"I don't know what he saw, but Bill was pretty shook up."

"Let's go."

The sheriff coughed into his handkerchief, then followed Whittacker out of the Night Owl Cafe and headed east on Main Street toward the Masonic Hall. Like many mining towns, Prosperity had cropped up in a canyon, with its main road, naturally called Main Street, running through the center of the community. About two dozen businesses, most located in stone or brick buildings constructed more than a century ago, lined each side of the street, and small wooden houses had been pitched on the surrounding hillsides. At the east end of town sat a two-story brick courthouse—said to have been the site of the last legal hanging in the state—which was adjacent to the Masonic Lodge building.

Sheriff Quilici and Charlie Whittacker entered through a side door. It was a squat, single-story brick building, constructed sometime in the 1860s, which had originally been built for the local newspaper, called "The Road to Prosperity." Shortly after construction was complete, the paper went out of business, and the structure was sold to the Fraternal Order of Masons.

Charlie Whittacker led the sheriff down a narrow set of wooden stairs leading to a dimly lit hallway. The two walked into a large room that contained rows of ancient, wooden, folding chairs. At the back of the room, Bill Morrow was standing, nervously rubbing his thick hands together.

"Thought we'd better call you when I found this," Morrow said, pointing to a dark cavity in the brick rear wall. The sheriff took a small flashlight from a nearby toolbox and walked to the black opening. He shined the light through the hole and was surprised to see that it was swallowed up by vast, inky space.

"Is there a cave or tunnel back in there?" he asked.

"Appears to be," Morrow said. "Remember all those stories about caves under the town? I never believed them until now."

Sheriff Quilici slowly pushed his upper body through the hole in the wall, shining the flashlight into the dark. Behind the wall was a huge cavernous space—so large it was difficult to see much with the flashlight's feeble beam.

As he swung the light to the right, he was startled to see what appeared to be the skeleton slumped against the other side of the brick wall. It was dressed in what appeared to be men's clothing: brown pants, a white shirt, and brown boots. A tan-colored cowboy hat lay flat a few feet away. As the sheriff continued to examine the body, he noticed a revolver next to the skeleton's bony hand. In a half-circle around the body were 10 or so small mounds of wax.

"Scared the hell out of me when I spotted it," Morrow said.

"That is the damnedest thing I've ever seen," Quilici said as he crawled from the hole in the wall. "Let's open this wall up and see what we've got here."

As Charlie Whittacker carefully chipped away at the brick to enlarge the opening, Quilici called the dispatcher on his portable radio.

"Susie, this is Sheriff Q, could you please call Doc Etchegoyan, and ask her to come over to the basement of the Masonic Hall as soon as she can?"

"Is it an emergency?" the dispatcher asked.

"No... tell her it's coroner business."

Quilici signed off, then began to help the two plumbers pull loose bricks from the wall. He noticed that at the base of the brick wall was a large sandstone block that looked like it had been jammed into place.

"That's damn strange construction," Quilici grunted as he pushed it aside.

Within a short time, the three men had created an opening large enough to walk through. The sheriff plugged in a corded work lamp, which he turned on, then stepped into the dark hole. He kneeled next to the skeleton and held up the light. From the body's position, it appeared that the man—he assumed it was a man—might have been sitting with his back against the wall before he fell over. He could see a large hole in the back of the skull. Examining the interior wall with the light, he saw a faint dark stain on the bricks. Being no stranger to suicides, the sheriff hypothesized that the man had killed himself with a single shot through the roof of his mouth.

Quilici stood and looked around the body. He studied the strange lumps of wax, then deduced they had once been candles, which had burned all the way down. A few feet from the skeleton, he found a hand trowel, a small pile of bricks, which seemed to match those used in the wall, and a tub filled with dried grayish powder. He paused and slowly ran his hand across the brick wall, then turned to examine the rest of the cave.

The ceiling was about 12 feet high and covered in places with pointed stalactites, which looked like jagged teeth. While the ground around the skeleton was fairly flat, in the distance he could see stalagmites growing out of the floor. In some places, the two had grown together to form pillars, which almost seemed to be holding up the ceiling.

The sheriff walked a few feet into the cave—as far as the cord allowed—and found the darkness extended far beyond the light's reach.

He breathed deeply through his nose and coughed.

The ACES Anthology

The cave smelled stale—like a newspaper that has been left in the rain or the moldy cork of an old bottle of red wine.

Quilici turned around to study the skeleton.

"So, who might you be, friend?" he mumbled to himself.

"You okay in there, Sheriff?" Charlie Whittacker called.

"Just talking to myself," Quilici answered, feeling a little embarrassed.

As he stepped toward the opening, he was momentarily startled by Doctor Roberta Etchegoyan, coming through from the other side. At just over five feet tall, she was nearly a foot shorter than the sheriff. And, despite being 66 years old, she still competed in the town's annual five-kilometer fun run, winning the women's senior division for the past six years.

"Sorry if I scared you," the doctor said. "I came as quickly as I could. Bill and Charlie filled me in on how they found him."

Holding a flashlight in her hand, the doctor bent over the skeleton, closely studying the skull.

"Male. Can't really tell, but maybe in his early 30s. Looks like a self-inflicted gunshot wound to the head—that how you read it?" she asked the sheriff.

He nodded and pointed to the pile of bricks stacked near the body.

"What do you make of that?" he asked.

"Weird. What do you think they were for?" she said.

"I'm no hod carrier, but it looks like this guy might have built at least part of this wall," Quilici said.

"He bricked himself in here?" the doctor responded.

"Appears that way. Then he laid out these candles all around him and shot himself in the head. Sure seems like a pretty strange way to kill yourself," Quilici said. "If you're done here, I'll shoot some photos, bag him, and get him over to your office for an autopsy."

As the doctor started to step through the opening, Quilici turned his head and barked a deep cough.

"Why don't we schedule an appointment so I can check that," she said. "Doesn't sound too good."

After the doctor was gone, Quilici stood over the skeleton,

deep in thought. Suddenly, he spun around, holding the light up in front of him, eyes searching the cave. His right hand automatically clutched his gun handle. He couldn't see anything but he'd *felt* something was there. He held his breath and listened. Nothing.

After nearly a minute, he relaxed. Once again, he turned to study the skeleton. He reached down for the cowboy hat and was surprised to find that it covered a small, black, leather-bound book. He picked up the book and carefully opened the front cover. The inside pages, still white, were filled with neat, almost delicate handwriting. Scanning the first few pages, Quilici saw that the book was a personal journal written by a young woman. The first entry was about arriving in Prosperity from San Francisco. He slowly flipped through pages and noticed that later entries had been written by someone else in strokes that were heavier and less neat. He started to read the second correspondent's words.

October 10

Julianne is dead. Her sickness finally took her away from me. I am lost.

The rest of the page was blank. Quilici looked once again at the skeleton. Was this the young man who wrote those words? He turned the page and read the next entry.

October 12

Another has died. First it was sickly little Timothy Stout, then my beautiful Julianne, now it is the Abbott baby, which had been born too early. Is it a coincidence that all of the dead had lived in the Brower Street neighborhood directly behind the courthouse and the new newspaper building? I will ask the doctor about this tomorrow.

Sheriff Quilici turned the page and felt warm in spite of the cave's dark coolness. He knew he should probably take some photos, but curiosity—a cop's best friend, he had always told himself—compelled him to continue reading the journal.

October 13

Today was Julianne's burial. I have written her parents and told them she died of consumption. Dear God, I miss her smile. I can still hear her sweet laughter. I do not know if I want to go on.

Doctor Spaulding told me it was coincidence and that all the dead were not well. That was certainly true of my Julianne, although the dry desert air seemed to make her stronger after we had moved here months ago from the cold and wet of San Francisco. I do not know what made her take such a turn for the worse.

"Sheriff, you need some help?" Charlie Whittacker called from the other room, momentarily startling Quilici.

"I'm okay, Charlie," the sheriff answered. He wanted to read more of the journal but knew he'd better get the skeleton zipped up. He slipped the book into his coat pocket and stepped through the opening into the Masonic Lodge basement, where Charlie Whittacker was standing.

"Bill had to go unclog Mrs. Peterson's toilet, but I decided to stay in case you needed anything," Whittacker said.

"You know, you can help me if you don't mind," Quilici said. "I've got to run over to my office to pick up a camera and some things so I can move this guy. It'd be a big help if you could keep an eye on things while I'm gone."

"Sure, Sheriff," Whittacker said.

Quilici pulled himself up the steps leading from the basement and into the bright sunlight. He blinked a few times, then slipped on a pair of wire-frame sunglasses. As he walked next door to his office in the county courthouse, he thought about the journal in his pocket. He pulled it out and started reading again.

October 14

 I do not want to seem obsessed, but I cannot understand what made Julianne's illness return so unexpectedly. I visited the doctor again today and asked if there was chance that she and the others might have been stricken by some new plague which preyed upon the weak. He said that was possible but was not eager to answer my questions. I fancy myself a most prudent and rational man, and perhaps I am growing obsessed, but I feel he is hiding something from me.

"Reading something good, Sheriff?" asked Melissa Loomis, the county recorder. She nearly bumped into him as he walked up the steps to the courthouse.

"Sorry," Quilici said and smiled. He slowly limped up the wide staircase to the Sheriff's Department on the second floor. He paused and nodded at the dispatcher, Susie Sloan, who was busy on the radio, then walked into his office. From a wall cabinet, he pulled out a gray, vinyl camera bag and several things he'd need to move the skeleton from the cave, then sat on the corner of his desk and opened the journal once again.

 Another has died. This time, it is Mrs. Klein, who had been ill following the birth of her daughter a few days ago. Like the others who died, she lived on Brower Street, a few houses away from our house. I still believe there is a connection.

 Last night, I wrapped myself in a blanket and sat under a tree in front of our house, not sure what I was awaiting. I had a box of matches, two candles, and my revolver. I do not know what I am hoping to find. I am not certain when I fell asleep but I was too tired to go to work.

 I very much miss my dearest Julianne. I find I cannot eat or sleep. I must find out what killed her.

Quilici looked at his watch and thought about Charlie Whittacker waiting for him in the Masonic Lodge. He knew he should return to the cave and get to work on removing the body, but the journal intrigued him. He decided the skeleton wasn't going to go anywhere and continued reading.

October 15

    I went to Doctor Spaulding to ask him about Mrs. Klein. He told me she had bled to death due to a complicated birth and assured me that there was no connection with the other deaths. He said I looked tired and suggested I get rest. He said he understood my pain at having lost my wife and warned that if I didn't take care of myself I might join her soon. He is right.

    I am so lonely without my beautiful Julianne.

The sheriff forced himself to close the book. He gathered the items he'd need in the cave and shoved them into a green canvas duffel bag. After lighting a cigarette, he walked from the courthouse to the Masonic Hall. As he opened the door leading to the basement, he began violently coughing. He tossed his cigarette away.

"Charlie, I'm back," he called as he came down the steps to the basement. He looked around the meeting room filled with chairs but did not see Charlie Whittacker. He wondered if the plumber had decided to explore the cave. He picked up the lamp and stepped through the opening in the brick wall. Shining the light around, he saw that the skeleton, bricks, and darkness were just as he'd left them.

"Charlie!" he called into the cave. "Charlie! It's Ray, you in there?"

He tilted his head in the direction of the darkness to listen, but there was no response. Quilici stood for a moment, pondering Charlie Whittacker's whereabouts. Perhaps there had been an emergency—another plugged-up toilet—or Bill Morrow had come back to get him.

The sheriff dropped the canvas bag next to the opening in

The ACES Anthology

the wall and pulled out the camera. "Smile," he said and began snapping photos of the skeleton. With each flash, the dark cave disappeared in the whiteness.

After he'd taken a number of shots from various angles, he pulled out a plastic, zippered bag in which to place the remains. He tugged on a pair of rubber gloves and kneeled next to the corpse.

"Did you ever find out what killed your wife, friend?" he asked the skeleton. He carefully laid the bones and pieces of clothing in the bag. He collected the cowboy hat, then picked up the revolver. It was an old Colt Peacemaker. He opened the chamber and noticed that all of the bullets had been fired.

"Either you were the world's worst shot or you were firing at something besides your brains," Quilici mused.

Suddenly, the sheriff felt something touch his shoulder. He jerked involuntarily and whipped the lamp around.

"Hold on, Sheriff, it's just me, Charlie!" Whittacker shouted. "I didn't mean to startle you again, but I thought I heard you talking to someone and was trying to see if everything was all right."

"That's okay, Charlie," Quilici said. "I guess I'm just getting too old for this shit. So, where did you go?"

"While you were gone, I decided to find that busted water pipe. Turns out it goes from the corner there up to the first floor. I found the break upstairs and fixed it," Whittaker said. "It's kind of funny, but we didn't even have to go behind this wall to fix the problem."

"Lucky for this stiff, you did," Quilici remarked.

"Well, Sheriff, if you don't need me anymore," Whittacker said.

"Sure, you go on. I've just a few more things to pick up and I'll be out of here," Quilici said.

The ACES Anthology

The sheriff heard Whittacker leave, then returned to his grisly task. After he had finished cleaning up the site, he stepped back into the meeting room and sat on one of the folding chairs. He pulled the book from his pocket and began to read again.

October 17

I could not sleep again last night and found myself wandering Brower Street. I did not see anything unusual and only heard cats and dogs. No more dead have been found, so perhaps the plague, or whatever it is, is over. We can only hope.

Perhaps Julianne's death was God's will, although I cannot believe a merciful God would torture me in this way.

My friend Paul Curtis stopped by my office today to kindly offer his condolences. He said it must have been horrible watching Julianne cough up so much blood before dying. I told him I had been working late at the newspaper and she was dead in bed when I came home. She had apparently died peacefully because there was no blood. He said he must have misunderstood because he thought the doctor had told him she had died from coughing up so much blood.

I do not think he misunderstood the doctor. I am now certain the doctor is hiding something.

Quilici looked down at the long, narrow bag containing the young man's remains, which he had pushed through the opening into the basement. Amazing how light a body is when it lacks flesh, muscle, and blood, he thought. He turned the page and read some more.

October 18

As I walked to the newspaper offices this morning, I stopped to see the progress on my new building under construction adjacent to the courthouse. The workers were excited about uncovering the entrance to a large cavern that apparently stretches a considerable distance beneath the town. Several speculated that it might contain gold or silver. I suspect if there is any gold it is of a fool's variety.

In the afternoon, I returned to Dr. Spaulding's office, but he did not want to see me. I insisted he talk to me about the cause of Julianne's death and told him what Paul Curtis had told me. After I threatened him, he finally told me he was trying to prevent a town panic. He said the deaths had not been caused by any disease he had ever seen. He said each of the deceased had experienced a mysterious loss of blood, which, he believed, caused death. I asked him what could be responsible, and he said he did not know. He asked me not to discuss this with anyone and reminded me of my responsibility to the town as owner of the newspaper. I agreed with him that the story would be bad for our young town and promised not to print anything.

Still, for Julianne's sake, for my sake, I must find out what is doing this.

Quilici forced himself to close the journal. Like you, my friend, I, too, fancy myself a most prudent and rational man—and I've got to get back to work, he thought to himself. He gathered up his bags, including the one containing the skeleton, jammed the journal into his pocket, and headed up the steps. Just as he got to the top, he heard a faint scraping sound below. He silently dropped the bags on the landing and crept down the stairs. He cautiously looked into the basement meeting room. He saw the rows of wooden folding chairs and the yawning hole in the rear brick wall, but nothing else. He crossed the room, picked up the flashlight, and stepped into the cave. The pile of bricks, tub of mortar, stalactites, and stalagmites all appeared as they had before.

"So much for being a prudent and rational man," he muttered.

Back at the top of the stairs, Quilici picked up the bags and stepped outside. He locked the outer door and pulled on it to make certain it was secure. He deposited the bags containing the skeleton and equipment in a locker in the basement of the courthouse then headed upstairs to his office. He lit another cigarette, inhaled deeply, and began coughing loudly. I've really got to quit, he thought, then pulled out the journal.

> *I have made a list of things I know and do not know.*
>
> *I know that a boy, a baby girl, and two women are dead.*
>
> *I know that all had been sickly.*
>
> *I know that all lived on Brower Street behind the courthouse.*
>
> *I know that all experienced a substantial loss of blood, which apparently caused their deaths.*
>
> *I do not know what might have caused the loss of blood.*
>
> *I do not know why only those on Brower Street are afflicted.*
>
> *I do not know what killed them.*
>
> *Today, one of the Irish, Timothy O'Hare, was badly injured in a cave-in at the Bellweather Mine. As he and his family live on Brower Street, I will keep watch on his house tonight.*
>
> *October 19*
>
> *I have seen the Angel of Death.*
>
> *This angel is not winged nor robed nor girded with a sword, and is like no creature of God that I ever imagined. I did not see it enter the O'Hare house but caught a glimpse as it departed. There was moonlight last night, and I could see well enough to know that the creature did not walk erect like a man but on all fours like an animal. Once, when the wind suddenly blew through the trees, it stopped, stood on its back legs, and seemed to smell the air. It is about the size of a large dog or a child, and its body is covered with slick, dark hair.*
>
> *I am haunted by what I saw of the creature. Its head is completely*

without hair, and its face is smooth, round, and beautiful, like that of a sweet young child. The thing opened its mouth and made a sound like the soft cry of a baby. The crying stopped, and I saw that it had a long, sharp tongue that flickered hideously in the moonlight. It may look like a child but it is unlike any child birthed by a human mother.

I silently slid my revolver from my holster. Before I could act, it resumed its journey. I followed it to the site of my new building, where it disappeared into the darkness of the large cave recently discovered by the workmen.

My God, it is true that we unleashed this hellish creation? Am I somehow responsible for these deaths, including that of my Julianne?

Forgive me, my love.

Quilici closed the book. He wondered what the man had seen. He also found himself starting to believe he was reading the ravings of a madman. What nonsense. But it makes for a good yarn, he admitted, and read on.

October 21

Since yesterday was Sunday and the workmen were not around, I went into the cave with my revolver. It is my solemn vow to kill this creature should I encounter it. My candle could not provide much illumination, but I did see that the entrance led into a labyrinth of passageways, some heading downward. Many times, I thought I saw the shadows move, but I did not encounter the hellish thing.

I believe the only way to draw the creature out is to offer it blood, then kill it when it appears.

October 22

Last night, I laid a freshly killed wild cat at the cave's entrance and waited, but the creature did not show itself. Perhaps it is only attracted to human blood.

The ACES Anthology

October 29

The workmen have completed my building, and I am ready. They were curious about my plans for the cave in the basement, and I told them I might use it for a wine cellar or sell tickets.

I have collected sufficient materials to seal the cave entrance but must be certain the creature is inside. I cut a deep gash in my left arm and dripped blood in a bowl, which I placed at the entrance. It is my hope that the blood will attract the creature, then I will kill it.

I waited for several hours, but the creature did not appear.

October 30

I returned to the basement this morning and saw the bowl was empty. Still, I cannot be certain the creature is inside the cave, so I have decided to go inside again to kill it. I have nearly completed work on the brick wall that will contain the creature once I am certain it is here.

Julianne, I will kill it for you.

October 31

I am sitting here, my back against my new brick wall, awaiting the creature. I should be frightened, but I'm not.

It was not my intention to die here, but the creature has made certain I will not be leaving. I went into the cave to seek it out but discovered that I, and not it, was the prey. Strangely, its bite was not unpleasant. Apparently, it injected me with a type of venom or poison that induces feelings of euphoria, followed by numbness. The creature disappeared when I fired the revolver several times.

After dragging myself to the entrance, I discovered I was too weak to move the heavy stone block that I'd placed in the crawl hole that was to be my escape route. I know I am probably dying, but I would like to have at least one more shot at the thing.

I set out all the candles so that I could see better in the darkness, but it seems like gauze has been wrapped over my eyes. I feel numbness creeping into my arms and fear that soon I won't be able to hold the revolver or this pencil. I do not want to be alive when it finally comes to finish me. I guess the last bullet won't be for the creature after all.

I hear a baby crying.

The rest of the pages were blank. Quilici tossed the journal onto the passenger seat and slowly shook his head. He pulled out another cigarette, lit it, and reminded himself that he needed to call the doctor to set up an appointment for a physical. A cough erupted from his chest and he spat out the window. Damn things are killing me, he thought.

The sheriff started up the Bronco and headed home. After a few blocks, however, he made a quick U-turn. He knew it was ridiculous, but he wanted another look at the basement of the Masonic Lodge before calling it a night.

He parked beside the building and walked to the side door leading to the basement. He pushed the key given to him by the plumbers into the lock but was surprised to find it was open. Flashlight in one hand, revolver in the other, he stepped inside and saw that the basement light was on. He crept down the stairs and into the main meeting room. He could see no one.

Cautiously, he crossed the room to the opening in the brick back wall. He stifled the urge to cough, then stepped inside.

"What the hell are you doing in here?" he boomed.

"Sheriff Quilici?" said a teenage voice.

"That you, Sam Whittacker?"

"Yes."

"Don't shoot, Sheriff, I'm here, too. Mike Whittacker," another, slightly deeper voice said.

"What are you boys doing in here?" Quilici asked.

"Don't tell Dad, but we heard him talking to Bill Morrow

about finding a cave, and we snuck over here to see it for ourselves," Sam Whittacker said.

"I ought to lock you boys up for the night for breaking and entering," Quilici said.

"We didn't touch nothing, Sheriff," Sam said. "We just wanted to see it."

"Let's get out into the open and talk," Quilici said.

The three stepped out of the cave and into the meeting room. The sheriff coughed several times, then looked at the two young men.

"I'm going to let you go home because you boys have never caused any trouble," he said. "But I'm going to remember this."

"Thank you, sir," the two said in unison.

Quilici watched as the two quickly walked across the room and scampered up the stairs. He smiled, remembering his own minor misdeeds as a teen. He lit a cigarette, inhaled, and coughed several times. He glanced at his watch, realizing he'd probably missed dinner again, then began walking toward the steps. Suddenly, he felt a prick on the back of his leg, but there was no pain. The basement light seemed to dim but he didn't feel particularly concerned. In fact, he felt strangely pleased with himself. His bad leg gave out, and he fell to the floor but even that didn't hurt. He rolled over slowly, feeling like the night that he'd had too many shooters at the Night Owl Cafe.

Why is that baby crying, he wondered just before he blacked out.

The ACES Anthology

The Culling is ©2023 by Richard Moreno. It appears here for the first time. The author has published 14 works, including "Frontier Fake News: Nevada's Sagebrush Hoaxsters and Humorists," "Nevada's Myths and Legends," and "The Roadside History of Nevada," which are available on Amazon (www.amazon.com/stores/Richard-Moreno/author/B001JP3UC0). The author is the former publisher of Nevada Magazine and writes a travel/history column for the Lahontan Valley News. You can follow the author at https://backyardtraveler.blogspot.com/.

Ashley Hanna Morgan

Not My Daughter

Today in the bath I practice
Looking at my body with
Kindness and ask
My brave strong girl
What do you like about
What your body can do?
At merely four (and thirty-two)
The answers stream forth
Soothing as a mineral spring:

My body can taste food!
My body can dance ballet!
My body can ride horses!
My body can paint with all the colors!
My body can tickle!

My body made you!

What towering sequoia ever accepted criticism for standing too

proud and tall?
What imposing oak ever believed the naysayer who said you take up too much space?
What lusciously fragranced lilac would tone it down for a picayunish passerby?
What extravagantly ruffled rhododendron would deign to draw near to hear
You're too much?
Don't overshadow us.

So why have we
Rooted and raised
In the patriarchy
Allowed others to take us down
For their own purposes
Branch by mighty branch
Leaf by luscious leaf
Until piece by precious piece
We have become former trees
Painting our stumps for their approval?

Not my daughter.

"Not My Daughter" is ©2023 by Ashley Hanna Morgan. The author is a resident of Reno, where she practices Clinical Social Work, and has published several other works, including a volume of poetry titled, "I Gave Birth to My Heart," and a Perinatal Mental Health Support Group Curriculum, available in the ACES bookshop at acesofnorthernnevada.com. Ashley is a passionate advocate for mental health and healing through stories. You can follow her at www.ashleyhannamorgan.com.

Marie Navarro

Friday the 13th

A black cat ran across the parking lot when Roger Morelli pulled his older-model Jeep Wrangler into the parking lot of Kelly & Kelly distributors. Roger laughed. "Good try kitty. But you are not going to ruin my Friday."

Roger parked in the back row assigned for employees. He whistled happily, as he slammed the door shut. It was mid-November and a Friday the 13th, yet the gloomy, cold, and overcast weather had no effect on Roger's mood.

He strolled toward the warehouse where he worked as a forklift operator, cheerful because he had plans for the weekend. The warehouse manager walked by just as Roger clocked in. "How's it going, Derrick?"

"Today is looking good, Rog," Derrick replied, checking his clipboard. I have you and Manny at door four. We've got a truck arriving right now. Looks like an easy offload."

"Sounds good." Roger poured himself some coffee and strolled through the cold warehouse toward his door. He hoped Manny had snagged the good forklift. He had.

The ACES Anthology

Manuel, aka Manny, was sitting in the forklift in front of their rollup door. He had one foot propped on the steering wheel and was sipping coffee as he waited for Roger.

"Morning Manny," he greeted. "Got the good one, I see. You the man." He gave his friend a thumbs up.

"Of course, you know me." Manny smiled proudly. "You still coming over tomorrow for the barbecue, right?"

"Wouldn't miss it for anything. And then Sunday I plan to..."

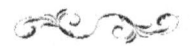

※

"Ay. Dios mio." Manuel sat up and clenched his chest, while interrupting his friend. "Roger, I'm in love."

Roger turned to face in the direction his coworker was looking. Walking toward them was the driver of the truck that had just backed in at their door. She was a very attractive driver. Her step was energetic and confident. She had medium-length dark brown hair tucked under a wool cap, and she wore well fitted blue jeans and a black zippered sweatshirt. As she approached them, Roger noticed her eyes were a beautiful dark green... and familiar.

"Hi," she said. "I'm Sam. Is this ...?"

Her voice trailed off, and Roger saw recognition in her eyes too.

"Oh wow. I don't believe it." She laughed excitedly. "Jack Taylor. It is you, isn't it? Gosh, it has been what? 12 years? It's me, Sam. Samantha Jones from high school."

The truck driver gave Roger a friendly hug. His arms automatically wrapped around her. He was just as thrilled as she was. However, he forced himself to lie to his old friend.

"Um, sorry, Miss Jones. You've made a mistake," he said, unwrapping himself from her embrace. "It is a pleasure to meet you. But my name is Roger Morelli."

Samantha blushed and stepped back. "Oops. Well, this is embarrassing. Er, here's the paperwork. I think I'll go and get some coffee and pretend I didn't just make a complete fool of myself."

She handed Roger the shipping papers. As he took them from her, she looked down at his right hand. He noticed her left eyebrow arch when she saw the scar that ran across the top of his hand from the forefinger to his wrist. Samantha looked up at his face and met his gaze. She gently caressed the scar with her thumb.

"I'll be in the driver's lounge, Mr. Morelli," she said coolly, emphasizing his last name.

She turned on her heel and walked off.

"Ay, Roger. You are a lucky man. Why couldn't she mistake me for someone she knew?" Manuel chuckled.

"Because Manny, you forget, you have a wife who would have to remind you that you have no recollection, whatsoever, of any pretty truck drivers in your past."

"Right. I keep forgetting about Linda controlling my memories." Manny nodded and smiled, referring to his very pretty wife, who Roger knew adored him. And he knew Roger adored her even more.

As Manny started the forklift, Roger looked down at the paperwork and his scar. Samantha knew he had lied. Roger knew in that moment that his life was about to change.

Twenty minutes later, Roger walked into the driver's lounge. Samantha was sitting at one of the tables, reading a magazine and ignoring her coffee.

"You're good to go," he told her. "Just need you to sign here." He put the paperwork and a pen on the table next to her. She looked up.

"Who are you hiding from, Jack?" Her voice was gentle.

His head jerked at his old name. He answered her question with another question. "Are you leaving town right away?"

"No, getting low on hours. Not leaving until Sunday morning."

"You going to park at Crossroads?"

"Yep. Only truck stop in town."

"I get off work at six. Want a break from truck stop food?"

"You inviting me to dinner?" The corner of her mouth twitched.

"Guess I am." He shrugged.

"But Mr. Morelli, I just met you." She feigned shock.

"I suppose it is rushing things. But I have this feeling we might have been good friends in another life."

Grinning, Samantha nodded toward the copies of the paperwork in Roger's hand. "You have my truck and trailer number. See you later?"

"See you later."

Roger watched Samantha as she walked out of the breakroom. She looked just as good as she did in high school. Actually, after the life he had been living the past few years, she looked better. Letting his guard down scared Roger. Still, he knew if there was one person he could trust with his life, it was Samantha.

After making plans with his friend, the workday could not go by fast enough for Roger. He tried to focus on his work, hoping he wouldn't notice the hours dragging by. Still, the hands on the warehouse clock didn't seem to move. It didn't help that Manny teased him incessantly about the friendly truck driver.

By the time Roger pulled into the truck stop later that afternoon, the weather had not improved. It was drizzling. He drove around the lot full of 18-wheelers and soon spotted Samantha's Freightliner. She had a good parking spot close to the building and next to a large parking lot safety lamp. He went to the other side of the travel plaza, where the parking for cars was located. Roger found a spot and climbed out of his Jeep.

He trotted across the large blacktop to Samantha's rig. He was feeling cheerful and nervous at the same time. He wondered how changed his friend might be. How did Samantha Jones go from graduating among the top ten of their class to driving a truck?

He knocked on the passenger door of her rig. She had her curtains closed, but he could hear the canned laughter of a TV sitcom playing. Soon her face appeared in the window. She smiled and opened the cab door.

"Come on in. I need to get my socks and shoes back on."

He climbed into the passenger seat while she went back to the bunk in the back of the cab. Sam closed her laptop that had been playing the show. She began pulling on her socks.

Roger looked around the cab. "Hey, this is very nice. You have what? Your laptop, microwave, refrigerator, Keurig coffee maker? Sam, your truck is nicer than my apartment. Wanna trade?"

She grinned. "Are you sure about that? At least at your apartment you probably have your own bathroom. Mine is over there." She pointed in the direction of the truck stop.

"You're right. I'll keep my place."

Sam and Roger laughed. Sam's face softened, and the two old friends silently looked at each other for a moment, seeing in each other the old and familiar, and at the same time, the changes brought by the passing of time.

"So, tell me 'Roger', what happened to Jack?" Sam no longer looked angry.

Roger exhaled. "It is a long story."

"Will it explain your blond hair turning dark brown and those silly phony glasses?"

"Yes." He gave her a wry smile. "But the glasses are real. I'm a little nearsighted now."

"Oops. Sorry."

"Do you remember Tami?"

"Sure, I half expected you two to get married."

"And you remember Pete?"

"Sure, I half expected him to be your best man. Wait. Did you finally marry Tami? How did I not get invited to the wedding?"

"Tami and I were engaged. Pete was going to be my best man. But it turns out that Tami considered Pete the better man. I came home early one day and found them together. I moved out that day and have not spoken to either since."

"Wow. Jack, I am so sorry."

Jack closed his eyes and exhaled.

"What is it?"

"It feels really good to hear you say my name." He continued his story. "Anyway, I didn't date for a long time after that. When I did start dating, I always kept it very casual. About four years ago, a coworker set me up on a blind date. The woman was pretty and..." Suddenly Roger's stomach growled.

Sam laughed. "Hey, why don't you tell me the rest of the story in the car? I'm hungry too." She laced up her boots and pulled on a light jacket. Then she turned off her dome lamp and grabbed her wallet and cellphone from the overhead compartment. Roger climbed out of the rig, followed by Sam, who locked the door.

Sam looked up, letting the drizzle hit her on the face. "Wow. Nice night, huh?"

"Know what this night reminds me of?"

"Uh huh. Prom night."

"I'll never forget it. Tami got sick. Strep throat, right? My date got drunk, and I caught him making out in his car with that cheerleader... what's-her-face."

"Lindsey. You and I left the prom early and went to the movies. We were very overdressed."

"It was raining when we left the movies. We got soaked."

Roger opened his car door for her. "It was a great night." His voice was soft. Sam looked up at him.

"It was a great night."

Roger could tell she was thinking the same thing he was. It was the only time they had kissed. Because Roger was still dating Tami, they agreed it was a mistake. Over the years, more than once, Roger had wondered if the mistake had been not choosing Sam over Tami.

He climbed in behind the wheel and pulled out of the parking lot. "Back to my story. My blind date turned out to be an obsessive and unstable young woman."

"Seriously? That sounds bad."

"It was. After our first and only date she decided she was in love with me. She told me that she loved me that very night."

Sam nodded but said nothing.

"I tried to be nice. However, I also made it clear that I didn't feel the same way. That didn't work on her. She constantly phoned me and messaged me. On social media, she put that we were in a relationship. She told the coworker who set us up that we were a couple. She would buy me romantic gifts. I told her to leave me alone. That just made her worse."

"What do you mean?"

"She would stop by my job and bring lunch. She would come by my apartment with takeout." He exhaled. "Then she booked us on a cruise. Obviously, I told her I wouldn't go with her."

"Couldn't you get some kind of restraining order or protection order against her?"

"No. She never threatened me or did anything dangerous. There was really nothing I could do to make her stop. She was unnerving and annoying. However, she didn't do anything exactly illegal. It wasn't even considered stalking."

"So then what happened?"

"I got rid of all my social media. I asked for a transfer and moved across town. I don't know how she did it, but she found me."

"Jack, I don't know what to say."

Roger sighed. "It feels good to finally share it with someone." He pulled into the parking lot of The Jade Dragon.

"Chinese? Yay. My favorite." Sam clapped her hands.

"Yeah, I thought it would still be." Jack parked the car, got out, and opened Samantha's door. "I think you will like this place. I know how much you love hot and sour soup and Szechwan chicken. They make the best in the area. You do still like hot and spicy dishes, right?"

"I sure do. Can't wait to try it.".

They walked inside, and a friendly server greeted them and showed them to their table. After they had placed their orders and their beverages had arrived, Roger looked across the table at his friend. "The insanity went on for months. She was relentless. I couldn't take it anymore. I didn't know what else to do. So, one day I just packed up and moved away and changed my name."

Sam blinked. "Oh Jack." Then she shook her head. "Wait. I guess you really aren't Jack anymore, are you?"

"No. I'm not."

"Are you okay with that? Does anyone else know?"

Roger sighed. "You know I have no family. I aged out of the

foster system. My only friends were a few old classmates and coworkers." He looked away and then back at Samantha. "I did regret losing touch with you."

"To be fair, that was mostly my fault. I never got into the whole social media thing." She shrugged. "And after I left for college, I just never went back home. You know how it was for me. School was torture for me, and home was worse."

"I still wish we had kept in touch." Roger poured tea into the two tiny cups. "I'm curious about what you've been up to. What's your story, Miss Jones? A truck driver? I thought for sure I would be watching you on the evening news one day. What happened to your journalistic ambitions?"

"I got a degree in Journalism." Sam sipped her tea.

"Well? Why no anchor job? No newspaper byline?"

"I worked part-time at a bar-and-grill during my senior year. That is where I met Eddie."

"He was a truck driver?"

Samantha nodded. "He and I started talking, and I found out I could make really good money as a driver and Eddie was looking for someone to drive team with him."

"Just like that you decided to do it?"

"Oh, no. No. I asked him a million questions. I researched it. I learned so much about the trucking industry that I wrote a feature paper on it. In the meantime, Eddie and I became good friends. Then one day he said something that really appealed to me. He said to give it a year, to just try it. I thought about it and realized it was a chance to see the country while being paid at the same time."

"So, you did it?"

"I did it, and I loved it. I made very good money. Eddie and I ended up driving together for six years."

"It seems like hard work. What did you love about it?"

The ACES Anthology

"There is a feeling of freedom with traveling. I saw so much of our country. It was an amazing experience." Sam gave Roger a smug smile. "And you need to read more. I did get my bylines. I have been freelance writing for the last four years."

"Why aren't you driving with Eddie anymore?"

Sam pushed her teacup away and took a swig of water. She was silent.

Roger noticed a tear running down her cheek. "Sam, what is it?"

"Jack, Eddie died." Sam's voice was barely audible.

Roger studied her face for a moment. "You loved him, didn't you?"

"Yes. Very much."

"Were you going to marry him?" Roger asked gently.

"Huh?" Sam looked confused.

"Huh?" Roger was confused by her confusion.

Samantha gave a small laugh. "Jack, Eddie was a good friend, but he had a boyfriend, Ryan. I did love Eddie, like a brother. I love Ryan too. He and I are still good friends."

Roger felt foolish and allowed Sam to thoroughly enjoy the confusion at his expense.

The food arrived, and Roger was thankful for the opportunity to change the subject to something not personal. For a few minutes they discussed the food, weather, music, and entertainment. Inevitably, the conversation came back around to their personal lives.

"So, did you finally get away from that woman, Jack?"

"Yes. I've not seen or heard from her since changing my name and moving out here."

"Would you rather I called you Roger?"

Roger considered his friend's question. He met her gaze and finally smiled. "No. I will always be Jack to you."

She rewarded him with a brilliant smile. "Yes. You always will be." She frowned thoughtfully. "Isn't it kind of strange running into each other like this?"

"Sure is. What are the odds of it happening? Finding each other in a warehouse, in a small town, in a different state?"

"And on Friday the 13th." Sam whispered in a mysterious voice. "Maybe it is a sign?"

"Ha. Ha. So, you never got a new person to drive team with you?"

"No, it can be hard to find a person you can trust and get along with. Think about it: You spend all day every day with the same person in a small space. It was easy to get along with Eddie. He was clean, professional, and was just a nice guy, you know?"

"I guess."

"You know, you could make more money driving a truck than a forklift. Maybe you should give it a try."

"Yeah, right." He laughed.

Sam did not laugh.

Roger went back to concentrating on his food. Samantha continued eating in silence.

Roger had finished most of his meal before he broke the silence. "Were you serious about me driving?"

"Sure."

"I couldn't stand to be alone in the truck for days. I need people. I need someone to talk to."

"So, team with me. You wouldn't be alone."

"Really?"

"Why not? I don't think you have changed that much. You are still the same guy I knew in school. I trust you. Jack, we've known each other since fifth grade. If there is one person, besides Eddie, that I could stand to be cooped up with, it is you. I do like team driving better than solo."

Just then the server arrived with the bill and two fortune cookies.

"Ooh, I love fortune cookies." Samantha immediately reached for hers.

"Remember how we used to force them into becoming true?"

"Well, they are always right when it comes to us." Sam grinned. "Think they still work?"

"You go first."

Sam opened her cookie, and it read, "Your inspiration will lead to success." She looked up at Roger. "See? The cookie knows. Now, your turn."

Roger opened his and stuffed half the cookie into his mouth; he nearly choked on it as he read, "You will travel far and wide for business and pleasure."

"The cookies have spoken," Samantha whispered imitating the voice of a carnival fortune teller.

"Let's get out of here."

Sam and Roger stood up. They both stuffed their fortunes into their pockets.

When they got in the car, Sam turned to Roger. "What do you think of the fortunes?"

"Coincidence?"

To quote Sherlock Holmes, "Rarely is the universe so lazy."

"Sam, do you know when you are going to be back through here?"

"I just started a dedicated route for the season. I'll be through here twice a week."

They were both silent until Roger pulled into the truck stop. He parked and shut off his Jeep. He turned to Samantha and, for a couple minutes, they just looked at each other. He reached over and pushed a strand of hair away from her face.

She smiled.

"Listen Sam, I've told no one the truth about myself. You are the only one who knows. I trust you; even though I haven't seen you in 12 years, even though I don't know anything about you except that you drive a truck and drove team for a while with a guy named Eddie. I trust you because of the girl I knew you to be."

"Jack, you know I won't tell a soul. I am that same person... just a little older." She reached over and brushed her hand against his stubbly cheek. "You've been hiding behind a dye job, a forklift, and a rented room long enough. It's time you lived again. Come see the country with me. It'll be fun."

"It does sound good." He ran a hand through his hair. "Manny at work is having a barbecue tomorrow. He told me I could bring a date. How'd you like to avoid truck stop food again?"

"Sure. Hey, should I give you my number?"

"Yes. Please." Roger handed Sam his phone, and she punched in her number.

Then Sam opened the car door. "I can pester you about driving with me some more at the barbecue. You will do it. The cookie said so."

Roger opened his door too. "Let me walk you to your truck."

As they walked across the parking lot, it started drizzling again. Roger took Sam's hand. "Let's talk again some more tomorrow."

"Okay."

Samantha put the key into the door and unlocked her truck. "Thanks for dinner, Jack, I had a great time. I'm so glad we found each other again."

"Me too. I knew it was going to be a lucky weekend." He took a step closer to her. "Is it okay if I give my old friend a good night hug?"

Sam didn't answer. She hugged him.

It felt right. Roger didn't want to let go.

Then she leaned in against him. Roger lifted his head and searched for her face. She looked up at him. He wanted to kiss her; he could see she wanted him to. He wondered if it would be as nice as the one kiss they had shared back in high school. He bent his head, and his lips met hers. This time, the kiss was even better.

She smiled. "Good night, Jack."

"Good night, Sam. See you tomorrow."

He waited for her to get safely back into her truck before he turned and crossed the wet parking lot to his Jeep. He sighed. Damn it. After the weekend he would have to come up with a new name and relocate again.

⚜

"Friday the 13th" is ©2023 by Marie Navarro. A former contributing writer for the San Jose Mercury News and staff writer for El Observador, she is the author of the FeyTerrah young adult fantasy series, which is available in the ACES bookshop at acesofnorthernnevada.com and on Amazon. **Marie serves in her community in Reno. She also spoils her grandkids, plants fairy gardens, and sings classic rock 'n' roll loudly and off-key.**

Janice Oberding
Gold Fish

She had nothing—except for two goldfish; two gold fish in a tiny globe fish bowl, always on the move. She came home from work every afternoon, pulled off her shoes, grabbed a book, or turned on the TV and talked to the goldfish.

They had no worries. Their food was in the little yellow box that God kept on the bookcase shelf where the fish bowl sat. She might be only a dispatcher for a local cab company, but to those two gold fish she was God—the giver of all good, light, water and food. God who had saved them from the crowded fish tank at Woolworths and had carefully brought them to their new home on the bookshelf they shared with an assortment of books.

She liked to read. Her books were mostly paperback, bodice-ripping romantic tales of long ago and faraway places of saucy maidens and fearless swashbucklers. While she read, the gold fish watched and swam. They were fed, their world was safe and clean; what did it matter what God did?

It didn't. And the gold fish saw it all—the way she stood in front of the TV every morning and half-ass exercised along with Jack LaLanne, the way she opened a can of chicken noodle soup for dinner, and the men she brought home from the bar out on South Virginia Street.

⚜

Neither she nor the gold fish knew it, but she had a reputation at the cab company. She was easy. Every new driver was invited to her little apartment. After a few drinks, she'd pull the hideaway bed from the wall, step out of her clothing and let it be known that the time for small talk had passed.

The man already knew what he'd come here for, and it wasn't the cheap bourbon. She was easy. He'd be quick to jump out of his clothes and into her old bed. When he was satisfied, he'd dress, and leave, shutting the door softly behind him.

Then God would cry. Curled up in a naked ball of despair, she'd cry herself to sleep. Tomorrow was another day—the gold fish saw and swam, safe in the knowledge that no matter what happened, God would be there with the yellow box in the morning.

⚜

By the time she got to the bar the rain had ruined her hair and sent rivulets of mascara running down her face. He didn't seem to mind. Seeing that she was alone, he took the stool next to hers. An hour and three drinks later, they were on their way to *her place*.

Thunder was roaring across the sky when she unlocked the door and led him in. God had returned. The gold fish saw and swam. She pulled the bed from the wall, and quickly undressed. He was here for *this*—what good were pretenses?

But this man was different. And neither she nor the gold fish understood. Once he was satisfied, the man jumped from the bed and dressed, all the while telling her how vile and worthless she truly was.

Whore, filthy whore—the words echoed through the little apartment.

No one should come into another's home and be so disrespectful.

"Get out!" she screamed.

But he was not finished with her. He slapped her, sending her reeling into the front door. As she stood, he grabbed her, pulling her to him. When she was close enough to feel his breath upon her, the man pulled a switchblade from his pants pocket. He thrust the knife into her—and twisted it.

God was dying. And as they swam, the gold fish saw it all, even though they did not understand it.

In her bathroom the man wiped himself clean and left her there, a bloody heap.

A no call-no show was not like her. The cab company called the police two days later. She would not be going back to work, nor would she be reading any more books. Once her body was bagged and taken to the morgue, two detectives came to the apartment to sift through her life—and death.

Neither of them asked themselves who could do such a thing to another human being. They'd long ago discovered that the world is full of monsters, hiding behind one mask or another.

Hers had been a life of deprivation—unless one considered gold fish, a television and a bookcase full of paperbacks luxuries.

Gold fish! The poor bastards must be starving about now. One of the detectives picked up the yellow box and sprinkled food into the fish bowl. The gold fish swam to the food and ate. *There was a new God.*

"This was no break-in." One detective said to the other. "She let him, willingly."

The ACES Anthology

The other detective nodded in agreement.

They'd seen it too many times in their combined years on the police force. *Too trusting, and middle-aged women were the worst.*

Once they'd gone through her paltry belongings, one of the men turned to the other.

"What about the gold fish?"

"The landlord will be in here next week to clean and paint."

"They'll be dead by then. Don't you need some pets?"

"The kids have a couple of cats and dogs and that's enough."

"We can't just leave them here."

"They're just gold fish for crying out loud. You can get all you want for a quarter apiece down at Woolworths."

"It just doesn't seem right."

"Right? I'll show you right," the other detective said picking up the fish bowl. In the bathroom, he poured the fish and their water into the toilet bowl and flushed the toilet.

There was no God after all.

Gold Fish is ©2023 by Janice Oberding. It appears here for the first time. The author is a resident of Reno and has published 45 works of fiction and non-fiction, including "The Big Book of Nevada Ghost Stories," "Murders Mysteries and Misdemeanors of Hollywood and Los Angeles," and "Haunted Las Vegas," which are available in the ACES bookshop at acesofnorthernnevada.com. Janice is a true crime buff who enjoys travel, cooking, history, and the paranormal. You can follow the author at https://www.facebook.com/JaniceOberding.

Sharon Marie Provost
The Shining Night

Gunter was difficult, to say the least. He was disruptive in class, a bully to all the other children, and destructive with school equipment. It seemed like nothing was safe from Gunter. He would either break, vandalize, or steal every item he encountered.

Gunter's mother had to work multiple jobs to pay the school back for all the damage he caused. Worse still, she had to degrade herself by begging the school regularly to keep them from expelling him. Gunter's mother was a proud woman whose self-worth was determined by her reputation amongst the townspeople as a hard-working Christian. She tried to pretend her heart was not hurt every time she heard the other women in town judge her parenting skills or seemingly threaten her precious son.

"Someday that boy will pay for what he has done, and it will be an awful sight to behold."

"She is so high and mighty, but someone needs to tell her how to raise a child properly."

Gunter heard them talk about him and his mother, but he couldn't be bothered to care what they said. He loved to torture the townspeople—young and old alike. He scared younger children with stories of monsters and ghosts, especially tales from local folklore, and threatened them with violence if they refused his demands. He knew these stories well because his own mother had used them for years to torment him for refusing to do his chores.

Gunter's mother doted on him. However, the stories she told him always warned that some evil entity—such as a witch, a wolf, or her favorites, Frau Perchta, or Krampus—would make him pay for his misdeeds.

Those warnings, however, had little effect.

Gunter still enjoyed tormenting every person he met, and more than anything, he enjoyed making his mother's life difficult. He knew she was a God-fearing woman, and that she worried about his soul. Yet he always managed to sneak away rather than attend church with her—to her great dismay. He never cleaned his room and rarely even attended to his own basic bathing and grooming. She often lamented that the barnyard animals in the village smelled better than he did, comparing his behavior to that of his "drunkard slob of a father," who had not been an influence, good or bad, in his life. The man had gone off one day into the mountains—drunk, as usual—to hunt. He had gone missing and was presumed dead when he never returned.

But his mother's dismay at Gunter's actions and her admonitions only irritated the boy.

Most annoying to him were her superstitious ways. She didn't just try to scare him with fairytales, she actually believed them: especially the local Christmas folklore regarding Krampus and Frau Perchta. To Gunter's utter embarrassment, she would stand outside church during the Yule season, admonishing the villagers—and especially children—to be kind and well-mannered, and reminding them of how important it was to keep their homes clean and their chores done. She even had a needlework decoration hanging in their home with the warning:

> *When Christmas draws near,*
> *Kind, well-behaved children need not fear.*
> *When slovenly, naughty children abound,*
> *Krampus and Frau Perchta come round.*

The Christmas season was Gunter's favorite time of year for two important reasons. The first was because he received many presents from his doting mother—both because she was afraid of him, and because he was her whole world. The second (and most fun for him) was because it gave him the chance to scare the other children and townsfolk.

On December 5th, better known as Krampusnacht or Krampus Night, he would run around town encouraging other children to misbehave with him, stealing food from the street fair, scaring old widows and spinsters, and vandalizing other villagers' homes.

His favorite malicious act was perpetrated on unsuspecting old ladies: He would knock on their door and run away around the corner so he could watch their reaction to finding a flaming bag of excrement he'd left upon their porch steps. When they screamed for help, fearing their homes might go up in flames, he would run back around and offer his own assistance... for a small fee. When they paid him, he would urinate on the bag to put out the flames and then stomp on it, spreading the mess across their meticulously cleaned porches before running off laughing.

After he had corrupted the other children with these misdeeds, he would terrify them by spewing stories of the terror, pain, and even death that Krampus and Frau Perchta could inflict upon them—the very same stories his mother used to torture him. He told them how Krampus, the horned half-goat, half-demon creature, would visit children that night with St. Nicholas and beat the naughty ones with birch rods. Sometimes, Krampus even took the worst children to hell with him or ate them.

Upon hearing Gunter's stories, many a child would run home on Krampusnacht, crying to their parents, confessing their wrongdoings while desperately looking for a way to repent.

Of course, Gunter's mother believed those stories too. She desperately tried to make him stay home and behave during the season to prevent Krampus from stealing her precious boy. But she was even more worried about Frau Perchta. Between Christmas and when Twelfth Night arrived on January 6th, she tried to ensure that the house was meticulously cleaned, that the flax was obtained and spun, and that a traditional bowl of porridge was left out for the Frau on that last night.

She tried to enlist Gunter's help in making sure the household chores were done to the Frau's satisfaction.

Gunter, however, delighted in evading all her efforts to protect him. Worse still, he even sought to undo what he viewed as her ridiculous attempts at saving them from Perchta's wrath.

Life in the village had shown him that there was no reason to worry about such "stupid" beliefs. Gunter never faced any consequences for any of his actions. On the contrary, his mother would still shower him with whatever gifts she could afford, especially at his birthday or Christmas.

⚜

Gunter's Uncle Otto—his mother's brother and the only other family he knew—was less understanding. He had come to the house for an overnight visit one evening before Christmas the previous year, and of course, he found Gunter up to his usual ways. The boy arrived late to dinner, even though he knew company was expected. He demanded his dinner as soon as he entered, without even saying hello to his weary mother or his uncle. When his uncle chided him for his bad behavior, he simply ignored the gruff old man and announced he was going to his room, without being properly excused from the table.

He did not, however, go to his bedroom.

Instead, he sneaked into *his uncle's* room, intent on finding some form of mischief to engage in as payback for his uncle's meddling. Rummaging through his uncle's bag by the bed, he found the man's most prized possession: a pocket watch from his dear departed wife. Gunter promptly threw it on the floor and ground it under his heel before picking it up again and carefully placing it back into the bag.

Later that night, he heard an angry cry when his uncle went to his room and found it. Moments later, the man stormed into his room and demanded that he confess to breaking it. But of course, Gunter lied straight to his face. He even had the guts to laugh at his uncle's reaction.

His uncle grabbed him by the scruff of the neck, prepared to "give him a beating he would never forget." As Gunter expected, he was saved when his mother ran in and begged her brother not to hurt him. She promised that Gunter would be properly punished the next day.

"Someday, you will get what's coming to you," his red-faced uncle had promised, warning him that Krampus would come for "evil little boys like him."

To his mother's dismay, his uncle immediately packed his belongings and swore he would never return to his sister's home again so long as "the devil's spawn" remained. As he stormed out of the house, he repeated his warning threateningly.

"Boy, one day you will go too far, and your mother will not be there to save you. You will rue the day you were born."

The year since then had gone as every other year had for Gunter, who was never held back in school, even though he barely passed any of his classes.

This time, he failed all of them—except for physical education. He liked to exercise and play. But even more to his liking, this particular class afforded him an opportunity to "accidentally" hurt other children in his zeal during games.

Yet despite his poor marks and violent behavior, he was promoted to the next grade as usual at the end of the year. His mother had overheard other parents discussing their theory that the school just pushed him through each year in an effort to be rid of him.

His instructors had tried everything they could think of to get him to behave, but they were not any more successful than his mother. At the start of the year, they had given him detention as punishment when he was caught doctoring another student's sandwich. Gunter hated Timmy because he was a "goody goody" who followed all the rules. He was the one kid Gunter could not convince to perform wicked pranks on other people. Gunter had been sent to the corner of the classroom to work alone after he was found berating Timmy during recess. Later, his instructor noticed him missing from his desk and found him putting Ex-Lax in Timmy's sandwich.

He went to the first two days of detention—just to see what problems he could cause—and, as usual, he was so disruptive and abusive that the teacher in charge finally threw up her hands and told him to go home. Nobody said anything when he did not return to the detention hall after that.

Gunter quickly learned that the harder he worked to make people hate him, the more he was shunned. And the more he was shunned, the more freedom he had to cause trouble. He had successfully alienated almost the entire town, and best of all, his meddlesome uncle had not returned to visit them since the previous year, just as he had promised. Not that he would have noticed, since he scarcely spent any time at home anymore.

One Sunday morning, however, he returned home and snuck in briefly to retrieve his slingshot, which he used to target store windows, other children, and small animals. He arrived to find his mother singing to herself as she busily cleaned their home. As usual, she was off-key as she sang that ridiculous, oft-repeated tune. He'd heard it from her for as long as he could remember—although he had never heard anyone else sing it—and it always made him laugh:

Through wintertide we don our cloak
And toil beneath the wizened oak

Day by day and into night
When daystar yields to pale light

Inch by inch and speck by speck
We scour ev'ry niche and crack

In hearth and home we render clean
The shadowed places in between

Unfortunately for Gunter, on this occasion, he laughed just a bit too loud, and when his mother caught him, she dragged him to Sunday school. However, he was determined that he would not be forced to stay there. After hitting the Sunday school teacher, making multiple young girls cry, and tearing up a Bible, he was sent home. His mother was "advised" that, in the future, he should perform Sunday school Bible readings on his own at home.

⚜

Once again, the Christmas season arrived with a flourish.

Gunter was up to his usual tricks and faced no repercussions. Krampusnacht passed with no sign of Krampus there to punish him. Instead, St. Nicholas left him small gifts, nuts, and other goodies stuffed in his shoes, which he had left by the window. On December 24th, his mother bestowed upon him many wonderful presents, as she did every year.

Of course, he did not reciprocate or even bother to thank her.

Instead of being grateful for her generosity, he grew more and more irritated with what he considered her constant nagging. Each year, as he got older, she demanded that he do a bigger share of the household chores in preparation for Twelfth Night, warning him more fervently than ever about what Frau Perchta would do to him if he refused.

But Gunter had reached his breaking point when it came to his mother's absurd superstitions. He *knew* that Frau Perchta was just a story parents told their children, trying to instill a strong work ethic in them—or so they said. He was sure that parents really wanted an excuse to be lazy and get their children to do all the work for them! And he was even more sure that *no one* was going to punish him or anyone else on the "Shining Night" when the star of Bethlehem shone down.

This year, Gunter decided, her lies had to end. He was not going to do her bidding now... or ever. It was high time she realized that. This year, he would do everything in his power to end this farce once and for all.

If he couldn't make her stop, he would avoid his mother altogether. He left the house each morning before she rose and returned after she went to bed; in between, he spent his time causing trouble or playing in the hills.

He did no work at the house to clean it.

He did not help his mother prepare or spin their allotted flax.

He did not go shopping in the village so she could prepare the Twelfth Night porridge for Frau Perchta.

The day before the Frau was to arrive, he peeked in through the window at his mother and saw that she had nearly completed her cleaning. Having grown hungry from a day of mischief-making, he decided it was safe to go home for dinner that night.

Since she was finishing the last of the day's chores, there was no need to avoid her notice by sneaking past her, so he came in with a clatter, tracking mud in as he headed to the table. The stew was ready, piping hot on the hearth, so he helped himself without waiting for her to join him. As expected, she was singing that dreaded song of hers as she swept and dusted the last of the dirt from the shelves and baseboards, but this time, he noticed, there was something different.

Inch by inch and speck by speck
We scour ev'ry niche and crack

In heart and home we render clean
The shadowed places in between

"You sang it wrong. You said 'heart,'" Gunter called out to his mother with a sneer on his face.

"Mmm hmm." She didn't even look at him as she focused on her mopping.

The next day, Gunter's mother begrudgingly and fretfully completed all the remaining tasks, ensuring that nothing was out of place. She hoped if the house were sparkling clean, the porridge hot and delicious, and the flax spun perfectly down to the last straw, that maybe, just maybe the Frau would skip their house.

Gunter did not lift a finger to help her.

He was gone as usual.

And at the end of the night, she went to bed full of fear because he had not yet returned home.

It was near midnight when Gunter quietly stole into the house—and immediately set out to undo everything his mother had done to prepare for the night. He "forgot" to wipe his shoes and tracked more dirt into the house, which, of course, he didn't bother to sweep up. He burned all the spinning his mother had done. He disposed of the porridge promptly. (It was certainly delicious.) He put the bowl in the sink, caked in dried porridge, and splashed water on the counter as he poured himself a drink. He sprinkled flour all over the counters. In short, he did everything he could to dirty the immaculate house his mother had painstakingly cleaned.

He wanted to show her once and for all that the Frau was just a figment of her warped imagination. Besides, it was fun!

When he had done his worst, he prepared for bed, exhausted, and fell into a fitful sleep nearly instantly.

About an hour later, Gunter awoke to a rumbling like thunder and the sound of the wind wailing around the house. This seemed quite bizarre because the weather had been perfect when he went to bed a short time earlier. He shook his head and turned over, throwing a pillow over his head, and he had finally started to drift back to sleep when he heard a rustling sound... inside the house.

His mother never got up in the middle of the night.

For a moment, he was concerned. Then he chuckled quietly and decided it must be a rodent enjoying the fruits of his labor.

Or was it?

A moment later, he jumped and sat up straight in bed: He was sure he heard his name quietly whispered—no, hissed—in the hallway. That was no rodent, and it did not sound like his mother's voice. Once again, he suppressed the fear that was trying to creep up on him, allowing himself to lean back on his pillow. Surely, this must be one of his so-called friends (who were really his reluctant minions), trying to get back at him.

As he lay there, forcing himself to calm his breathing, he saw the doorknob start to turn.

His apprehension faded, turning to anger.

SOMEBODY dared to come into HIS room. This was really just too far. Who did they think they were? He would show them!

Gunter jumped up, ready to pound them into submission. He ran to the door and yanked it open, expecting to confront some neighborhood boy who'd snuck in to spook him. But he saw before him someone—a creature; an old hag in tattered rags with stringy black hair and a pale complexion that made her look barely human. She stared out at him through laughing, vacant eyes over a hooked nose as she balanced herself easily on the uneven floor, even though one foot was obviously larger than the other.

Gunter couldn't believe his eyes. Surely, he must be dreaming. It couldn't possibly be! Yet, it must be... it had to be! There, standing in front of him, was the exact image of Frau Perchta, just as he had heard her described so many times by his mother and others in the village.

She grinned at him threateningly.

Gunter backed away, tripping and falling back onto his bed.

The Frau lurched menacingly toward him. "You... you are the evil little boy I have heard so much about these past few years," she hissed.

Gunter stammered unintelligible guttural sounds as he shook his head back and forth vehemently.

"No! No, it is not me. I am a good boy," he whined.

"Then who made the mess in the kitchen and all through the house?" she demanded. "Who ate the hot, delicious porridge that your mother made for me? Why do I find ashes in the hearth, instead of freshly spun flax?"

"I didn't mean... I didn't know. I'm sorry. I won't do it again. I will be a good boy from now on. I will go clean..."

"Stop! I don't want to hear it! Lies... it is all lies," Frau Perchta declared.

She advanced on him menacingly, brandishing a long, sharp blade as Gunter mewled hopelessly. He rocked back and forth like a toddler as his eyes glazed over, realizing his fate was sealed. The neighbors later recalled hearing grunts and cries of pain issuing forth from the house, but they were much too afraid to investigate. Everyone knew this was the night that the Christmas witch Frau Perchta rode through the skies, so they barred their doors and stayed inside.

A short while later, the rumbling and wailing winds receded, and the oppressive darkness that had surrounded the home lifted.

It was early the next morning when Gunter's mother crept down the hall to her son's room. She was sure Frau Perchta had paid them a visit, yet she herself had escaped the Frau's wrath. She could envision in her mind's eye what terrors the Frau might have visited on her beloved son.

But any horrors one might have imagined could not compare to the sight she beheld when she opened the door to his room. There, propped up on the bed, was her beautiful boy. His now-lifeless body had been disemboweled; his organs and entrails lay spread out across the bed. In their place, the night visitor had stuffed his abdomen with straw and small pebbles, leaving it open for the world to see the intruder's frightful handiwork. His hand clutched a small note with a single word written across the top: "Slovenliness." Scrawled at the bottom was the signature of Frau Perchta, along with a short postscript: "Krampus sends his regards as well."

Gunter's mother ran to the door, and the whole village heard her cry out for help. Women ran to her side as she broke down sobbing and told them her worst fears had been realized.

"Why didn't he listen? Why?" she sobbed as they took her into their arms.

She had warned him so many times. She had done everything she could to keep him on the proper path; to dissuade him from the evildoing that could only have ended the way it did... just as it had for his father.

The men in the village helped remove Gunter's body and took him to be prepared for burial.

The ACES Anthology

Once they had carted him away, his mother's demeanor immediately calmed, and she began to re-tidy her home. She started a fresh pot of porridge on the hearth as she worked, humming her familiar tune. The villagers in the town were bewildered by her stoic behavior, but they chalked it up to shock. They left her in the capable arms of her brother, who had just arrived unexpectedly.

Everyone in the village learned a lesson that year, especially the children. No one wanted to be the next victim of Krampus or Frau Perchta. Likewise, though, no one mourned the loss of young Gunter, except for his mother.

Or did she?

"The Shining Night" is ©2023 by Sharon Marie Provost. It appears here for the first time and will appear in the forthcoming collection of short stories "Shadow's Gate," of which she is the co-author. The author is a longtime resident of Carson City, where she works as a veterinary office manager. She is the owner of champion of dog-trial poodles, and the creator of handmade dreamcatchers and chainmaille jewelry. Sharon is also the co-editor of this volume and provided the foreword to Stephen H. Provost's "Sierra Highway." You can find her at local craft fairs, author events, and at "Sharon's Dreams" on Facebook.

Stephen H. Provost
Ghostbusted!

Rick Piersall hadn't made his reputation backing away from a challenge, and this certainly was... different. His assistant had handed him a letter from a viewer in Mound House, Nevada, named Adolph Sutro, claiming to have knowledge of the "most haunted place in the entire U.S. of A." That was how he'd put it.

That part wasn't different.

Hundreds of places claimed to be the most haunted this or that, and Rick had visited dozens of those since his show, *Haunted Havens*, went on the air six years ago. But this letter wasn't flagging him to some haunted hotel or opera house or abandoned mansion. Instead, it claimed an entire town was haunted—so much so that no one dared live there... or even visit.

Of course, the letter said, some folks might have just left once the cyanide mill closed: It had opened in the early 1920s to process silver, only to close a few years later when the price of the metal fell. Now, the letter claimed, it was totally sealed off to the outside world. The government had made sure of that, supposedly to protect trespassers from the mill's ruins, which had lately been demolished. But it remained a hazard thanks to the number of deep shafts in the area.

That was the government's story. But this mysterious viewer, this Adolph, had a different take: The government wasn't just keeping people out, it—or something—was keeping the ghosts in.

Rick wondered how effective such an effort could be or whether it was even needed. He could have told you that ghosts were often tied to a place anyway—most commonly, their old residence or the place they died. And if they did decide to get out, he didn't see how the government could stop them.

"You can only get to American Flat through my private tunnel, and I am the only person who can grant you access," Adolph had confidently stated in his letter. "If you seek to enter the town through any other means, you may be well assured of failure. What you will find on the other side is, I give you my word, nothing short of astounding, and, I dare say, terrifying."

It was that last word that hooked Rick Piersall. Whoever this Adolph was, he'd obviously seen *Haunted Havens*, which put a premium on making each locale appear as scary as possible. That's what kept viewers on the edge of their seats.

When Rick had first pitched the show to The Horror Network, he'd played to his strength as an investigative journalist. He'd vowed to place a premium on scientific evidence, supported by credible witnesses. Each episode, as he envisioned it, would conclude with a verdict:

The site in question would be declared either "haunted" or "safe."

THN had liked the concept, in general, but had told him the audience wasn't looking for Scooby-Doo-type ghostbusters. Viewers wanted to be scared. They wanted to believe. And that meant Rick would have to convince them that the places he visited were haunted—or at least very likely could be.

He was "encouraged" to stumble across a number of unexpected surprises during each episode to keep the viewers on the edge of their seats. (These "jump scares," as the network called them, would invariably be edited to occur just prior to commercial breaks.)

"It's just business," the network honchos had told him. "Like in those *Scream* movies. They're full of jump scares and gotcha scenes, and they always set up a sequel. That's why they work."

"But this is reality TV, not a film script." That had been Rick's argument. Besides, he thought, *Scream* was part satire, a sendup of horror films. It wasn't meant to be taken seriously. And Rick wanted to be taken seriously.

But they had set him straight: "Who told you reality TV was all real? It's edited like any other show. We show them what we want them to see—and what they want to see. There's nothing wrong with that."

Rick hadn't liked any of this—not at first. But he figured it was the price for having a show on cable TV. When *Haunted Havens* became an unqualified hit, he no longer questioned the network's ground rules—especially when the execs allowed him to keep producing the show himself. They obviously knew what they were doing: Who was he to argue with success?

Instead of interviewing skeptics, he confined himself to "true believers." And he learned how to act suitably distressed (read: scared shitless) at a sudden temperature drop in a drafty old mansion. Naturally, the temperature did drop when there was a draft, but Rick knew better than to mention that on camera. And he hyped it up if his EMF meter suddenly picked up a "spectral shadow"—a term he'd coined himself. Or if his flashlight started flickering. Or if there happened to be a sudden noise off-camera.

Skeptics, of course, said the EMF readings weren't ghosts, the flashlight's batteries were loose, and Rick's assistant, Faith Woolridge, was the one who made things go bump in the night.

The network bosses didn't care, and Rick told himself he didn't, either: The skeptics watched, too (so they could try to debunk him) and ratings were ratings. Still, deep down, he always felt a twinge of guilt about playing fast and loose with the facts. That's why, whenever he heard about something that sounded legitimately scary, he jumped at the chance to investigate it.

That way, he didn't feel quite so guilty.

This letter from Adolph had that ring of legitimacy to it. Who named their kid Adolph these days, anyway? Even the language of the letter sounded... spooky.

So Rick packed up his equipment and chartered a flight to Reno along with cameraman Cory Ainge, co-producer Skip Hathaway, and on-camera partner Faith, who routinely played the part of "damsel in distress" at the appearance of any grouchy ghoulies.

It was Cory who had given him the letter from Adolph; he and Rick weren't on the best of terms—Cory had made it clear he wanted more time in front of the camera and that he thought Rick was a control freak—but the show was a success, and Rick was the boss, so he stayed in line. He even brought Rick show ideas from time to time.

Mostly, Rick just tossed them, and Cory wasn't happy about that either. So it was natural that he seemed especially pleased at his boss's response to the Adolph letter.

The ACES Anthology

The flight to Reno was uneventful—with one exception. When the plane hit some pretty bad turbulence in its descent to RNO, Rick found himself wondering if the ghosts from American Flat had sent a welcoming committee. But Faith (who'd grown up down the road in Verdi) said this was typical.

"If you don't like wind, you won't like Nevada," she told him.

Even with her reassurance, Rick didn't breathe easy until the plane landed safely at the airport, where they picked up their rental car for the drive to Mound House, a small town just east of Carson City, a little more than half an hour away from where letter-writer Adolph had said he'd be waiting.

Mostly, it was known for its four legal brothels.

Adolph met them just outside one of them: the Moonlite BunnyRanch just off Highway 50. Adolph hadn't mentioned the brothel in the directions he'd sent; he'd just asked Rick and his team to meet him at "the old Pony Express stop"—which happened to be on the brothel property. When he greeted them, he ignored the brothel entirely, although Rick suspected the man was a regular. Attired in a double-breasted suit and decorative cowboy hat, he looked very much like the kind of gentleman who would find something he liked on the BunnyRanch "sex menu," even if his overgrown mutton chops made him seem a little old-fashioned.

Okay, a lot old-fashioned.

The way he talked only confirmed that impression.

"Good day, sirs and madam," he said, extending a hand. "I trust this day finds you well. I see you have brought with you one of Mr. Edison's Kinetographs. Grand! They certainly have advanced further than I suspected. You will want to record this for posterity!"

"Kinetograph?" Faith said, puzzled.

Adolph pointed at Rick's video camera, which he was using

to film the exchange.

"Ah," she said, not looking any more at ease with her new knowledge.

Rick looked at her and shook his head slightly. Whoever this man was, he was obviously playing a role. He'd heard about Chautauqua performers taking on the personas of historical figures in nearby Virginia City—site of the biggest strike in mining history—and he felt sure that Adolph was doing just that. Rick just couldn't figure out who he was supposed to be.

It probably didn't matter.

He climbed into their rental car, and they drove him toward the private tunnel he had referred to in his letter, which was less than ten miles up the highway. Once they reached the property, he directed them past a fence and onto a dirt road that wound up toward a low line of hills. At the end of the road lay the tunnel, framed by brick covered in white plaster. The wide entrance was surmounted by a signboard shaped suspiciously like a headstone that read "Sutro Tunnel" along with the date 1888. It had been commissioned, the signboard revealed, on October 19, 1869, which meant it must have taken a long time to complete.

The Sutro name sounded vaguely familiar, so Rick got out his smartphone and tried to google it. Unfortunately, however, he had no reception this far out.

"What's that contraption?" Adolph inquired.

He certainly was playing the part of the 19th century gentleman.

"I've heard that name somewhere," Rick said, pointing above the tunnel. "I was just trying to figure out how I knew it."

Adolph chuckled. "Of course you have, my friend," he said. "Sutro's my name. Adolph Sutro. I told you it was my tunnel in the missive I sent you. I finished it just before I went back to Frisco. I'm the mayor there now, you know. Just on a little sabbatical this weekend. It's a shame my old friend Samuel no longer lives in these parts. I would have liked to tip a glass with him."

"Samuel?" Skip asked.

"Clemens," Adolph said. "Goes by Mark Twain these days. A genuine chucklehead coffee boiler if ever there was one. Once tried to joke about a friend of mine being bald." He tipped his cap, revealing his own hairless pate. "That was taking things a little far, especially since the man in question was not bald. His name was Ball. Clemens thought that was funny. But when I refused to laugh as he expected, he had the gumption to label me as 'insensible to the more delicate touches of American wit.' In the press, if you can believe that. But I eventually forgave him. He's more famous than I am these days, and funnier now than he was then, so how could I not?"

Skip just stared at Rick, as if to say, "Is this guy for real?" But he and Cory both ignored him. This was great stuff. Either this Adolph guy was acting—and doing a great job of it—or he'd gone round the bend more times than a NASCAR driver. Whichever it was, it made for great TV.

"So," Rick said, adopting his serious TV ghosthunter voice, "if we go straight through this tunnel of yours, we'll reach the ghost town you told us about, American Flat."

Adolph nodded. "That's what the letter said, did it not? Well, I suppose that it isn't entirely accurate. The tunnel goes to Virginia City.

"That's what I built it for: to drain water out of the mines up there. But there's a side tunnel about halfway up that goes off to the left. That will take you to American Flat."

"You'll show us this tunnel when we get there?"

He shook his head vigorously, looking both determined and a little scared. "Me? Go back there?" He acted as though it was self-evident why he would want to avoid doing so, but the team's puzzled looks persuaded him to explain. "Most of us ghosts never get out of American Flat. Those of us fortunate enough to do so are most definitely not going back. I'll never set foot in that tunnel again."

"You're saying you're a ghost?" Faith said.

"Quite so, I'm afraid."

The man was certainly not a ghost, Rick felt sure. He was obviously an actor—probably planted by The Horror Network to spice things up. Without bothering to tell Rick, which was taking things a little far. Rick was fine with playing the part of the spooked spook-hunter, but he didn't like being played for a fool or wasting his time on a wild ghost chase. So he did what any veteran ghost-hunter would do: He sought confirmation the whole thing wasn't a hoax.

Pulling out his temperature gauge, he waved it in the air a few inches from Adolph's face.

"What in tarnation...?" Adolph leaned back abruptly, taken by surprise, but Rick still got his ambient thermometer close enough for a reading.

It was well over 80 degrees outside, it being summertime in the Nevada desert, but to Rick's surprise, the thermometer read 42.

Forty-two!

Any ghost investigator will tell you that a sudden, highly localized drop in temperature indicated the likely presence of a ghost.

Rick did a double-take, but he wasn't convinced. Still, whatever trick this Sutro character—or whoever he was—had pulled made for great TV. Rick shot a glance at Cory to be sure he was getting the footage, and a quick nod confirmed that he was.

Rick hammed it up, stepping back and opening his mouth wide for effect.

"O... kay...," he stammered, feigning the kind of fear he manufactured every week for the camera. "We... believe you. Just tell us where to go, and we'll be on our way."

Adolph shook his head. "In through there. I told you," he said, pointing at the tunnel. "Just watch for that side passage I told you about."

Rick nodded, still pretending to be scared out of his wits as he backed up toward the tunnel.

"You'll be wanting these," Adolph said, producing four lighted mining helmets, as if from out of nowhere. Rick had been counting on the lighting from Cory's video camera to help them navigate the tunnel, but he made a show of accepting the helmets anyway and having everyone strap them on. It heightened the sense of theater. Frankly, he wished he'd thought of it.

"Be careful," Adolph added. "Time's a funny thing in there."

The four of them made a show of moving quickly toward the tunnel, with Rick taking the lead, followed by Faith and Cory, and Skip bringing up the rear. Skip's schtick was to scream at the appropriate time to remind the audience just how dangerous ghost hunting was, even though the team never seemed to "discover" why he'd raised the alarm.

Sure enough, they'd only gone a few steps into the tunnel when Skip let out a scream: one that sounded much more intense and heartfelt than usual. It wasn't just a cry of fear, but of pain.

"Fuck!" he shouted, and Rick uttered his own silent curse because they'd have to edit that out.

"Watch the language." Rick said, but as he turned back toward Skip, he saw the man writhing on the ground, wincing in the shadows near the cave mouth as he grasped his ankle with both hands. Rick's questioning look was met with more cursing.

"Snakebite, you asshole! Fucking rattler. Where's the med kit?"

Rick froze.

He looked helplessly at Cory, then at Faith, but he knew the answer before he saw them shake their heads.

"What the fuck?" Skip half-shouted, half-whined. "We're in fuckin' Nevada and you didn't bring a snakebite kit?!?"

"We'd better go back," Faith said.

Rick knew she was right, but something in his head was making him hesitate, pulling at him to go deeper into the tunnel.

"Rick!" Faith shouted.

"She's right," said Cory. "We need to go back."

But it was Adolph who spoke next, his tone oddly cheerful and detached considering the circumstances. "I've got a snakebite kit right here," he said. "I always have one handy. It is Nevada, after all."

The quip wasn't lost on Rick, but the pull of the tunnel was still just as strong. He looked at Adolph, then back into the blackness.

"Never you worry," Adolph said. "Go on ahead. I'll have him fixed up in no time."

That was all the encouragement Rick needed. "Thanks," he shouted back, then turned to Faith and Cory. "Come on. We should get through this tunnel while there's still enough daylight left to film."

"But...," Faith began to protest.

"Who's in charge here?" Rick snapped, surprised to hear the impatience in his own voice. Then, more softly: "C'mon, guys. Skip's in good hands." He was trying to convince himself of this, but the pull of the tunnel was stronger than his level of reassurance about Adolph. Hell, he didn't even know the guy. But why would he say he had a med kit unless he really did? Besides, he was right: This was Nevada. Everyone here had one. Except Rick and his team.

He could tell Cory and Faith were reluctant to leave Skip, but they knew who the boss was, and they followed his lead. It was a good thing too. The tunnel turned out to be longer than he'd expected: nearly two miles before they reached the side passage Adolph had told them about. Covering those two miles took a lot longer than Rick would've thought; he told himself it was because they were moving more slowly through the darkness, with only the camera light and helmet lamps to guide them. But Adolph's warning kept echoing through his head: "Time's a funny thing in there." Had he been referring to the tunnel or the ghost town... or both?

The drip-drip-drip of water and the trickle of a stream through the tunnel heightened the sense that their journey was interminable, like Chinese water torture.

Rick tried to calm himself: It always seemed to take longer to get to a place—especially when you didn't know the way—than it did to come back. But his nerves weren't having it.

It was a relief when the three of them finally stepped out into sunlight, which blinded them for a moment before their eyes adjusted to the unexpected scene before them. They hadn't expected to find much in American Flat, if anything. The city itself was long-since gone, and even the cyanide mill had been razed nearly a decade ago. But what they saw flew in the face of everything they knew or expected.

There before them was a bustling town, filled with buildings in various stages of completion. None of the ones that were complete looked to be more than a year old; most were constructed of wood or, in a few cases, brick and mortar. Dozens of people were out in the streets, hurrying this way and that, but there wasn't a car in sight: just a number of horse-drawn wagons and carriages.

A sign on one of the buildings read "American City Hotel," while another proclaimed itself the Eureka Hotel, "Theodore Gosse, proprietor." Both were hubs of activity, but neither more so than Brown's Exchange Saloon, where a sign promised that the "best quality of wines, liquors etc" was "always on hand." From the number of customers entering the place, and leaving in various stages of inebriation, Rick surmised that living up to that promise might be a challenge.

It wasn't the only watering hole, either. The Willows Saloon looked just as popular—perhaps even more so, since it advertised having a race track out back.

Faith pulled Rick close and whispered in his ear: "We must have come out in Virginia City. That's where Adolph said the tunnel led."

Rick shook his head. He'd been to Virginia City for an early episode of *Haunted Havens*, before Faith joined the team, to investigate the haunted Washoe Club there. He knew this place looked nothing like Virginia City.

Come to think of it, though, Faith should've known too. Shouldn't she? She'd grown up in Nevada, barely an hour away from here. There wasn't anything to indicate that they were standing in Virginia City. Besides, there were plenty of signs that said "American Flat" or "American City."

"It's a movie set," Cory offered, not bothering to whisper.

But Rick didn't think it was that, either. He'd never seen a movie set so elaborate that it went on for blocks in every direction.

They were still trying to get their bearings when a man wearing a bowler hat ran up to them and thrust a piece of paper in Rick's face. "You gentlemen look like you know a good opportunity when you see one. Get in on the ground floor, my friends. Invest now, and you'll make a killing. It's the new Virginia City! It's bigger than Aurora!"

"And you are...?" Rick asked.

"Buddy McGursky, at your service," the man said, tipping his hat. "Representing William Hunt, broker and mining secretary of six mining concerns, hereabouts. But I'm sure you know the name. He's on the level, I assure you."

"Hey," said Cory, looking at Faith. "Weren't you a Hunt before you married...?"

She scowled at him, a reminder that she didn't like to discuss her former husband. She'd only kept the name because she'd started doing the show when she was still married, and Rick had insisted she keep it. If it had been her show...

Cory shrugged. "Maybe this William guy's your great-great-something-or-other."

She wasn't any less irritated at this. "It's a common name," she spat.

Rick ignored their exchange and took the flyer. "We'll keep it in mind," he said in a polite tone that failed to mask his suspicion.

"You do! You do!" said McGursky before quickly hopping on down the road to accost another pedestrian.

Rick noticed Faith shivering.

"Cold?"

"Aren't you?" she answered.

Come to think of it, he was. The sun was still high in the sky, and the dust on the streets made it clear that the place hadn't seen rain in some time. He looked around at the people coming and going: Some were dressed in summer attire, and the rest looked very uncomfortable in their formal clothing. There wasn't a wool coat or a pair of gloves to be seen. It didn't make sense, unless...

Rick pulled out his ambient thermometer and began walking around, staring at it the whole time. He was nearly knocked off his feet by a horse-drawn carriage, whose driver shouted at him: "Somebody steal your rudder, ya half-wit?" But he was too fascinated by what he was seeing to care. The thermometer wasn't fluctuating wildly, as it did when you encountered a spirit. It was steady. But the reading was too low.

In fact, the reading was 42—the same temperature it had shown when he'd waved it near Adolph.

"What? Is it broken?" Cory asked.

Rick stuck it under his armpit to be sure, and when he removed it, it was close to his normal body temperature. He shook his head. "Take a look." But as he held it out in front of him, the reading began to drop rapidly until it settled once again at 42.

"Huh. Jackie Robinson's number," said Cory.

"Or," Rick offered, "the answer to the ultimate question of life, the universe, and everything."

Cory just laughed. "More questions here than answers."

"You can say that again," said Rick.

But Faith was shaking her head in exasperation. "Sports. Science fiction," she said dismissively. "The answer is obvious: Adolph's a ghost, just like he said he was. And everyone here's a ghost too. This isn't just a ghost town. The entire town is a ghost."

Adolph had said the entire town was haunted. That had been part of what intrigued Rick in the first place.

It made sense in a twisted sort of way, but it also seemed absurd. Rick remembered reading a quote from Sherlock Holmes: "Once you eliminate the impossible, whatever remains, no matter how improbable, must be the truth." But Holmes was a fictional character, and this situation was very real. Far from eliminating the impossible, Faith seemed to be suggesting the impossible. And they hadn't eliminated everything else. Not yet.

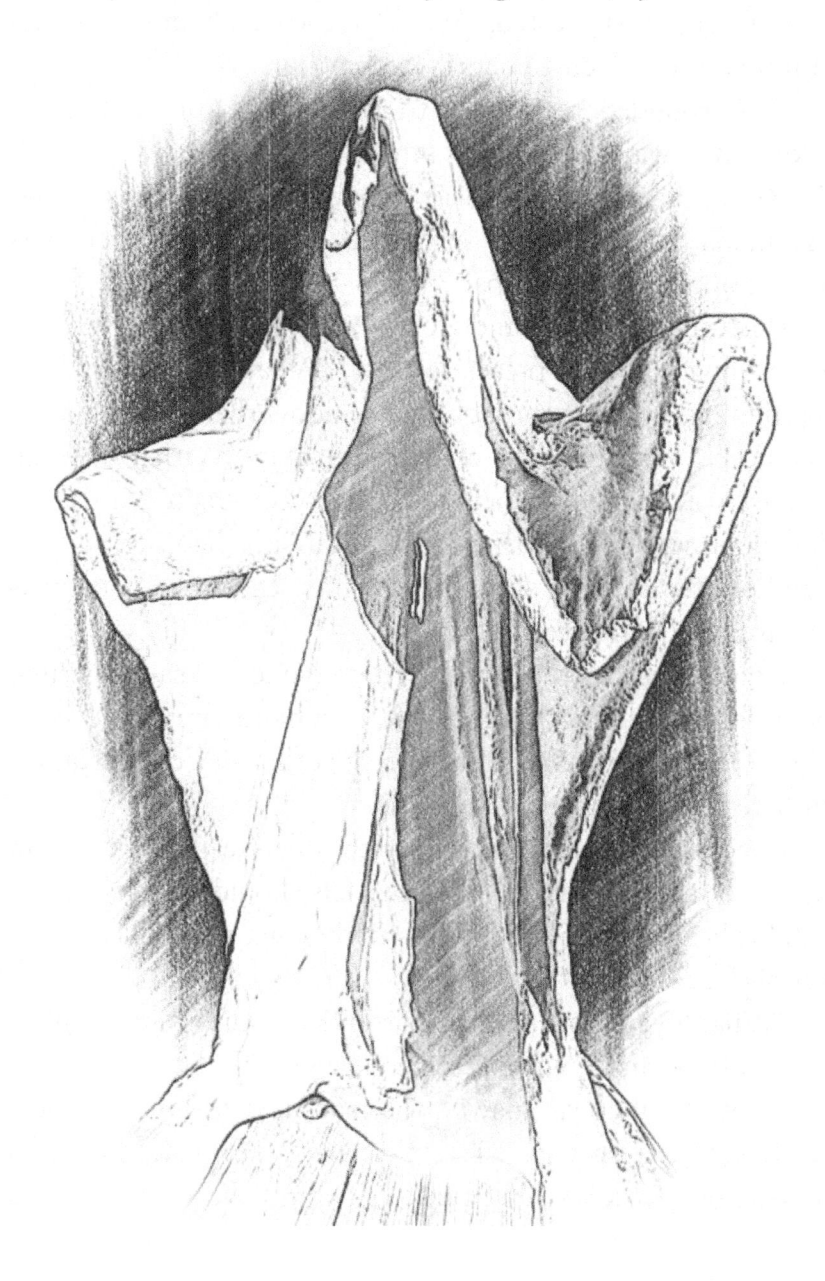

"Maybe," he said, unconvinced. "Where do you think we can find some answers around here?"

Cory shrugged and pointed to the Willows Saloon across the street. "Bartenders know pretty much everything that goes on in a town," he suggested. "And what they don't know, you can get from one of the customers if you buy him a drink."

That sounded reasonable to Rick, who lost no time in making his way across the street to the Willows, which advertised itself as "a place of resort, amusement and refreshment." There weren't any tables available, and there was just one open space at the bar.

He turned to Faith and Cory: "You two wait outside," he said, adding under his breath to Cory, "Whatever you do, don't stop filming. Zoom in through that window there." He pointed. "And keep the mic boom pointed straight at me. With luck, you'll be able to pick up what's being said." He wasn't sure of this last: The saloon was filled with boisterous cussing, hooting, and the sound of glasses being slammed down on the tables. Rick was surprised he hadn't heard a gunshot.

He was even more surprised that no one had said anything about the videocam, although it stuck out like a sore thumb. Even Adolph had remarked on it back on the other side of the tunnel. But here, it was as though it didn't exist.

Cory nodded, and Rick claimed the open seat, next to a man who sat hunched over a mug of beer. His shoulders rose and fell with his heavy breathing, and his cowboy hat was pulled down over his face.

"What'll ya have?" said the bartender, adding, "and drink it down quick or make way for someone who will."

Before Rick could answer, the man next to him wheezed, "He'll have the special, J.T. I'm buyin.'" The voice sounded familiar, but Rick couldn't place it behind the wheezing and sputtering of the man's obvious drunkenness. Besides, who would he know in this place?

"Thanks," he said, turning to the man.

The cowboy didn't look up.

The bartender, a tall but wiry man with a big shock of golden hair, stepped to the back shelf and pulled down a dusty, unmarked bottle. He opened it and sloshed some of its contents into a shot glass, then set it on the counter in front of Rick.

"Down the hatch," he said with a humorless smile. "I'll get you another if ya want it, but ya won't need it. It's powerful stuff."

Rick stared at the shot glass for a minute, then decided he'd better do what he was told if he wanted time to ask his questions. He put the shot glass to his lips, threw his head back, and downed it in one swallow, wondering what it was. It tasted like shit, the way he imagined turpentine or motor oil or formaldehyde might taste. Not like any whiskey, rum, or bourbon he'd ever tasted.

He made a face and looked up. "Tell me...," he started to ask the bartender, but J.T. was gone.

"He won't say shit," wheezed the stranger sitting next to him.

Rick turned to look at him, but the man was staring down at his beer from underneath the wide brim of his hat. Yes, he seemed drunk, but he hadn't touched his drink since Rick had come in.

"How long have you been here?" Rick asked him.

"Just got here." The voice did sound familiar, but it was clipped and his breathing was labored, and he wasn't saying enough for Rick to place it. Yet. He told himself to listen more closely and tried to ask a question that would get more out of the man.

"Where from?"

"Sutro."

That was no help.

"And this is American Flat?"

He shrugged. "Signs say."

"Who all lives here?"

For the first time, the stranger said more than a few short words: "Nobody lives here, Rick. Nobody's lived here for 100 years. They're all dead. So am I, now, thanks to you."

The man knew his name. And the voice... It couldn't be...

The stranger finally turned to him, raising the brim of his hat to reveal his face. "That's right, Rick. It's me. Skip."

Rick felt his chest pounding. He was having difficulty breathing. "God, it's good to see you're okay. How'd you get here ahead of us? Where'd you get those clothes?"

Skip curled his lip up in a smirk. "The town gave 'em to me. The town provides."

Rick had no idea what that meant. Skip couldn't have been here long enough to change clothes, let alone get drunk.

"Shouldn't you be resting?" he suggested, not knowing what else to say.

But Skip ignored him and slammed his hand down on the bar. "Another for my friend here, J.T.!" he shouted at the bartender.

The saloonkeeper reappeared and hurried over to refill Rick's glass.

"Drink it!" Skip demanded.

The bartender nodded. "Now. Or clear the seat."

Rick downed the shot.

"Good man," Skip said. "But you weren't listening, Rick. I'm not okay. I'm dead." He growled the last word. "You didn't bother to listen to Adolph before you left me behind back there. He told you he'd never set foot in that tunnel again."

"You mean he didn't get the snakebite kit?"

"There never was a snakebite kit. He said he wanted me to die. No, he needed it, because he needed someone in here to take his place. If he hadn't, he would have been forced to go back. American City must have a stable population. Exact numbers. The population as it stood on this exact date in 1864. When Adolph escaped, he had to send someone back. To be a ghost here in this ghost of a town. That someone was me."

"What about the government? Adolph said..."

"Crock of bull," Skip said. "The government has nothing to do with it. It's just the rules of the game. The way things operate. An eye for an eye, a tooth for a tooth... a life for a life."

Rick's breathing was becoming more labored, and he could tell it wasn't just at the shock of what Skip was saying. His head was pounding, and his hands were shaking. The room was spinning, and when he looked up at the ceiling to gain his bearings, that was spinning, too. He retched, but nothing came up.

"J.T.!" Skip shouted. "Another! That should do him!"

J.T. refilled Rick's shot glass again, but he shoved it away and off the back of the bar.

"That's bad manners, Rick," said Skip.

"Get your ass outta here!" J.T. yelled. "Now!"

Rick had never wanted to vomit, but he was trying to puke now. Desperately. But his body wouldn't cooperate.

He turned to Skip and tried to stand, putting out a hand to steady himself on the barstool. "What's in that shit?" His voice sounded to his own ears like a gurgling whisper. He felt like his heart was about to go through his chest.

Skip grinned. "Didn't you hear Adolph talking about the cyanide mill?"

Rick's body convulsed, and he fell to the floor.

"Now you'll be the ghost, but there'll be one too many. Which means I can go back! I'll still be dead, but I won't be stuck forever in this godforsaken hellhole." No sooner had he said this than he made a beeline for the door, with several other people in the bar sprinting after him, throwing down chairs and knocking over tables as they tried to beat Skip to what they all craved.

Freedom.

There could be only one.

Rick looked frantically toward the window for Cory and Faith, but they were nowhere to be seen. He wondered how cyanide from a mill built in the 1920s had made its way into a drink served in 1864. Or did it just seem like 1864? Was it really 2023 after all?

"Time's a funny thing in there."

The echo of Adolph's words was the last thing Rick ever heard.

Before he died, that is.

⚜

Cory and Faith made it back safely to The Horror Network's studios in New York, where they presented the videotape of their experiences to the producers. They looked shocked to discover that the tape was mostly blank. The only thing on it was a brief scene showing Rick Piersall's body lying on the bare earth of American Flat.

A forensics team found the corpse at that very spot.

An autopsy revealed that Rick had died after ingesting cyanide, and investigators suspected foul play. Skip's body, meanwhile, was found just inside the entrance to Sutro Tunnel, where he died as the result of a rattlesnake bite. Investigators questioned Cory and Faith in connection with both deaths before releasing them. Cory, however, was taken into custody a week later after police searched his email and found an incriminating exchange with Skip. The pair had apparently been plotting to take control of the show and force Rick out. "By any means necessary," one of the emails said.

Was this evidence of a murder plot? Investigators thought so, but with Skip deceased and his death ruled accidental, there was no one to corroborate their theory. They went looking for Adolph but came up empty. It was as though he had never existed. They couldn't even find the tunnel to American Flat that Cory and Faith both swore they'd taken.

⚜

So the charges were ultimately dropped, and the episode, such as it was, never aired. *Haunted Havens*, however, can still be seen in reruns, and The Horror Network recently announced that new shows will be produced to air this fall, under the revised title *Haunted Havens with Faith Hunt*.

⚜

Historical background

Adolph Sutro really was the mayor of San Francisco and really did build the Sutro Tunnel to drain water from the mines at Virginia City. His lack of wit was the subject of a letter by Mark Twain published in the Virginia City Territorial Enterprise during the winter of 1863-64. American Flat, aka American City, was a real boomtown in 1864, and the businesses mentioned in this story really did operate there; the business slogans were taken from the 1864 city directory. J.T. Keepers was the proprietor, with his partner Barton Lee, of the Willows Saloon. American Flat experienced a brief revival in the 1920s when a cyanide mill known as the United Comstock Merger Mill operated there, but the government razed the abandoned mill in 2014 and subsequently restricted access to the area.

BROWN'S EXCHANGE SALOON,
AMERICAN FLAT.

BEST QUALITY OF WINES, LIQUORS ETC, ALWAYS ON HAND.

"You will find Brown as snug as a Bug in a rug, And snugger than any other Bug-ger."

"Ghostbusted!" is ©2023 by Stephen H. Provost. It appears here for the first time and will appear in the forthcoming collection of short stories *"Shadow's Gate,"* of which he is the co-author. A California native, the author is a resident of Carson City and has published more than 50 works of fiction and nonfiction. His books include several fantasy and science fiction novels, along with history books on Mark Twain, America's highways, and 20th century history. All his books are available in the ACES bookshop at acesofnorthernnevada.com. Stephen is a historian, photographer, and former newspaper editor. You can follow him at stephenhprovost.com.

Peggy Rew
Selected poems

Running from the Red

Fear incessantly rushes through crimson
veins pumping a sad, carmine
heart into my throat as a rag-top cherry
T-Bird races through stop
signs of a contradictive
Catholic childhood.

Scraped elbows on redwood
divided our lives – fences skinned our knees, raggedy
as wild minds wander back, sweet maraschinos
submerged in Shirley Temples, as sunburn
made cheeks of rose
in our backyard of thorns.

The ACES Anthology

>Whispering, garnet
>oak leaves shadowed jealousy and scarlet
>anger of divorce, but daydreams of ruby
>slippers pacified sisters and brothers, any cheap burgundy
>soothed the parental demon
>until morning sky red.

>Crossing against her vermilion
>hand often triggered tormented, bloody
>nightmares, curdling screams of puce,
>even teachers ignored our obvious youthful secrets
>whilst veracity stung
>as did our bruises.

>Tenaciously, I twirl my strawberry
>curls, another horrific flashback, I sip my Coke
>and stare: do I need a black or blue
>pen to wrangle this negative
>balance in my checkbook.
>I blush.

New York City's People Processor

We descend into a cold, damp passageway
where hundreds of jet-setters, military populace,
cranky baby strollers and old folks tramp
this way and that on gum-spotted concrete.

Our journey begins like the gut rumble
you get after a forbidden meal, lackadaisically
we grip filth-infested handrails, our heads bob,
bumping against graffiti-scratched windows.

The people-moving missile launches, gaining speed, shooting recklessly through the underbelly world of darkness as if it were spicy indigestion passing through the intestines of the city.

The ACES Anthology

Heads and stomachs turn in a death chamber
of fumes where silent, passive passengers
read their newspapers on this rolling coaster,
we look away and lock our lids to avoid nausea.

Our racing projectile sprints, then slows, dashes,
and speeds up, jerking us back and forth,
then stops as the monotone voice articulates
each destination and for this, we pay to exit.

Walking Backwards

Wisdom: infinite, retrospective or possible
Audaciousness clouds judgment causing us enabler and
caretaker types to
Loiter in exhausting situations while our emotions are
Knitted into complicated apprehension. Mental commotion
Interlaces crisis and tension, wreaking havoc that may
Nullify the only chance at survival, a throbbing numbness
burrows in, so I
Guard my heart, secure my spirit from theft, now an intense
battle.

Breathing new life into myself, I must
Act on a promise to resuscitate my soul before the warranty
expires,
Calculating a cathartic cleansing, though all the way I'm
Kicking and screaming, achieving the
Weaving out of tangled webs. Excited, yet
Armed, my backwardsness glimpses the lighted tunnel ahead,
allowing me to

The ACES Anthology

Recoil my fortitude and regenerate the essence within as I
Dawdle in the aroma of Blue Girl roses, then step forward, I
Sashay through a rainbow of tulips to rekindle thyself.

When Poets & Porn Stars Align

Progressive thinkers will command and control
the superficial world we recognize when poets and porn stars
align.

A day of reckoning, of calculated conclusions,
the parallel of such vocations and professions, a resolve emerges.

The mirroring of intimates: trade secrets, whispers,
and expressions are appreciated, but only by genre-specific
addicts or admirers.

Heroic couplets and heroic couples are revealed by disregarding
limits while solitary inner courses access the depths of the
imagination.

Both artisans struggle equally with exhaustion,
mental practices tax the physical, isolated existence, a bridge of
souls.

Groins of their minds birth anxiety for conversation and
miasma of guilt lurks, a sinister sky lulls each too much needed
slumber.

The ACES Anthology

In the blink of an eye, fatigue evaporates, free verse and free love splendidly splice into epic, rhythmic proportion—vignettes and fishnets appear.

So no matter what professional modus operandi is chosen, sensuous scenarios will be fleshed out when poets and porn stars align.

"Running from the Red" is ©2003; "New York City's People Processor" is ©2009; "Walking Backwards" is ©2010; "When Poets & Porn Stars Align" is ©2009, all by Peggy Rew. A professional nanny, published wordsmith, copy editor, and pet care educator, the author has been a pet rescuer since the 1970s. She is the author of "Dog Bite Prevention: Don't Be Scared, Be Prepared," which is available in the ACES bookshop at acesofnorthernnevada.com.

Abby Rice
Miracle in the Rain

I hadn't meant to come here again today. But somehow, as the summer days faded into fall, I'd found myself here more and more often.

There was an anniversary of sorts coming up. So maybe that was it.

Whatever. Here I was again this morning, even though it was starting to rain. As if the place called me. As if there was nowhere I'd rather be. Except, of course, I'd rather be *anywhere* else.

Anywhere, just so long as he was with me one more time.

The grass was wet from the combination of overnight dew and this morning's intermittent rain, soaking into my sandals as I trudged across the perfectly manicured lawn to the grey granite marker. I hadn't bothered with a hat or raincoat, much less an umbrella. Because, why?

Duane Hebert Anderson. The rigid letters mocked me with their familiarity. Their finality. Almost exactly a year since he'd been gone: September 17th. A date carved in stone, right?

I needed to just accept it, everyone kept saying. Stop coming here. Maybe go out once in a while. Have fun. Live a little.

Except all that felt so *wrong*. What exactly was "living" supposed to look like, without my best friend, my other half, my husband-to-be?

A gust of wind blew my hair across my face, a warning sign that the clouds soon would fully unleash their full cargo of moisture. Already, a soft staccato of raindrops was hitting my hair and shoulders. Big, fat drops cooling my face, my arms.

Luckily there was no matching dampness in my eyes. I'd long since cried out all the tears. I'd even stopped asking *why*.

I knew why. The cops had explained it all to me as they stood on my porch—our porch—that horrid night nearly a year ago. To them, it was just a job. To me, it had been the end of life as I knew it.

The shorter cop had shifted awkwardly from foot to foot as he imparted the tragic news. The road slick with rain. Duane heading south: driving home after work. Speeding a little, of course, as usual. Something could have startled him; a deer in the road, a raccoon, who knew? No one had seen a thing. Nothing except twin black arcs on the pavement and the crumpled remains of his car off the side of the road. When the cops arrived, the engine had still been running. But for Duane, it was already too late.

I bent, my fingers tracing the letters of his name etched solidly into the granite. "I miss you," I whispered.

Off to my left, I caught a discreet cough. My head snapped around. A lone figure stood a dozen feet away, sheltered a bit from the rain beneath a tree.

"You're Duane's girl, aren't you." It wasn't a question.

The man pushed himself away from the trunk. Dark hair, dark eyes—from a distance, I could almost have mistaken him for Duane, though a closer glance showed he was likely a few years older. The same slim hips and strong shoulders, though; the same habit of rolling the ends of his sleeves up, leaving wrists and forearms exposed. Raindrops had left dark, blotchy polka dots on the faded denim shirt.

I didn't recognize him, but his mention of Duane brought a small surge of warmth to my belly. Duane's girl? Yes, of course. Always was, always would be.

I didn't say that, of course. I just nodded, keeping my features even.

"Thought so." He inclined his head to the left as he slowly approached, thumbs hooked in the front pockets of his jeans. "I keep seeing you here. Noticed the name on the stone."

Really? Was that the world's strangest pickup line? If he'd been here at the cemetery when I came before, I'd never noticed him.

I glanced down at the wet stone again, darkening in the rain, then back up at the stranger's face. He stood a polite arm's length away now. Crinkles around his eyes told me he spent time in the sun, and that he laughed a lot. His cheeks were growing wet, but he didn't seem to notice.

"Duane—did you know him?" I hoped so. Oh, how I hoped he'd have a memory or two to share with me.

"Not exactly." A hand came up, his right thumb and forefinger slowly stroking the line of his lower jaw, as if he was working out exactly what to say. "But I think I know what Duane would say to you right now."

I shivered in a way that had nothing to do with the rain.

Those dark eyes settled gently on mine. Calm. Warm. Reassuring.

"Name's Travis." He extended his hand to me slowly, the way you would greet a skittish dog. I took a step back, not quite ready to shake.

"Look, I know this seems strange, but something told me I should talk to you." Hooking a thumb over his shoulder, he pointed toward a headstone near the tree where he'd been standing. "Lost my dad last year. Same month you lost your Duane, it looks like. I know. It sucks."

My eyes dipped to Duane's stone again. Solid. Familiar. Grounding. Just like Duane had been.

"I'm sorry to hear about your dad. And yes, it does. It totally sucks."

His voice was a low rumble. "You gotta hold on to the good. Not the pain."

A shock of what felt like recognition ran through me.

"What did you just say?"

"That's what I think he'd try to tell you if he were here right now." He cocked his head toward the stone. "I never met Duane. But I'm pretty sure that's what he'd want to say if he could."

I hissed in a breath. How could he know? That was *exactly* the expression Duane would have used. *Hold on to the good.* Accompanied by the same tiny smile just lifting the corners of this man's lips. I looked closer. Yes. This stranger even sported a similar dimple in his right cheek when he smiled.

Wishful thinking, I chastised myself firmly. There was no way this handsome stranger was actually channeling Duane for me.

And yet, he had. That expression sounded like Duane, exactly: *Hold on to the good. That was Duane to a T.* Always smiling, always looking on the bright side. Always doing his best to cheer me up when I was down.

I fixed my attention on the headstone, suddenly uncomfortable about noticing how another man looked. Only because he reminded me so much of Duane. That had to be it.

"What happened with your dad?"

Out of the corner of my eye, I watched his smile droop a little. "Cancer."

He allowed a beat to go by. "What happened to your Duane?"

"Car accident." I'd told the story too many times to want to repeat it. Thankfully he didn't prod for details. He just nodded.

His hair was getting plastered to his forehead by the rain. Mine probably sported the same drowned-rat look. A cold droplet of water trickled down my neck and made its way beneath my collar. I shivered.

"Like to get a cup of coffee?" That charming smile was back at full wattage again.

And that's how I found myself with damp hair in a red vinyl booth at Cuppa Joe's, stirring a spoonful of sugar into a steaming mug and staring across the table at Travis Stapleton's charming dimple, rain pounding the window beside us.

With the beginnings of a matching smile on my lips.

The ACES Anthology

"Miracle in the Rain" is ©2023 by Karen Dustman, writing as Abby Rice. A former prosecutor and now freelance writer, she is the author of over 25 books ranging from non-fiction history to time-travel romance. Her articles have also appeared in both national and regional publications. Karen wrangles an active history blog for her indie imprint, Clairitage Press, and she's currently working on the third book in her "Blue Moon" time-travel romance series (writing as Abby Rice). Her books are available in the ACES bookshop acesofnorthernnevada.com.

Ken Sutherland

SWOOP!

An odd little story

Dash Hooper took the pistol out of his mouth and let it drop into his lap. The Old West Colt .44 left a metallic taste behind. He'd worn the gun on his hip for four years on the set of *Dash Hooper Rides*. The producers had objected to the use of a real gun on the show, but Dash had insisted.

"Real cowboys carry real guns," he'd told them. "Not props." Back then, Dash was popular enough to make it stick. Of course, the bullets were blanks.

The gun had been displayed in a glass case on the wall of Dash Hooper's Ranch House Motor Court for nearly sixty years. Of course, the gun was empty.

But on this lonely, rainy night, the gun was loaded and the bullets were real. Dash Hooper had come to the end of his lariat.

Another wife had deserted him. This one, Number Three, had run off on a gray Nevada morning with a truck driver who'd stayed only one night at the motor court. Number Two had at least faced him to announce she was unhappy before she left.

Number One wrote him a note in lipstick on the bathroom mirror, like a scene from a bad soap opera. *Goodbye, Dash. Paperwork to follow.*

He'd survived the first two just fine. And marriage Number Three was never anything to live or die for, so that wasn't really the issue.

He listened to the rain, sitting on the orange and red plaid sofa that looked like a horse blanket. Dash scanned the motor court lobby, filled with memorabilia from his television days as a rootin', tootin', shootin', singin' cowboy. The knotty pine walls were covered with pictures of Dash and the Amazing Trick Horse, Starr; Dash with his gun drawn; Dash posing with the other cast members; and his favorite, Dash at the White House, receiving a special honor from President Lyndon B. Johnson. A Texan, Johnson loved cowboys.

His trademark ten-gallon hat had its own lighted, locked glass case in the center of the room. Like his wives, it was the third replacement, the first two having mysteriously wandered off. Hence the lock. His guitar, the same one he played in his *Singin' in the Saddle* segment that closed the show each week, was also in a glass case. This case was never locked, because Dash took it out and tuned it up every single day.

No, the problem wasn't the abrupt loss of three wives, or the fact that his children didn't care enough about him to visit.

The problem was nothing. All the fame, all the adoration of his fans. Worth nothing now. He wondered if it had been worth anything then.

He thought about the children who once came to his personal appearances to see the fast draw that made him famous. "They probably all draw Social Security now, if they can still draw air," Dash said aloud to nobody.

All this had come to nothing. Just an empty motor court

with empty cabins. And an empty heart.

He couldn't see the point of continuing. But for some reason, he couldn't pull the trigger, either.

Dash heard the eighteen-wheeler coming. Somebody dodging the scales, he thought, or they wouldn't be on this road. Lost, maybe. They almost never stopped anymore. But the sound of the air brakes was unmistakable. He slid the Colt under a cushion on the sofa and went to the front desk. Be nice to finally have a customer.

Outside, a metal door slammed, and the truck slowly pulled away with a diesel clatter and roar. He heard it splashing through puddles on his gravel lot. Curious.

The little bell jingled when the door flew open. A young woman, barely out of her teens, stood in the lobby, soaking wet. Dash couldn't help but notice she was dressed in white from head to foot. White sneakers, white socks, white pants, a white turtleneck sweater, a white windbreaker, even a white wool stocking cap. She had big, bright eyes and a huge smile.

"Welcome to Dash Hooper's Nevada Ranch House Motor Court, conveniently located in the middle of nowhere."

She smiled enthusiastically and faced him, eyes shining. "What a beautiful night!"

Dash shook his head. "No it ain't. It's raining like hell."

"Yes! Don't you think that's beautiful?"

"I don't." He reached under the counter and came up with a towel. "Here. You're soaking wet."

She took in a deep breath and let the air out slowly. "Even the air is spectacular! It smells like... I don't know, like *hope*."

"Dairy farm down the road. Rain makes it worse."

Dash watched her pull off her stocking cap and shake her head like a puppy, giggling as water sprayed everywhere.

"This ain't our regular weather," Dash said. "Hardly ever get rain in the high desert."

"It must seem silly to you," she said. "Where I come from, we don't have any rain at all. It's always so hot, and there is no water anywhere."

"Las Vegas?"

"I'm from Joy. That's my name, too. I'm Joy." She extended her hand, and Dash shook it cautiously.

"Pleased to meet you. I'm Dash."

"Oh! You're the man on the sign. Cowboy star of the Old West! Were you in the movies?"

"Television. Before you were born. I was the youngest cowboy on TV. And I made some records of songs I wrote. Roy Rogers and the Sons of the Pioneers recorded one of my tunes, *Campfire on the Plain*."

"I don't think I know that one. How does it go?"

"You really want to hear it?"

"Yes! That would be wonderful."

While Dash walked over to get his guitar, Joy toweled off her face, beaming like an excited child.

Dash sat on the arm of the plaid sofa, strummed once, then began to sing.

> *"Like a candle in the window*
> *to a stranger in the rain,*
> *its flame a glowing welcome to*
> *his trouble or his pain*
> *Like a candle in the window*
> *like a campfire on the plain."*

Joy clapped her hands. "That's so beautiful."

"Simplistic. They said all my songs were simplistic. Like advertising jingles, is what they said."

"Well, I don't know who *they* are, but *they* don't know what they're talking about. That is a terrific song, and I'm sure that's why this Roy Roberts guy recorded it."

"Rogers. Roy Rogers. He was a big cowboy star, like me. Are you a musician?"

"I don't have to be a musician to know when something comes from deep inside. From the heart. I know a little about *that*."

Dash didn't feel like discussing his heart tonight. "So where is Joy? I don't think I've heard of it. I'm not aware of any Joy in Nevada."

"Oh, you can't see it from here. It's two galaxies over. Humans can't possibly imagine how far it is."

Dash nodded. "Ahh, I see. So you're on a very long trip. You must be tired."

"Doesn't really take too long. I just left this west-morning."

"Excuse me? I thought you said *west-morning*?"

She smiled patiently. "Yes. We have two suns, and that means two mornings. West-morning would be like late afternoon on Earth."

"Mm-hmm. You must have a pretty fast rocket ship, I guess."

"Ships would take years."

"Yeah, I suppose so."

"I came by swoop."

Dash clapped his hands once and smiled. "Damn! I was gonna say swoop. It's just that the diesel rig you arrived in threw me off."

"Once we get to Earth, we have to take regular ground transportation. After we get a body, that is. On Joy, we don't have bodies."

Dash looked her over. The sleeves of her jacket had ridden up, and he noticed bandages on both her wrists. "You do seem to have a body."

"I do *now*. But you can't swoop with a body. It would fall completely apart on the journey. We have to find one after we get here. That part isn't hard. The problem is getting lost when we hit your atmosphere. Once I landed on the wrong continent. I had to go through immigration and everything. What a mess *that* was. You simply can't plan for it."

"Course not."

"I got pretty close this time. Idaho Falls."

"Lucky for you. I mean finding a body nearby and all."

Joy began to notice the memorabilia in the lobby. She walked around looking at the displays. "Not really," she said. "There's always a body somewhere. Humans have a pretty high mortality rate."

"Yeah, I suppose you need that kind of positive outlook if you're gonna go swoopin' around the galaxies."

"You have to be optimistic, that's for sure." Joy pointed to a photo on the wall. "Is this you?"

"Long time ago. I was only about twenty in that one."

"Isn't that young to be a big star? I mean, even by Earth standards, that's *young*."

"Start young, finish young. I was a has-been before I was twenty-five."

"What happened?"

"Cowboys went out of style. At least that's what the big shot TV executives said. And then they had the nerve to tell me I was such a good cowboy I could never be anything else, so good luck and goodbye and please get lost."

Joy put her hand on Dash's forearm. "And they just abandoned you? That is so sad."

"It was rough for a while, but then an advertising company asked if I could write them a jingle. They wanted their laundry soap to sing and dance. So I stayed on television another way. I did dancing cigarettes and singing refrigerators. One outfit had cartoon singing alligators to sell shoes. The advertising people liked my songs *because* they were simplistic."

"So you won."

"After a while, that ran out, too."

When the room went quiet, Dash realized he'd been going on too much about himself. "Look, you didn't come in out of the rain to hear all that baloney. You need to dry out and get some rest. Let me get you a cabin. Plenty to pick from tonight."

"Well, I..."

"Don't tell me. You left all your money in your other space suit."

"I don't have any money. I planned to keep going until I got to Reno, but I saw you on that big sign in that gigantic cowboy hat and I felt like I *needed* to come here, so I made the driver let me out. He didn't want to stop."

"They don't want to stop here. Only use this road to duck the scales. Legal trucks are all on the interstate."

Joy slipped out of her wet windbreaker. "This *is* a pretty quiet road."

Once her jacket was off, Dash noticed a large plastic button pinned to her sweater, and bent to read it. "'It's not odd to vote for God.' What's that about?"

"I think we should elect God to be our president. It was my idea, so I'm going to run the campaign personally. From Reno."

"I wasn't aware God made his residence in Reno. Or do you think you'll maybe get better odds there."

"Actually, I'm the one who picked Reno. God only told me Nevada."

"God sent you to Nevada? You sure? Now, is this the same God we have locally, or is your planet in some other fella's jurisdiction?"

"There is only one God in all the universe, and next November, He's going to be elected President of the United States."

"Well, that'll sure be different."

"It'll be better."

Dash had begun to notice a fragile center in his enthusiastic visitor. "I guess it will be pretty interesting to see how he handles those Philistines in Congress. And if we're lucky, maybe we'll get a shakeup at the D-M-V."

"I'm sorry you're so cynical. God can be trusted. Men can't."

"Men can't be trusted? And you call *me* cynical?"

"I had to leave where I was. I took a long journey on pure faith, and God gave me the answer. You just don't understand, that's all."

"Let me see if I do. You're from another planet where they have two suns and no water..."

"It's called Joy."

"Okay, Joy. And you came here by swirl..."

"Swoop."

"Swoop, right. And you stopped to pick up a body in Idaho."

"That was the freshest one."

"Of course. And now you're on your way to the sacred city of Reno to run God for President."

"Probably Reno. He only told me Nevada."

"Now really, is this God's idea or somethin' you cooked up yourself?"

"Everything is God's idea. God gave me that one while I was swooping."

Dash shook his head. "You should probably give it right back It ain't ever gonna work."

"I would never second-guess God!"

"And what if God doesn't want to be President? You ever think of that?"

"Then why would I even get the idea?"

Interesting logic, Dash thought. He took a deep breath. "Listen. You seem like a sweet kid. I like you. But you have to think this through. Assuming there actually is a God out there, and frankly I have my doubts, and assuming he toils away as Master of the Universe, working out the rotations of the stars and the blossoming of the flowers, and swooping people around from planet to planet, why would he *ever* take a demotion to President of the United States?"

Joy's jaw dropped in shock. "A *demotion?*"

"The president answers to the people. God won't ever do that, never has. And the atheists will drive him batty. They don't even believe God is God. They're certainly gonna have trouble believing he's moonlighting as president."

"How many people believe in the president you guys have now. Or the one before him?"

Dash chuckled. "Okay, I'll give you that one. Let's see how you do with this. If God was the President of the United States, would that make Americans the chosen people? Because I can think of a bunch of other countries who might have somethin' to say about *that*. Canadians, especially. We're always draftin' their best hockey players and such. And don't you think it might be just a little bit frustratin' for the poor ol' Pope?"

"You're joking, but you'll see. God will use the presidency to unite the population so we can all be one people. And we'll be happy. Pretty soon everybody will want to vote for God."

"All I see is greedy, self-centered people who vote their own special interests, and me among 'em. I voted for Ronald Reagan because I thought he might remember what it was like to be a broken-down, has-been old actor. Turned out he couldn't remember anything at all."

"You sound like you regret being an actor. Can't you just think of it as a wonderful experience and move on? It was years ago."

"You're right. The single achievement of my life ran past me more than sixty years ago. I went from being a big television star to plunging toilets in a dilapidated old motor court. And I'm still here, doin' it!"

"Maybe you'd be happier if you tried something different."

"You're trying something pretty different. You think you'll be happy if you get a bunch of people to vote for God?" Dash heard the sarcasm in his own voice. He regretted it while he was still talking.

"It's not about making *me* happy. It's for everyone," she said. "For you. For the girl who had this body. Everyone."

"Why would it help her?"

"She was so sad. She didn't know God. She couldn't find love. She lost all her hope, and she had to leave the life she had. She cut her arms open and got in the bathtub and she died."

"That is sad. I guess she didn't have any family she could go to for help."

"Her family lied to her. They betrayed her. They said they were there for her, but all they thought about was themselves. Not one of them cared about how she felt."

"How do you know that, Joy? Unless you're that girl?"

Joy folded her arms across her chest and took a step away from Dash. "I'm not her. Of course I'm not! But I was there. Waiting, while she decided. I knew what she was thinking. She could have gone back. People can do that. They can go back, if they really want to. But she had no reason to go back to them. None. They only made her sad. So she left. She had to, it was all she could do."

Dash thought about this for a moment. "I always thought dying alone would be the most terrible thing. Somehow it doesn't seem so bad if you have people there with you. Even if they're not exactly the right people."

"It's no better, believe me."

"But she could have gone back, you said. Maybe if she tried again, I mean, after nearly dying... her family..."

"Well, it was her choice, and that's what she chose and that was it. I took over her body."

Dash chuckled. "Bet the family didn't expect a space alien to show up."

Joy smiled, remembering. "When she left, the doctor pronounced her dead. Right at that second, I took this big, deep breath and sat straight up on the emergency room table. I blinked my eyes and said, 'What nation is this? What Earth-language do you speak?' I thought the doctor was going to need emergency treatment!"

Still laughing, Dash said, "That had to be quite a sight. What did your family do then?"

Joy turned serious. "*Her* family, not mine. I already told you I don't know these people. They said she was crazy. They tried to put her in an insane asylum. Only it wasn't her anymore, it was me, and I didn't want to be locked up! Then God spoke to me clear as day. He said, 'Joy, run away! Go to Nevada right now.' And that's what I did."

"I think I'm starting to understand this swooping thing a little better now."

"People say God works in mysterious ways, and they're right."

"Here's one of God's mysteries for you. Down the road in Winnemucca, a baby boy was born with a hole in his heart as big as your thumb. Last year, it was. They figured the poor kid wouldn't still be alive by the end of the day. But they flew the little guy to some high-powered heart surgeon in San Francisco, and he installed a monkey heart in that baby. Made all the newspapers. Later that doctor said he felt the presence of God standing right at his side during the operation."

"And you still question the existence of God? Do you believe in anything?"

"I believe this: God or no God, it was the doctor who gave that child a chance to live his life. The doctor didn't *put* the hole in his little heart."

Joy stared into Dash's eyes. "You obviously think God is cruel."

Dash pondered this. "I've been on this planet a lot longer than you. In more ways than one, maybe. My money would be on cruel."

"God is just. He only causes pain for people who do bad things."

"What did that little baby do?"

She sighed. "You must have a very unhappy life. Do you think it's God's fault?"

"God doesn't allow for mistakes. A priest will go down to Death Row to keep a killer in the church right up to the minute they give him the needle. But let a man marry a woman who runs off with a truck driver, and they never want to see his face in church again."

"Is that why you're so cynical? Because your wife left you?"

"Nah. Took three of 'em runnin' out to turn a tough old buzzard like me."

"Did you go after them? Any of them?"

"Go *after* them?" Of course not! They want to leave, let 'em go. If they don't want to live with me, I don't want 'em around here anyway."

"Maybe if you went after them, they would know how much you cared."

"Or, it might have made everything worse. Makes no difference now, anyway."

"But it was a choice, see? You make your own choices, then

blame God when it doesn't work out the way you want. If something good happens, who gets the credit?"

"Something good would have to happen."

"You lost your career as an actor, but you said yourself you didn't pursue it. Maybe if you had..."

"Yeah, well, it's a little more complicated than that."

"You still have choices. You could do advertising again. Or you could live the life you have."

Dash had reached the end of his patience. His voice filled the room. "That what you did? Live the life you had? Or did you just run away like women always do? You're so damn pious, but you still ran away, didn't you? And you have the gall to say God sent you!"

This outburst from Dash frightened Joy, and she backed away from him. Dash matched her step for step.

"That's not fair! You don't know what it's like," she said.

Dash leaned into Joy's space, his voice booming. "I certainly know what it's like to have people walk out on you. Abandon you without another thought. I'm an expert at that one, little lady. When somebody you care about just... just gets in some stranger's truck and doesn't even say why!"

"I'm sorry. I shouldn't have said anything." Joy, on the edge of tears, continued to back away. "Your life is none of my business."

But Dash hadn't finished. He couldn't stop now. "Seems like your own life is none of your business, either. You wanted out so bad you had to turn into somebody else!"

"No! That wasn't me. That was another girl!"

Joy had walked backward halfway across the room, and bumped into the sofa, causing Dash's Colt .44 to clatter to the floor. Joy, tears streaming down her face, picked it up and stared at it."

"Careful! That thing is loaded. You could kill yourself."

At this, she laughed, but there was no humor in her cynical bark. "Ha! Can't kill *me*. I'm not from your stupid little planet anymore! I'm from a planet God cares about. And I'm indestructible now!" Joy put the barrel of the gun to her temple. "I could shoot myself, and I'd still be here for everyone to torment. I could open my veins and spill my blood out all over the bathroom and *still* be here. I can't even *die!*"

Joy collapsed into sobs, and Dash reached for the gun. "You'd better give me that."

He took Joy gently by the shoulders and eased her down onto the sofa. He walked over to the registration desk to put the gun into a drawer and picked up a clean towel.

"Uh, here."

Wiping her tears, she said, "Thank you. I should go. I'll just go now."

"You think that's a good idea? It's pouring out there. You should probably stay here tonight."

"No! I have to get to Reno. I'll just catch a ride."

"But..."

"There's nothing for me here. I'm going."

"Okay, sure. Go ahead. Means nothin' to me."

Joy shook her head, frustrated. "You never believed anything I said, did you? You were making fun of me the whole time. You're just like them! Just like everybody!"

Dash, standing at the window with his back to her, studied the rain. "Think what you like. You're on your way down the road anyway. Don't matter what I think."

Joy stood and picked up her jacket. Her voice had lost its confidence. Trying to pull on the jacket, she kept missing the sleeve. "I have to go."

"Suit yourself. Might be tough to catch a ride, though.

Maybe you didn't notice, but the last truck to come down this road was the one you came in. Could be morning before another one comes along."

"I'll be all right. God is watching me." Joy said this more to the floor than to Dash.

He followed her to the door. "You don't have to, you know."

"I can't pay for a room anyway. I'll get a ride. God will send somebody for me."

When the door closed behind her, Dash moved to the window. He watched her walk in the rain to the edge of the highway.

Barely a moment went by before a large truck approached. Joy stood erect and put her thumb out. But the truck didn't stop. It raced by at a high rate of speed, throwing water in its wake, drenching Joy.

The rain picked up, pounding against the roof. A brilliant flash of lightning preceded a loud thunderclap, and Dash decided to try one more time.

He walked out to the parking area in his shirtsleeves, immediately getting soaked. He shouted to be heard over the roar of the rain. "Hey! It's raining too hard to be out here. Come inside and I'll give you a place to stay."

She folded her arms across her chest and looked down at the gravel. "I'm all right. Really."

"I've been thinking about your campaign."

"Can't hear you over the rain," she shouted.

Dash moved closer, the raindrops coming faster, slapping hard against his head, stinging his face. I have an idea to help you. Please. Come back inside and let me tell you about it."

"Why would you help me? You think I'm crazy, just like everybody else."

"Who knows who's crazy? Maybe we disagree on a couple

of things. Look, I'm sorry I yelled. I wasn't mad at you, I was mad at my own life. I didn't mean to hurt your feelings."

Dash gently put his arm around Joy's shoulders and led her to the door.

When it closed behind them with a little jingle from the bell above, Joy said, "So...what kind of an idea?"

"I was just thinkin' I could write a song. A God for president campaign song. You, know, like an advertising jingle. Couldn't do as much harm as those dancing cigarette ads I used to write."

Dash watched the idea cross her face. Her exuberance brightened her demeanor, and Dash handed her another towel.

"Ohh! A jingle." Smiling now, she said, "That would be nice."

"Well, it's just somethin' I know how to do, is all. It ain't like I'm lookin' for a cabinet post."

"Oh, I don't think I could promise anything like that."

"I'm sure God will want to make his own choices."

"Exactly. So you said I could stay here tonight? I don't have any..."

"I know, I know, you can't pay. You'll just have to earn your way. The cabins are kinda dusty. Some sheets to wash."

"You need a maid. I can do that."

"Pays minimum wage. You'll get an employee discount on the cabin, and you should come out okay on payday."

"But, I told you I have to go to Reno. God sent me."

"I seem to recall you saying God sent you to Nevada, and you came up with Reno on your own."

"Well, I..."

"Well nothin', you're *in* Nevada. And didn't you say you felt you *needed* to come here when you saw my billboard? Maybe that was a sign."

"So you think God sent me to Nevada to meet... *you?*"

"I'm saying nothin' of the sort. All I mean is you're here now, and one of the best jingle writers in the history of advertising jingles just offered to write you a campaign song. For free."

Joy took a moment to consider the idea. She looked around at the museum that passed for a motor court lobby, and back at Dash. She sighed and nodded. Then she smiled.

"When do we start on the campaign song? What do you think it should say?"

Dash pointed at the big plastic button on her sweater. "You already wrote a good slogan. That'll start us on the lyric. We can work on the rest of the song in the morning. Come back around nine. I'll make some breakfast and we'll talk about it, then you can get to work on the cabins while I write somethin'."

Joy's excited smile returned. "Thank you, Mr. Hooper! Um, Dash."

"Thank *you*, Joy. I hope we can be friends." Dash handed her a key. "Cabin 3 is all made up. It's the third one down. Looks like the rain is gonna let up for a while. Better hurry."

Joy, smiling, took the key and went back outside. Dash noticed the spring was back in her step.

After the door closed, he went to the drawer and retrieved his Colt .44. He opened the chamber and shook the bullets out, then returned the gun to its display cabinet on the wall. He took his guitar out of its display case, pulled the strap over his head, and sat down on the horse blanket sofa. He strummed a C chord and hummed a tune for a second.

Then he sang...

> *It's not odd to vote for God,*
> *If you're not con-tent.*
> *We all win if you vote for God,*
> *To be the pres-i-dent.*

Smiling, Dash put his guitar back into the case and headed for his apartment, humming his new composition and turning lights off as he went.

The ACES Anthology

"SWOOP!" ©2023 by Ken Sutherland, who lives in Reno. This is his first published work and appears here for the first time. He has three novels currently awaiting publication. Ken is a graduate of San Jose State University and Cal Lutheran University, and a retired broadcaster who has written and produced thousands of broadcast commercials, programs and documentaries. When it was time to write a novel, his lifelong love of mysteries left him no choice but to work in that genre. You can visit his website here: https://kensutherlandauthor.com/.

Richard Thomas
Bury Me Deep

The stranger rode into town on a horse that was nothing more than dried skin stretched taut over creaking bones, one eye glancing back over his shoulder watching the devil that he knew, the other wandering forward to spy the one that he didn't. He slid off the horse, a layer of dust and grime coating his torn clothes—lanky and disoriented, his lips chapped, torn and bleeding from riding into the wind, his yellow teeth chewing on them to slow his worried heart. He'd left the shadows in the mountains, their stench still in his bandana—the cloth around his neck damp with sweat, covering the thin slash marks that ran a red line from ear to ear. Peace was all he sought, and perhaps forgiveness for his done deeds. Whether the legs that were roasting on the open spit had two legs or four, a man had to eat, regardless of the cries that echoed through the whispering pines—his eyes twitching, bony hands trembling, his swollen gut twisted in knots.

The town had no name that he knew, but the sign at the crossroads pointed this way, offering work, and maybe a place to rest his head. He closed his eyes for a moment and prayed for forgiveness, and then he prayed for a glass of something dark and hot, a bit of amber to coat his throat and wash away his sins. The hefty woman in the doorway of the saloon had no hair on her shiny bald head, hands on her hips, apron straining over a faded blue dress, but her smile was as white as bone, beckoning him inside with a nod of her head and a wave. He went to tie his steed to the rail and wondered what was the point. The mare would be dust soon, drained of its life over the trails these past few months. It was better that the horse should close its eyes and forget what it had seen.

He found his way to the bar, slid onto a stool, and exhaled all that he had carried over the hills and dry, empty land. She poured him a short glass, asking for no payment, simply walking back toward the mirror that reflected his shaking hand rising slowly to his lips.

"You come over the mountains, through the pass?" she asked.

"Yep."

"How long? Weeks maybe? Did you miss the snow, or catch it?"

"Months, I reckon. No snow when I passed through, just a bitch of a wind—no offense."

"None taken." She smiled. "Your horse is dead," she muttered.

The stranger glanced out the door. "I know," he said. "She just doesn't know it yet."

The empty bar was nothing but tables and chairs, a small piano by the back wall, and rows and rows of shimmering bottles sparkling in the gleam of stray sunlight beams, the woman polishing a tall glass nearly to dust.

"Thanks for the drink," the stranger said.

"First one's always on me," she said. "I'm Sadie."

He nodded.

"Much obliged."

"You looking for work or moving on?" she asked.

"Not sure—just trying to keep breathing, ma'am. But I suppose the work will find me, it always does—one way or another. Can't seem to shake nothing these days. Must be getting old."

He grinned in her direction, brown teeth filed down nearly to points, a cough and a hack filling the dusty room, spitting toward the floor, the blood-stained mucus holding their attention.

Her smile faltered, and she placed the glass on the shelf.

"Well, stranger, maybe there is something you can help me with after all," she said. "We don't have a lot of folks here in town, or even on the farms still. Hard to raise much of anything here."

He nodded, licking his lips. She wandered over and refilled his drink.

"That's for the work, what I'm about to tell you about," her eyes turned to steel, and then blinking, back to light brown.

The straw man knocked it back and nodded.

"Go on," he said.

"Kids wander off," she sighed. "They run to the hills, wanna get nekkid or maybe just shoot something. Sometimes they come back, sometimes they don't."

She rubbed her neck and eyeballed the man. Taking a deep breath, she went on.

"Same with the cattle, the dogs, the chickens, the hogs. Don't know what draws them up to them damn mountains, but take your eyes off them for a moment, and they gone."

The double-doors to the saloon slapped open, and a pale young boy bounced in, took one look at Sadie, and the stranger, and stopped.

"Go on, Jeb, get out of here. We're talking business."

The boy turned and fled, eyes wide. The stranger didn't move, didn't turn his neck, or blink his fading eyes. Instead, he swallowed what liquid was left in his mouth and stared into his mangled hands.

"I got a well out back, and somehow a calf fell down it, just happened before you wandered in here, in fact. If you listen, you can hear it crying out there. Broke its legs in the fall, I suspect."

The man craned his neck and listened, and sure enough there was a low bleating moan, drifting on the wind.

"Help me out, stranger? I got rope, the men are all busy harvesting or hunting, some two towns away selling seed and corn, nobody giving a shit about Sadie until they want to wet their whistle."

The man picked up the glass, licked it clean, what was left of the brown liquid, and stood up straight.

"Sure, Sadie, I'll help you out. Then we can talk about what other forms of compensation y'all got around here."

She smiled a wide grin, her face nearly folding in half, running her plump hands over her slick, bald head.

"Deal," she whispered, and topped off his glass one last time. He knocked it back, hitched up his jeans, and headed for the back door.

Sadie followed him out, the wind picking up, the sun sliding behind the heavy clouds. He could hear the noises seeping up from the bottom of the well, and on the wind, they changed, from bleating calf to crying child to weeping man and back to farm animal, a low guttural moan.

"How deep?" he asked.

"Not far," she said. "Enough to snap a thin leg, like my calf, but not that far, maybe fifteen feet? Not sure, it's been here longer than me."

The man stared at the stones that formed a ring around the hole, dust and dirt, a chip here and there—dark stains splattered now and again, water perhaps. There was little fear in him, because there was little life left in his weary bones, so he hopped up on the lip of the well, grabbed hold of the rope, nodded once to Sadie, and down he went.

Above, the sun held a fading gray light, his boots on the stone, looking down into the darkness, looking up to the circle of sky. It grew colder the deeper he went, and then it grew colder still. And yet, a sheen of sweat coated his back and neck, the stench from the bottom of the well growing, the fading bleat rising up to meet him.

He landed on the bottom with a wet slap, bones snapping under his feet, the dank mossy smell mixing with copper and rotting flesh. As he knelt to grab the calf his hands found a shoulder and a skull, thin arms and wet denim running down worn-out boots. The dying man moaned, took his last breath, and expired. Glancing up to the darkening circle above, the stranger watched as Sadie leaned over the hole, a cast of shadows standing tall beside her, her long arm pointing down the hole toward him, and the shades spilled over the lip, finally catching up to him, and the town of Redemption moved on.

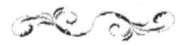

"Bury Me Deep" is ©2014 by Richard Thomas. The author has published four novels, four collections, with over 175 stories in print, and has also edited four anthologies. He has been nominated for the Bram Stoker (twice), Shirley Jackson, and Thriller awards. You can find him at www.whatdoesnotkillme.com.

Kitty Turner
They Call Me Will

Late June wasn't a sensible time to start west. When the party finally crossed into Wyoming territory, the long summer days had lost their sweltering dullness and turned sharp with the September chill. Thunderstorms moved across the plains like lumbering grey beasts bristling with malice as our covered wagons made painstaking progress. Each rut and rock slowed our oxen to the pace of a lazy walk. Winter would be upon us long before we reached California.

I'm a stout woman. Pleasant to the eye and clever enough. My name is Willette, but my husband, John, called me Will. He was among those who didn't survive the trail. There was room for me under the bowed canvas shade alongside the hardtack, dried meat, grain, and calico quilts, with John now a seeping corpse under a cairn of stones a hundred miles behind. The pregnant, the sick, and the grieving were allowed to ride, but I chose to walk with the men and able-bodied women.

I strapped John's six-shooter to my hip. The Colt .44 gave me a sense of security and independence. The scorn for a woman with a sidearm was palpable, but I didn't let the disapproval discourage me. Back on my sister's crowded Missouri homestead, I couldn't hit a barn door with a shotgun, not that I had even tried my hand at shooting. But now, power coursed through my arms when I lagged behind the group to practice. The smell of black powder and the ring in my ears pushed away a John-shaped hole that hovered near me and filled me with fear. Within a month after my loss, I regularly shot rabbits for my evening meal. It was a small act of defiance, a reminder that I could take care of myself.

Owen and Murray had taken it upon themselves to shadow me after honoring a reasonable time of grieving, at least for the trail. The mismatched men were friends. Murray was ten years older than me, while Owen was younger, barely out of his teens. Owen had a beautiful singing voice and a meatless frame. Murray was a skilled hunter, tall and robust—a no-nonsense man. Across the evening bonfire, the odd friends whispered and made eyes at me.

Owen was the first to cross around the fire to the women's side after weeks of glances. I often sat slightly apart, and the girls and women tittered at our first interaction, especially since Owen was at least ten years my junior.

"Hey ya, Will," Owen said.

"Nice evening," I replied.

Bolstered by my not-off-putting response, both men approached me the following night at the community fire. We chatted about the day's events, and Owen boyishly retrieved his cigar box guitar and played me a tune, which the others enjoyed as much as I did.

Owen's skills of distraction proved more useful than Murray's marksmanship when we veered off the Oregon Trail at Fort Bridger, following a shortcut that turned out to be folly. The path was little more than an Indian footpath, nearly impassable by wagon. We lost weeks and precious food supplies to busted wheels, a conman's map, and off-course bearings. Not a rabbit or deer was seen for weeks. As the first snow fell, we were hungry and still had five hundred miles before we reached our promised paradise. That's when Owen's songs had the most value. They soothed our collectively aching hearts.

At the far edge of the Great Basin Desert, our supplies dwindled to moldy feed for the oxen, but turning back was not an option. More corpses were left where they fell, with only a walking prayer to mark their passing. We had no time to bury the dead. Buzzards circled above, ready to feast on the remains of our ill-fated journey. If we didn't return to the main trail by the end of fall, none of us would ever be claiming our land grants. I padded my corset and added an extra petticoat against the cold and inquiring eyes.

Relief coursed through my changing body at the sight of the mountains. From the desert, a deep purple line formed under a sky the color of a sunburn. The next day, substantial snowfall was visible on the crests of the hills. A treacherous path forced us to make camp at the summit of a lesser range that lay between a high dale and the Sierras. The grass of the valley floor, turned autumn drab, was cut through by winding silver streams. Beyond, majestic peaks stood tall, their ice-mirrored flanks reflecting the fading rays of the day. Nestled at the base of those towering mountains were paddocks, low buildings, and a gleaming white church.

That night, the moon punched a hole like a biscuit tin in the rising dome of disordered stars. The Paiute scout came silently upon our camp to give the news of the late season. He told us the twinkling of lights in the valley below was a settlement that could house us for the winter. The dark-skinned man said the crossing to California would be perilous, if not impossible. That night, as laughter and music filled the air, Murray and I huddled together over the crackling embers of my cooking pot.

"I don't know if the baby is yours or Owen's, but we can't cross to California until next spring," I whispered to Murray. "If we all stay in Nevada, we'll lose our claims. After everything we've been through, we can't give up on our dreams. Murray, marry me. Send Owen to secure the best parcels of farmland for all three of us. Can you do that for me?"

"I will," Murray replied without hesitation. "I don't care if the baby's not mine."

The next day, we were welcomed in the buzzing foothill settlement with open arms. A feast was laid in the impromptu commons—a bounty of cornbread, roast venison, mustard greens, and hopped ale. This was a place I could build a life and raise a family. I wasn't sure I wanted to claim John's promised land any longer, but the date of the rush to claim the parcel would pass if we all waited to cross.

Most of our group prepared for the treacherous climb ahead despite warnings from the townsfolk and the neighboring Paiutes. Snow had already locked the higher peaks, and the air was as cold as tart apples. The only guides willing to lead our party were two outcasts from the Miwok tribe down south.

"Owen," I said, pulling him aside as the departure preparations unfolded. The sadness in his eyes clawed at my heart as I told him my decision. Murray stood silently at my side.

"I need to stay here with Murray. I need his protection. You are younger and better suited for the climb. Secure the best land for us, and Murray and I will meet you in Sutterville next year."

Murray patted Owen on the back like a father and called over George Donner, our trusted leader, and relayed our plan.

"Will and I have made a decision. We're staying behind. Owen, our brave companion here, will continue with the Donner Party to California to stake our claim."

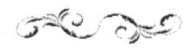

The ACES Anthology

"They Call Me Will" is ©2023 by Kitty Turner. It appears here for the first time. The author writes dystopian tech thrillers, short stories, and an occasional western. Her work explores the intersection between art, commerce, and purpose. Rooted in the philosophical and social commentary of Huxley, Camus, and Pynchon, her latest novel, "Zone Trip," is available in the ACES bookshop acesofnorthernnevada.com and on Amazon.

Kristina Ulm
Nevada Sonnet

In the sweet, wide open, just barely ruined
solitude, Nevada, if you're from
around here you know that dusty brown
mountains turn pink and purple, true and
perfect empty. People leave people here.
I've been left to find the longest
union of mine is the wild song
of Nevada. Brown, yes the soft brown sheer
beauty of a blank page. To stay here
is all that's left, I'm way too West
to make it away from home, my regrets
long dried up and hardened into fierce
love. A dusty, crazy, lonely state.
Unwritten land, unwritten fate."

"Nevada Sonnet" is ©2023 by Kristina Ulm. As Kristina Charles, the Reno resident is the author of "Murder on the Mesa," which is available in the ACES bookshop acesofnorthernnevada.com and on Amazon.

The ACES Anthology

The ACES Anthology

Made in the USA
Monee, IL
14 October 2023